END OF
INNOCENCE

K. J. HARTLEY

End of Innocence
Published by The Conrad Press in the United Kingdom 2016

Tel: +44(0)1227 472 874
www.theconradpress.com
info@theconradpress.com

ISBN 978-1-78301-875-8

Typesetting by:
Charlotte Mouncey, www.bookstyle.co.uk

The book cover and The Conrad Press logo were designed by Maria Priestley.

Printed by Management Books 2000 Limited
36 Western Road
Oxford
OX1 4LG

1

At a quarter to eight on an already warm April morning in 1939, Michael Harrington walked briskly along Rua da Rosa, the sun touching the tops of the buildings on the far side of the narrow street. The rain he'd heard falling during the night had served to wash the tessellated pavement, leaving the air clean, with only a hint of wood smoke from the bakery round the corner in Rua dos Mouros.

For Harrington this was the best time of day in the best of all places to be. Lisbon was his city, and the Bairro Alto, with its Renaissance churches, public squares, fine mansions, crowded tenements and narrow winding alleys, had been his world ever since he'd arrived in Portugal, close to twenty-seven years before. The Bairro Alto was occasionally disreputable but always friendly and fascinating; what more could anyone want from where one lived? Just lately, however, he'd become aware of scattered seeds of disquiet beginning to take root; tiny, hesitant shoots, not yet readily identifiable, but already disturbing his hitherto tranquil life.

At the entrance to the little corner grocer's shop on the corner, whose window was hung about with sheets of *bacalhau*, the dried cod that was a staple of the Portuguese diet, a thin stick of a woman swathed in a black shawl fiercely wielded a broom, as she always did at this time of the morning. Harrington waved her his usual cheery greeting, and she lifted her broom in response.

His attention was drawn to the rattle of cart wheels coming up the cobbled street behind him and the agonised scream of a mule being beaten by a labourer in stained work clothes.

Harrington could see the cart was heavily loaded with dripping tubs of white paint, destined no doubt to colour the stucco walls of some nearby building.

He knew it wasn't his place to remonstrate, but the poor animal's distress was so obvious, the man so callous that, distracted by the sight, Harrington found himself almost bumping into a plump little man who was stepping into the street from the doorway of a recently opened printer's workshop.

'I beg your pardon,' Harrington said, instinctively choosing English. Though his own Portuguese was very fluent he knew very few foreigners spoke the language and the man couldn't be Portuguese, not in that elaborately constructed suit with its complication of buttons and flaps, those stray blond curls escaping from the tweed hat adorned with a little feather in the band.

The stranger stared at him. 'You're British!'

'British? Yes, I am as a matter of fact.' Harrington was conscious of being closely inspected in his turn. Measured against himself, he reckoned the man was nearly a head shorter, which made the stranger not much more than five feet tall.

'You must forgive my curiosity,' the man said, 'but, with your black suit and your collar? Someone told me that there's a college for priests near here, and I just wondered.'

Harrington gave a faint smile. 'Yes,' he said. 'You mean the English College. I teach there. We educate young men for the priesthood. I'm Father Michael Harrington. You've probably seen our students walking around the town in their black habits and red stoles. The locals call our place *o colégio dos Inglesinhos,* the college of the little Englishmen.'

He hurried to explain the diminutive: 'It's just a Portuguese way of expressing affection. We've been a feature of Lisbon life for centuries. We take the students as youngsters of twelve or thirteen, and the ones that stay the course leave us when they're ordained priest at twenty-five.'

'Fascinating,' the stranger said. 'I'm Heinz Koenig.' There was a bob of the head and a click of heels. The men shook hands. 'I represent the Augsburger Druckmaschinen A.G. here in Lisbon. Our office is at the top of the Avenida da Liberdade.'

Harrington frowned at the German name.

'You've never heard of our famous Augsburger printing machine company?' Koenig asked. 'Our machines are the best of their kind in the world, like your Rolls-Royce motor cars, you know.'

'I'm sorry,' Harrington apologised, 'I don't know much about technical matters. I teach moral theology to our senior students, with Latin and English Literature thrown in for the younger ones.'

He'd heard there were increasing numbers of Germans in the city. The last time he'd been to the British Embassy on the corner of Rua Francisco de Borja and Rua da Arriaga in the aristocratic Lapa district on the other side of town, to have his passport renewed, he'd noticed that the nearby German Legation in Rua do Sacramento was adorned with swastika flags. The pleasant young woman in the consular office of the Embassy, who'd introduced herself as Miss Singleton, had made a wry comment about what she'd called 'the local decorations around the corner' as she dealt efficiently with his application.

'You shouldn't apologise,' Koenig assured him. 'Directing the minds of your students in moral matters is important. Especially at this time.'

'Why d'you say that?' With breakfast on his mind he'd spoken more sharply than he'd intended.

'Because of the way things are,' Koenig said. 'Our two countries, with so much in common and yet so far apart. Chamberlain's trying for peace, Churchill's making warlike noises, while we Germans,' Koenig sighed, 'what can I say? I know the Führer isn't everybody's cup of tea. Maybe there are wrongs on both sides.'

'I don't know. Perhaps.' It seemed to Harrington far too early in the morning to be engaged in a political discussion with a total stranger, and a German at that. He couldn't help thinking though that Koenig was right about Churchill. Years of being out of the limelight had put Winston's nose quite out of joint and now he was making up for lost time with his belligerent talk.

Harrington knew most of his own Portuguese friends, the ones who thought of anything beyond their own backyard, would share the German's view. Only the other week, Antonio Fonseca, whose family owned vast estates in central Portugal and who had his ear close to the ground in matters political, had put it bluntly to him: 'Churchill's a bloody fool to want a war.'

War, he thought, *the last thing any of us want.* As a student, he'd lived in Lisbon through times when violence had stalked the streets and civil war was always just around the corner, until Dr Salazar had been called from teaching at Coimbra university to bring sense to the economy and, as prime minister, had brought political stability to the country, modestly declining the presidency while ensuring that every nugget of power remained firmly in his own capable hands.

'Well,' Harrington conceded, 'it's not all one-sided, I suppose. The English can be an arrogant lot at times.' With memories of family stories about his uncle Séan Corrigan and the siege of the Dublin Post Office in the 1916 Easter Rising – he'd been in Lisbon at the time but his parents had kept him informed of the tragedy - he sometimes felt more Irish than English. His father, who'd migrated to England from Kerry before the turn of the century, had always insisted you didn't bite the hand that fed you, but even as a boy Harrington had found that to be cold counsel when sitting in the outside lav of a Salford back-to-back in the middle of winter. And as he recalled, the feeding hadn't gone as far as luxuries on the pay a docker earned on the Manchester Ship Canal. Only an unusually caring parish priest and a scholarship to the Lisbon college had opened the way for young Michael to escape from a similar servitude.

'I've offended you, perhaps?' Koenig asked anxiously.

'No, no,' Harrington protested, 'not at all.' It was difficult to explain to a foreigner. 'I've Irish roots, you see. One can't help but be critical, from time to time. And what,' he said, seeking rapidly to change the subject, 'might you be doing in this part of the city, if I may ask?'

'I'm visiting one of our clients.' Koenig gestured through the open window of the print shop from where the busy clack-clack of machinery could be heard. Harrington could see a poster tacked to the door, advertising *Every kind of circular, wedding or funeral announcement, in black and white or in colour, in small or large quantity. Enter without obligation.* The whole thing was very neatly printed in a variety of typefaces, illustrating the scope of the firm's abilities.

'I used to represent Augsburger Druckmaschinen in London, until I was sent here a year ago.'

This answered an unspoken question; Harrington had wondered how it was that the man spoke such excellent English.

'I did good business there. Your English printers have great respect for our machines.' Koenig hesitated. 'I had a lot of friends in London. I wonder, here in Lisbon, despite the blunders our wonderful leaders seem intent on making, perhaps we could meet occasionally, as friends, for a drink?'

Harrington shrugged. 'I don't see why not.'

'Well, then,' Koenig beamed, 'I've got to get on now, but tomorrow, how about the Cervejaria Trindade? You know it?

Just round the corner from here, in the Rua Nova da Trindade. My treat. Say, at six o'clock, for a beer?'

They shook hands and Harrington echoed, 'Tomorrow. I'll be there.' It was always good to meet fresh faces, make acquaintance with someone from a different background. They shook hands and each turned to carry on their separate ways.

2

Harrington resumed his walk along Rua da Rosa, his regular route back to the college from the convent of the Sisters of Divine Mercy on Rua Luisa Todi, where every morning he said the seven o'clock Mass.

His thoughts were on the man he'd seen beating his poor mule, and that led on to thoughts of Dona Elisabete. He knew she wouldn't have liked to have seen that. Harrington remembered how the first time he'd met her she had waxed indignant about the treatment of beasts of burden in Portugal. 'It's disgraceful,' she'd asserted, her cheeks flushed pink. 'We're supposed to be a Christian nation and yet the animals so many of us depend on for our livelihoods are treated in the most unchristian way.'

This had been at a dinner party given by Dona Maria Winter, the matriarch of the Anglo-Portuguese community in Lisbon, whose house overlooking the greenery of the Praça do Principe Real was the venue for soirées with her favourites.

Dona Maria was a formidable woman. If Harrington were asked to describe her, he would have suggested the enquirer should imagine a plump-faced rounded little body, a slimmer version of Queen Victoria's Jubilee portrait, minus the crown. He wasn't sure of her exact age but she had to be in her seventies, and she was as robustly imperious in her manner as ever the old queen-empress had been. He liked to imagine her as a spider in the middle of her web, minutely informed of all that was going. The college staff were frequently invited but that evening Harrington had come alone.

Dona Elisabete's outburst had been met with some amusement around the table. Someone asked whether she thought almshouses should be established for mules and donkeys. 'And what about superannuated bulls?' another wit had added. It was common knowledge that although the fighting bulls were not killed in the Portuguese *corrida* they were afterwards slaughtered and the meat distributed to the poor. An animal that had endured the torments of the arena knew too much to be allowed back in a second time.

Dona Elisabete had flushed a deeper pink at the ribaldry and, his chivalrous instincts aroused, he'd come to the lady's rescue. 'Dona Elisabete is right,' he said. 'You can't cure all the ills in the world all at once but you should in duty bound do what you can where you can.'

Dona Elisabete's grateful smile had been a reward to make him blush himself. Harrington hadn't known it at the time but it happened that her father's cousin ran a stud farm somewhere in the Alentejo whose animals were renowned for their ferocity.

Harrington suspected Dona Elisabete was being assessed as a suitable match for one of Maria Winter's tribe of unattached nephews. About thirty years old, he reckoned, the lady certainly was a very Portuguese beauty; of medium height and strikingly good looking with her jet-black hair, brown eyes and the sort of warm complexion that carried a hint of Moorish ancestry. He didn't know anything about women's clothes but even he could tell that the cut, style and quality of what Dona Elisabete wore were above average.

Dona Elisabete's hands displayed several jewelled rings but there was no sign of a wedding band and at their first meeting Harrington had been distinctly surprised that such a stunning woman wasn't accompanied by a husband. Was she a widow? he'd wondered. Her full name, he knew, was Dona Elisabete Louçá e Medronho but though Harrington had now known her for around six months she'd never confided what precisely had happened to Senhor Medronho and he didn't like to press the matter.

Harrington was finding Dona Elisabete Louçá e Medronho entering his thoughts more and more frequently, at moments he'd least expected and for reasons not unconnected with those sprouting little seeds of doubt that were beginning to disturb his life. He'd even begun dreaming of her recently; generally nothing he could remember with any clarity - nothing more than a vague impression of a warm and tender presence. Last night's dream, though, had been much more specific. She'd appeared in a sunlit woodland glade, wrapped in something diaphanous, at once hiding and revealing her supple body as she danced lightly towards him over the grass. There had been more of that he was sure, but what exactly Harrington didn't want to recall, ashamed of finding himself awakening in such an aroused state.

When he'd mentioned to her that his duties took him to the Convent of Divine Mercy and he'd explained the work the nuns did among the poor in the city, Dona Elisabete had insisted there and then on emptying her purse, instructing him to give the money to the Mother Superior and promising she would set up an arrangement with her bank for a more permanent contribution to the Sisters' work.

The Sisters, familiar figures around the city in their distinctive grey habits and wide-brimmed coifs, relied entirely on the munificence of Lisbon's leisured classes to fund their work. Harrington had been tending to their spiritual needs for several years, greatly admiring their single-minded devotion to duty.

Admiring the nuns' work didn't extend to accepting their daily offer of breakfast, though. A stale roll and a cup of weak coffee, to be taken in solitary state in a cubicle not much bigger than a phone box and served by the humourless Sister

Assumpta, wasn't Harrington's idea of a pleasant, or nourishing, start to the day. The professors' dining room in college, with its dark furniture and marble floor, didn't offer luxurious fare but the bread was always fresh from the bakery next door and there might be English marmalade on the table as well as Portuguese quince jelly.

3

It occurred to him that London must surely be a far more important place for the sale of printing machinery than Lisbon could ever be. So Koenig's move to Portugal could hardly be by way of promotion. Hadn't there been a faint hint that he wasn't in the city by choice? Perhaps he'd blotted his copybook in some way. Harrington supposed if Koenig had been shunted to Lisbon because of some inappropriate behaviour or sharp practice in London it was understandable the German should now think of himself as an exile. *But if he thinks I'm an exile too he's completely off track,* he reflected.

His own history was quite different. He'd arrived in Lisbon on a muggy, hot September evening back in 1913, aboard RMS *Hildebrand,* a Booth Line boat. The voyage from Liverpool had taken four days. He retained a vivid memory of saying farewell to Britain as he stood on deck, looking down at the diminutive figures of his parents standing forlornly amid the bustle of the dockside. After all these years he still felt a twinge of conscience at the ease with which he had turned away, more eager to be making friends with the three boys who were to be his companions for the next twelve years than to wave a last goodbye to mum and dad.

An elderly priest, himself a former student of the college, had undertaken to be their guardian on the voyage but the old man had taken to his bunk the moment *Hildebrand* encountered the first ocean swell and for four days Harrington and his new friends had had the run of the ship, being spoiled rotten by a Portuguese lady who bought them sweets and chocolate from the purser's store.

He turned into the Travessa dos Inglesinhos, *the street of the little Englishmen,* named for the untold generations of young men who had found their way to this corner of the Bairro Alto, and hurried along towards the college.

Not for the first time, he thought the place resembled a fortress, its high stone walls protecting the inhabitants from the world of the Bairro and its sometimes raucous population. Round the back, where the kitchen was situated, there were heavy wooden gates leading into the yard but here at the front the only way in, apart from the steps up to the chapel, was by way of the narrow door he now used, opening onto a flight of steps at the top of which the college porter, Manuel Cordeiro, had his cubbyhole.

'*Muito bom dia, o senhor padre Arrington,*' Cordeiro greeted him in his usual cheery way. A wiry little man, his hair liberally sown with grey, a little bent now; he'd been a college servant as long as Harrington could remember.

Harrington wished Cordeiro a very good morning in return and asked him how he was. 'Your back isn't troubling you too much?' Cordeiro had been complaining about his arthritis recently.

Cordeiro gave a resigned shrug. 'I suppose I mustn't grumble, senhor padre. We're all getting older, even you. Yes, yes, padre, I remember you when you were no more than a nipper.'

Harrington couldn't help but smile. It was true; he recalled that first day in college, catching sight of Cordeiro, who had only been a *moço* then, one of the kitchen staff, but who'd seemed very grown-up to a mere lad.

'I've taken the letters up to your room, senhor padre. I say, I've taken them already.'

'Very good of you, Manuel. Keep up the good work.'

What would we do here in college without our servants? Harrington wondered. Their pay was pitifully small, he knew, but their loyalty was unbounded. He felt privileged to have such people looking after him.

Passing through the vaulted hall called the Arches whose large windows looked out over the garden with its carefully tended beds of flowers, palm trees and shady walks, he turned up the stairway leading to the broad first floor corridor. There, opposite the stairs, was the room that had always been called the college President's Parlour; while on the left, next to the door into Harrington's own quarters, stood a grandfather clock, *Thomas Clapton, Oswestry 1789* inscribed across its yellowed face. It only kept anything remotely resembling good time by being constantly corrected, usually by Harrington himself. He checked with his wristwatch. 'You're slow today, Thomas,' he said, and nudged the minute hand on another five minutes. The clock must have been quite a novelty when it was introduced to an establishment that was then already a hundred and sixty years old and now, like so many things about the college, regardless of its usefulness, the old thing was part of college tradition.

He opened the door to his quarters, no more than a book-lined office-cum-sitting room whose tall window overlooked the street below, with a little bedroom and bathroom behind. On his desk he found the pile of correspondence Cordeiro had placed there earlier. Most of the English letters - Harrington squinted at the Post Office date stamps - were at least a couple of weeks old. There were hopes the mail service might soon significantly improve. He'd been told British Airways Ltd had recently made a couple of experimental flights from Croydon to the Averca aerodrome near Sintra and, if it became a regular run, he guessed they might one day be getting letters within a couple of days of posting.

One of Harrington's duties at the college was to censor the students' incoming mail, a responsibility he'd had for several years. He imagined the censorship of the students' mail must have originated in the dark days of the college's seventeenth century beginnings, when a Catholic priest returning to England to minister in secret could if caught, be found guilty of treason and suffer the appalling punishment of being hanged, drawn and quartered. It must have been a time of dreadful fear of infiltrators, who might in reality be English government agents out to trap the unwary. Perhaps too, Harrington reflected, in more recent days the college might simply have been concerned about girls writing to students who were destined to live celibate lives.

On taking up the duties of censor he'd been presented with the ivory letter opener his predecessor had used, but Harrington didn't take this responsibility very seriously and certainly didn't practise it with any energy. It was enough, he thought, to give the envelopes a cursory glance, and not even bother to open them, let alone read their contents, before handing them over to one of the senior students for distribution. He heard the old clock strike eight-thirty. Late for breakfast, Harrington darted into his bedroom, shrugged into his cassock that had been hanging on the back of the door and took a quick look at himself in the mirror, deciding with a touch of pardonable vanity that the tinge of grey in the dark-brown hair above his ears lent a certain gravity to his rather pale face.

Conscious he hadn't prepared much for his morning lecture to his Upper House students, some of whom who were in their final year before ordination to the priesthood, he grabbed the textbook, a nineteenth century work of moral theology by a Jesuit priest named Hieronymus Noldin, to take down to the dining room so he could riffle through the pages over his coffee. They'd been looking lately at the chapter on the commandment: *Thou shalt not bear false witness.*

Was there ever an occasion, he would ask his students, when withholding the truth could be justified? To illustrate the point he could set them one of his ingenious case-studies. *Honestus, a priest persecuted by reason of the cruel laws of his land, dresses in fine clothes and wears a dagger at his belt. He has been arrested in the house of Lucida, a widowed noble lady, who shelters him in the guise of tutor to her children, Obnoxius and Candida. The magistrate Perfidius demands that Honestus confess to being a priest, but he insists he is merely tutor to Lucida's children and has no knowledge of what Perfidius is demanding.*

With any luck the students would go on a wild goose chase after some detail or other, distracted by the fine clothes or perhaps by Lucida's widowed state. One of them - Charlie Russell probably, he'd never shown much promise of intellectual rigour - would question why a priest should be wearing a dagger. Harrington hoped it would be Peter Fielding who pointed out that Perfidius, implementing an unjust law, had no right to the information he was seeking and thus Honestus was justified in concealing his true identity. One way or another, it would keep them all busy for a half hour or so.

He deposited the mail on the shelf beside old Thomas and hurried along the corridor and down the stairs to the dining room. It was wrong to have favourites, Harrington knew, but he regarded Fielding as one of his brightest students: intelligent, alert and cooperative, and surely destined for great things, at very least a degree from one of the Roman universities, and after a few years working in a parish, a call to higher things. It would be a pleasure to be able to boast having had some small part in his development.

4

That Easter, the task of supervising the students for their week's break on the other side of the River Tagus at the college's holiday house in Pêra became the responsibility of Bob Knox, the professor of Scripture and Church History, leaving Harrington free to accept an invitation to the Quinta de Laranjeiras, Antonio Fonseca's ancestral property outside Sintra, some twenty miles north of Lisbon. *Michael, do come and stay with us for a few days,* Fonseca had written. Harrington suspected the wealthy landowner - they'd met the previous year at an Elgar concert sponsored by the British Council - regarded him as a bit of a trophy, his 'English priest.'

The dramatic Moorish-style façade to the Rossio railway station in the city centre always reminded Harrington more of a theatre than the entrance to a mundane transport system. He climbed the steps, bought his ticket and went to platform two. He was only just in time. Within seconds of finding himself a seat, the engine issued a huge belch of smoke and steam and they were off.

The carriage wasn't crowded and the half-hour journey into the countryside north of Lisbon was pleasant enough, apart from having to listen to a party of American tourists who spent their time complaining loudly that the aftermath of the civil war in Spain had stopped them taking in the glories of Toledo and Salamanca.

Harrington knew the quaint little town of Sintra fairly well and he'd never ceased to marvel at the Paço Real, the royal palace which monarchs had transformed over nearly a thousand years into a fairytale conglomeration dominated by the two gigantic conical chimneys featured in all the guide-books. Like any tourist, he'd done the tour of the palace and had speculated on what gargantuan feasts must have been prepared in those kitchens to require such spectacular smoke holes.

There was no time for sight-seeing this Easter Monday though. Fonseca was waiting for him in his immaculate open-topped cream-coloured Hispano Suiza K6 motor car, dressed in what Harrington imagined Fonseca probably believed to be the country outfit of an English gentleman: a jacket of loud check, dark green trousers and a loosely knotted vibrant yellow scarf. His dark hair gleamed with what, to judge by the discreet perfume, must have been an expensive dressing. He gave Harrington an enthusiastic handshake and relieved him of his suitcase, tossing it on to the brown leather of the back seat.

'I could do a hundred and fifty kilometres an hour in this beautiful beast,' Fonseca confided as they roared out of the station forecourt, 'if there were any roads in this country that would permit it.' It was his latest favourite toy. 'Six cylinders, one hundred and twenty horsepower and four-wheel drum brakes. Marvellous!'

All of which meant nothing to Harrington. Though he appreciated the exceptional comfort, the massive vehicle that was Fonseca's pride and joy seemed to Harrington out of all proportion to the narrow roads they were negotiating.

Harrington wondered what his parents would have made of the Fonseca residence. The Quinta de Laranjeiras was practically a palace. The rambling three-storey building, on the outskirts of the village that gave its name to the property, was painted a pale pink which, Harrington reflected, would have looked ridiculous in Salford but was perfectly in keeping here in Portugal. The mansion dated from the eighteenth century and replaced what had doubtless been a fortified manor house in earlier times. Everything hereabouts had been Fonseca land from earliest recorded history. From what he'd been told, Harrington gathered the entire neighbourhood still lived in a state not far removed from medieval serfdom.

Fonseca brought the car to a halt at the foot of the shallow steps leading to the main door where Dona Carmelita, Fonseca's wife, slender and elegant in a becoming blue dress, her light brown hair betraying her origins in the north of the country, a ready smile on her heart-shaped face, stood to welcome him with the twins, Carlos and Daniel, beside her. At five years old they preferred to hide behind their mother's skirts when Harrington came up the steps but Carmelita gently pushed them forward so they could shake hands with the visiting priest and whisper a shy '*bom dia*' before running back to the shelter of their mother.

'It's always so good to see you, Father,' Carmelita greeted him in turn, offering her cheek for a kiss. About Dona Elisabete's age, she was, Harrington knew, the product of the Irish Dominicans' convent school of Bom Sucesso in Belém, some ten miles down the coast beyond Lisbon's south-western suburbs. She spoke delightful English, with just a hint of the soft accent she had unconsciously picked up from the nuns who'd taught her.

'And it's so good of you to invite me,' Harrington said. The invitation had come officially from Antonio but he guessed it was Carmelita who had inspired it. 'And the boys! Just look at them. They must have grown an inch since Christmas.' Quite at ease with his students, Harrington was never quite sure how to treat little children.

Carmelita sensed his discomfort and smiled. 'Oh, just ignore them, Father; they'll come out when they're ready.'

She was a good mother, thought Harrington. When he'd been at Laranjeiras at Christmas he'd seen her chasing them with shrieks of laughter around the gravelled paths between the box hedges of the formal garden behind the house. She was firm but patient with the little boys, like now; not forcing them to be on parade but neither letting them run away.

Harrington also appreciated the way Carmelita ran her household. If previous visits were anything to go by, his room would be immaculate, the sheets on the bed turned down in readiness and, a charming feminine touch, a flower of some sort on the pillow. Fonseca was a lucky chap, Harrington reflected. Celibacy and the priesthood went necessarily hand in hand and he knew he had chosen the more noble path, but all the same, at the age of forty, he sometimes felt a pang of jealousy when he saw Carmelita and Antonio together.

Carmelita's charm only served to remind Harrington of his increasing sense of losing some significant control of his life; Dona Elisabete was becoming a disconcerting and growing presence in his thoughts, as those dreams only went to show. It wasn't, of course, the first time he'd met a woman he found interesting and attractive. But this was something different, something that touched him personally in a way he'd never known before, something he knew to be at once enticing and risky.

Watching Carmelita and Antonio together made him suddenly feel something he'd never felt as intensely before; like some lonely outsider, doomed as he grew older to an increasingly desiccated, arid and solitary life.

He envied the easy familiarity between the beautiful wife and the handsome husband. Antonio Fonseca put on a manly show of being the head of the family and in charge of things but Harrington could see how subtly and neatly Carmelita deferred to her husband while keeping her fingers firmly on the household pulse. What would it be like, he speculated, imagining himself in Antonio's place, to have Dona Elisabete as his Carmelita?

Inevitably, such thoughts led to guilt kicking in, the guilt bred into him by the Church, the *mea culpa, mea culpa, mea maxima culpa,* of the Latin confession of faults he recited daily at Mass.

Soon after his arrival, luncheon was served on the broad south terrace overlooking the acres of orange groves that gave the village its name.

'It's rather early in the year to be eating outside,' Carmelita explained, 'but the weather's so beautiful at the moment and with the orange trees in blossom the air is delightful.' It was true, the orange groves surrounding the estate were in full flower, though privately Harrington found the perfume slightly cloying.

The main dish, after an elegant little parcel of poached fish in a delicate buttery parsley sauce, was a delicious Alentejano-style pork stew, flavoured with a wonderful garlicky tomato sauce - Harrington reflected that Fonseca's French chef had clearly learned to adapt traditional Portuguese menus.

The twins joined them for the meal, as was the custom, and English was the language spoken round the table. Harrington couldn't imagine how much the little boys could understand but Carmelita claimed it was good training for them. Her own English was perfect and Fonseca had a forceful and ready, if accented, command of the language.

Fonseca himself was full of a reception he'd attended at the German Legation the previous week. 'You know, Father, I can understand the Germans' ambitions,' Fonscea declared. 'They're entitled to expect their place on the world stage. Portugal was a great nation once, as you know, and we're going to be again, now Salazar's got a firm grip on things. After all, we've still got our empire. We may have lost Brazil but we still have Angola, Mozambique and Timor, Macau and Goa. The secret, you know Father, is to make sure we keep the natives under control, just as Herr Hitler plans to do with the *Untermenschen* in Eastern Europe.'

Harrington willingly accepted the servant's offer of a second helping of the stew. 'Our own black pigs,' Fonseca explained, 'from our Alentejo estate. It's the acorns they feed on there that gives the meat that depth of flavour.' The rich stew was dotted with tiny clams. 'They add the finishing touch, don't you think?' Fonseca asked as he in turn loaded his own plate. Carmelita shyly remarked she thought the garlic might be a little overdone for English tastes but Harrington asserted loyally that the dish was perfect.

'That word you used just now,' he asked Fonseca. '*Untermenschen.*' Instinctively, Harrington found the word repellent even though he didn't know what it meant. 'It's German, isn't it?'

'*Untermenschen?* Yes. "Lesser breeds" I suppose you'd say, in English. I know the Germans tend to have a feeling of superiority about themselves but being Portuguese, I know I too want to feel proud of my own nation and, all right, I admit it, share also a sense of superiority. Let's remember, Father, the very name of those Eastern Europeans, "Slavs", gives us the word slave in English, and of course, in Portuguese, it's *esclavo*. I'm not suggesting the lesser breeds should be held to blame for being such, but the fact remains that's what they are and they need to be controlled. Mussolini has much the same idea in Africa.'

Harrington gave a polite nod. He felt distinctly uneasy with this whole subject. He didn't pretend to have any understanding of eugenics but he'd never trusted the Germans' automatic willingness to take for granted they were a special race and that other people should pay them something like homage. He wanted to argue against the things Fonseca was saying, but he liked Antonio and he also understood that Portugal had indeed once been a major nation of the world and that many Portuguese felt sad because it no longer was. They even had a word for it: *saudades*, a melancholy nostalgia for the irretrievable past.

Harrington knew most Portuguese thought Franco's campaign against godless socialism in Spain had been justified; it had certainly met with general approval in the *Diário de Notícias*, the daily newspaper that was the unofficial mouthpiece of the government, and all the other Portuguese newspapers he'd read had followed suit. The same newspapers said little of Portuguese policy in Angola and Mozambique, but reported in great detail Mussolini's conquests in Libya and Ethiopia, and it troubled Harrington to think Fonseca might condone anything like such brutal behaviour in Portugal's colonies. However, 'you can't make omelettes without breaking eggs', as his host reminded him when he ventured to make a mild criticism.

And what do I know about politics on the world scale? Harrington thought. He knew Fonseca moved within the corridors of power in Portugal and, to judge by the names he dropped in casual conversation, he was in contact with people of influence across Europe.

Perhaps Fonseca was right; in the long run the benefits did sometimes outweigh the violent means adopted. Ireland was a case in point, Harrington supposed. After rebelling against English rule, people like Michael Collins and de Valera had fought a bloody civil war against each other, from which a free Irish State had at last emerged.

So he learned to keep quiet. He celebrated Mass each day for the family in the exquisite little Baroque chapel attached to the house, did his best to play with the children, strolled around the orange groves, chatted with the estate workers, and at the end of the week Fonseca invited him to come back and spend some of the summer break at Laranjeiras. 'You can be our chaplain for a week or two, a month, why not?'

'Do come, Father,' Carmelita joined in, 'and that way you can get to know the boys a little better and help them practise their English.'

Fonseca offered to drive him all the way back to the college in the Suiza but Harrington declined, conscious of the likely effect the arrival of such an exotic vehicle would make in the narrow alleys of the Bairro. So he took the train from Sintra to Rossio and then a taxi up to the Travessa dos Inglesinhos.

5

Harrington could hear the commotion even before he walked through the open gates into the college yard where the students were unloading the cart that had brought up their belongings from the ferry terminal at Praça do Comercio, the vast riverside space he, like all the English in Lisbon, called Black Horse Square on account of its dominating central equestrian bronze statue of King José I.

They were like boisterous kids, he thought, after their free time at Pêra and being let loose on the wild coast of Caparica, their sunburned faces bearing witness to long treks along the miles of beach, into the countryside and up into the heights of the Arrabida mountain range. For a whole week they'd been able to wear what they wanted and spend their days more or less at liberty; now they were back in their sober black habits as they manhandled suitcases, boxes, pots and pans.

Not that the sober black habits always made these boys and young men behave in a sober way, Harrington reflected. He watched as Will Thompson, a lanky eighteen-year-old who'd just moved into Upper House, energetically defended his twelve-stringed guitar from being damaged in the scrum. Will, who'd taught himself to play the difficult instrument, had no doubt kept the community entertained of an evening under the stars in the farmhouse courtyard.

Peter Fielding, five foot ten, tall, solidly built, with a mop of black hair and a permanent faint shadow of a beard, almost Portuguese in appearance, stepped out of the mêlée holding a lump of rock. 'Look what we found. I reckon it's a fossil. What do you think, sir?'

Harrington examined the stone with polite curiosity. About six inches long, it looked like a monstrous growth of some sort. A bit of enormous vertebra perhaps, or some peculiar knuckle bone? He had no idea.

'I've brushed all the loose stuff off,' Fielding was explaining, 'and I was wondering, could we put it as an exhibit in the Natural History cabinet?'

Harrington knew he was referring to the cupboard on the second-floor landing containing a variety of odds and ends: a human skull, some folders of dried plants, books of geography, atlases, a tray of Roman coins and an eighteenth century model of the planetary system, probably introduced by the same college president who had built what they called the Observatory, the flat-roofed tower that provided panoramic views over the city and the river.

'It looks interesting, Mr Fielding, I agree, but you'll have to ask Father Pargeter,' Harrington told him. Pargeter was in charge of Lower House Humanities. The senior students assisted him, another college tradition, in supervising the young ones' evening studies, providing a modicum of extra tuition and correcting their prep. It was supposed to teach them responsibility, though Harrington realised the system also reduced the need for the extra staff the college could ill afford.

Fielding smiled. 'I'll do that, sir. But,' he persisted, 'don't you think it's interesting? Just think: weird and wonderful animals roaming about the countryside millions of years ago. We ought to know more about these things.'

'A very worthy thought, I'm sure,' Harrington said, then instantly regretted his rather patronising tone. For all he knew the lump of rock he'd just been shown might really be a piece of an ancient beast. Who was he to discourage another's enquiring mind? Fielding might be on the first steps to making a name for himself in palaeontology. After all, in its long history the college had produced alumni who had distinguished themselves in many disciplines; philosophy and mathematics and horology, as well as theology.

Charlie Russell, his fair cheeks burnt red by the sun, joined them at that moment, suitcase in hand. 'It's rubbish, isn't it, sir? I told him to chuck it in the river as we came over.'

'You never know,' Harrington retorted, determined to redeem himself in the eyes of his students. 'Mr Fielding might have something important there. A missing link of some sort.'

'Some hope!' Russell laughed and then fell serious. 'We've been cut off for a whole week, no newspapers, no wireless. Has there been any more news, sir? About how things are going? You know, Hitler and all that.'

Harrington hesitated. Fonseca had told him something about the Führer rejecting the Anglo-German Naval Agreement regulating the size of the Kriegsmarine, claiming it was the Germans' right to build a navy fit to protect the nation's interests. 'He reckons it belittles the nation to restrict their right to re-arm,' Fonseca had said, 'and, you know Father, I can understand how he feels.'

'There's nothing much new to report,' Harrington replied to Russell's question. There was no point, he thought, in spreading yet more doom and gloom.

'That's good,' Russell said carelessly. 'It won't come to anything, anyway, life will still go on as before.' He turned back to his friend. 'You aren't really going to ask Father Pargeter to make room for that rock, are you?'

Harrington left them to their wrangling. *Was I like that once?* he asked himself as he walked up the stairs to his rooms, *still acting like an adolescent in my twenties?* Fielding and Russell would soon be back in England as ordained priests and yet could still at times behave like children. The threat of an impending war seemed to mean little or nothing to them.

Perhaps he'd been just as immature himself in his own student days, Harrington reflected. He'd developed an interest in chess, and had spent more of his time poring over the chessboard than running wild on Caparica beach. His mentor and principal opponent had been Frank Hardacre, who left the college precipitously a couple of years before he was due to be ordained. Harrington remembered vividly the day Frank had barged into his room, declaring, 'Sod this! I'm off to do something with my life.'

The last Harrington had heard, Frank had been making a name for himself in the City. *Might these lads not be better off following Hardacre's example?* Such a treacherous thought surprised and alarmed him, but his week away from the college had left him in a strangely dissatisfied mood.

He got back to his room to discover the heap of mail that had been piling up in his absence. There was nothing for him, which hardly surprised him; he'd more or less severed what few ties he had back home. His mother, still in the old Salford house, wrote rarely and when she did put pen to paper her letters had little to say. He was conscious that his own replies were equally meagre in content. One or two of the students would be able to catch up with the fortunes of their favourite football teams to judge by the rolled-up sporting papers he saw among the letters. Much good may that do them, he thought as he put everything on the ledge outside his office next to the clock.

Harrington was aware his encounter with Fielding and Russell only served to deepen the sombre mood he'd fallen into, the result of his week at Laranjeiras, observing the easy give-and-take, the subtle interplay of each other's qualities, that made Antonio and Carmelita's marriage so much to be envied.

Thinking about Done Elisabete hadn't made life any easier either. Late in the day - too late, Harrington was beginning to understand - he was being made to confront what celibacy demanded of him. Fielding and Russell, what did they know about anything beyond the shelter of the college walls? What did he himself know, really, about anything? Scraps scavenged from Maria Winter's table-talk, fragments gleaned from Antonio Fonseca's political pronouncements. The world, the real world was as much a mystery to him as it had been when he'd been a student. *Shelter*, he asked himself, *this place is more like prison.* It shocked him to be thinking like that; not so long ago he would have refuted any such derogatory comment about the place that had for long been the centre of his life.

6

At their next meeting in the Cervejaria Trindade, Koenig was anxious to quiz Harrington about college life. 'Didn't you long to return to your native country?' Koenig added after Harrington had explained how he'd arrived in the city and the years he'd spent as a student. 'It seems monstrous, to tear a boy away from his parents at such a young age.'

'You may be right,' Harrington replied thoughtfully, 'but you have to understand the college was founded in the days of religious persecution in England. At first they only took grown men who had managed to escape the authorities in England.'

'How did they escape?' Koenig asked.

'You needed written permission from a magistrate to leave the country in those days. Or you had to find a way to get out secretly.'

'Is that so?' Koenig said, sounding definitely interested.

Harrington nodded. 'Yes, and as for accepting youngsters, well, a Catholic parent who wanted his son educated had a choice; either let the boy be brought up by Protestants or send him abroad where he could be taught according to Catholic principles. So the college began to accept boys whose fathers had found ways to get them out of the country. Some of them stayed on to train for the priesthood. We still take boys but, of course, the lads who come to us now are all intending to carry on to ordination. That's the way I came here. As for being homesick, yes, at first, it was only natural,' he admitted, 'but then you soon got used to the way of life; it became part of you. I can't say I miss England much.'

'What about missing women?' Koenig asked. 'What's it like to live without female companionship?'

It wasn't a question he'd ever been asked before. Harrington was silent for a moment. 'You get used to it,' he replied, with a shrug. He stopped there, unwilling to reveal anything of his own recent doubts on the wisdom of such an upbringing.

'When I said your native country,' Koenig said, 'I was thinking of Ireland. You mentioned earlier - your roots, I think you said.'

'Oh, I see. Well, my father was Irish. My mother was born in England. And that's where I was born, too.'

'But your mother, was she of Irish parentage, too?'

Harrington nodded.

'We have a saying about this in my country. How does it go in English? Ah, yes: *If the cat has her kittens in the oven, she doesn't call them biscuits.*' He saw Harrington's puzzled frown. 'The little ones, they are still kittens wherever they are born, you see. So,' Koenig concluded triumphantly, 'It's the blood that counts, my friend, not the place your mother gave birth to you. At heart you're Irish.'

Harrington wasn't sure. True, it had been drummed into him as a child that Ireland, the country he had never visited, was home in a way the grimy streets of Salford never could be. 'Remember where you're from,' his father had never failed to remind him.

It had been the same at school; shamrock and the green, white and gold for St Patrick's Day, with snatches of Gaelic patriotic songs to season the feast. The Irish knew well how to do their own version of *saudades*. Even here in Lisbon the entire college trooped down every year on the seventeenth of March to the Irish Dominican church in Rua do Corpo Santo, to celebrate St Pat with sung Mass, wine and cakes and Sweet Afton cigarettes.

But, in the end he had to accept that England was the country which had nurtured him, however poorly, and the college was an English foundation through and through. He tried to express something of what he felt but he could see Koenig looking at him quizzically. 'I know, I know,' he said, 'I sound confused and I suppose you think I'm simple-minded.'

'My friend, I think we have much in common. Our nations may soon be at war but I wouldn't question your moral values, any more than you'd cast doubts on my engineering abilities.'

'Are you an engineer, Heinz? I thought you were a salesman.'

'I'm both, my friend,' Koenig conceded with a smile. 'I find that I can only be a good salesman of the products I'm selling if I understand how they work, how all the little wheels go round. At which point,' he raised his glass of beer an inch or two from the table, 'I ought to say *Heil Hitler*! There's a portrait of him in my apartment,' he told Harrington solemnly, 'which I salute every morning. The portrait's provided by the company. My devotion's quite personal, I assure you.' The irony in his tone was emphasised by the way his solemn expression devolved into giggles. 'Your King George is, of course, of quite a different calibre. What a shame things didn't work out differently, though. You might still have had Edward on the throne.'

'It was the question of divorce,' Harrington told him, wondering why foreigners were so obsessed with the man who so shamefully had abdicated the throne. 'It wouldn't have done, you see, not at all.' It was a point on which his own Church and the Anglicans both agreed.

'You know your former king has been to see the Führer?'

'Yes, there was something about it in the *Diário de Notícias*.' Along with the occasional English newspaper and the nightly ritual of tuning into the BBC's short wave Empire Service broadcast in the President's Parlour, the *Diário*, a staunch supporter of Salazar's New State, was Harrington's regular source of information, a very reliable newspaper. Although other journals frequently appeared with half the front page reduced to white space by the censors, there was scarcely ever the slightest gap in the *Diário*'s news columns.

The last time the matter of the abdication had arisen at her dinner table, Maria Winter had been trenchant in her condemnation of the luckless former king. 'The man's a bounder,' she'd declared, 'and it's not by the nose the Simpson woman leads him. Quite another part of his anatomy.'

According to Maria, who seemed to know everything there was to know in the way of gossip, Mrs Simpson had spread her favours widely both before and after striking up with the man who had been briefly king. 'He's half German of course,' she declared decisively as though that adequately explained his delinquency, 'and some of his cousins are close to Hitler.'

It had occurred to Harrington that if the now Duke of Windsor were to be condemned for being half German, the same charge would logically lie at brother George's door, but it seemed more prudent to keep such a thought to himself, especially in Maria Winter's presence.

'Ah well, the English,' Koenig said lightly, 'there's no accounting for them.'

'Indeed,' Harrington replied in what he hoped was the same vein, 'And where would we be without them?'

7

Nuns as a tribe, Harrington had discovered, generally took a disconcertingly dictatorial approach to the running of their affairs, and the Sisters of Divine Mercy weren't an exception; their chaplain was at their bidding, an assumption conveyed with such beguiling charm as to warrant no refusal.

On arrival at the convent a couple of days after his meeting with Koenig in the Cervejaria Trindade, Harrington was surprised to find Mother Teresa, the Convent Superior, waiting for him just inside the street door. 'Forgive me for intruding, senhor padre,' she said, her voice more animated than Harrington was used to hearing, 'but before you begin Mass there's something you should know.'

Bad news? he was about to ask but sensed the excitement in her voice wasn't to do with death or sickness.

'We have a new member of our congregation this morning. An eminent personage. I wonder if you've heard of her?'

'Oh, who is it?' Harrington asked, not really all that interested.

Mother Teresa smiled faintly. 'Dona Elisabete Louçá e Medronho. She's become one of our most generous benefactors.'

'She has?' he responded blandly, aware his heart had begun beating a good deal faster at the mention of her name.

'Yes,' Mother Teresa replied. 'She's graced us with her presence in chapel today and she tells me she's going to come all the way over from Lapa each morning in future.'

Harrington wondered exactly how much Dona Elisabete had pledged, or already given, to the convent, but his puzzlement on that score was already overwhelmed by the realisation he was about to offer Communion to the woman who was stirring his heart in a variety of ways he found most disconcerting.

'I'll leave you now,' Mother Teresa said, 'but I'd be grateful for a word in the parlour after Mass.' With a swish of her long grey habit, she turned and made her way into the depths of the convent.

Harrington had always thought the Sisters' chapel was nothing more than a poor miniature imitation of the magnificent city churches. The plaster walls of the sanctuary were crudely painted to resemble costly marble; instead of pure gold leaf, yellow paint decorated the twisted columns on either side of the altar and the altar itself was nothing more than painted wood. The covering of the steps leading to the altar was so threadbare that any pattern the carpet might once have carried was long-since worn to little more than vague arabesques of dusty blue and brown. In the nave, standing on cracked stone flags, there were enough plain wooden benches to accommodate perhaps thirty people and in the far corner stood a rarely used harmonium. The narrow windows on either side of the nave were only frosted glass instead of the glorious vibrant coloured panes a wealthier church might boast.

But that morning, the moment he stepped out of the sacristy in his Mass vestments and saw Dona Elisabete kneeling in the second row of the congregation, it was as if the place had instantly been transformed. She was wearing a dark grey dress, suitably demure for the occasion, and on her head she wore a black lace mantilla fringing her forehead and draped over her shoulders. She glanced up as he approached the altar steps and her lips creased into a tiny smile he hoped no one else could see.

At the beginning of the Mass, standing at the foot of the altar with his back to the congregation, Harrington was keenly aware of Dona Elisabete's presence in the chapel. As the Latin responses came pat he was sure he could hear her voice, a tone higher, clearer than the nuns. Coming to the most sacred moment of the liturgy the familiar words of the ritual, *hoc est enim corpus meum, hic est calix sanguinis mei,* 'this is my body, this is the cup of my blood', seemed today to be charged with a new meaning verging on the blasphemous.

Finally came the moment for the distribution of Communion. Dona Elisabete did not come up to the altar rails immediately but out of deference allowed the nuns who were there, seven or eight of them in all, to receive the sacrament before her. She came only in the second wave of devotees. Administering communion was usually a purely routine matter to Harrington, but when he came to Dona Elisabete, his whole being became electric. He took the small white circular wafer from the silver ciborium and with his right index finger and thumb placed it on Dona Elisabete's delicately protruding tongue. She had her large brown eyes fixed on him as she daintily withdrew the wafer into her mouth, appeared to chew it very briefly and then swallowed it.

Still unable to get Dona Elisabete out of his mind, he returned to the altar, put the ciborium back in the tabernacle and went through the mechanical actions of purifying the chalice, pouring in the water and then drinking it, drying the inside of the cup and placing the veil over it. Still with his back to the congregation, he read the final prayer and then turned – he saw Dona Elisabete's eyes meeting his own – and, aware his voice was wavering slightly, gave the blessing of dismissal.

After taking off his vestments, Harrington went in search of Mother Teresa. The parlour where the nuns entertained visitors, was a room Harrington had never thought exuded the least charm. The chairs grouped around the little table draped in blue oilcloth were hard and seemingly designed to ensure the sitter maintained a painfully upright posture. On one wall there was a large painting of a pale-faced Jesus surrounded by ragged but immaculate children of varying ages gazing up adoringly at his blue eyes. The facing wall featured a saccharine portrait of the Virgin, hands joined, eyes lifted heavenwards. And dominating all, on the wall above the door, hung a hideously realistic tortured Christ figure carved out of ivory, with red globules of what might have been rubies but were probably glass, set into the wounded flesh to represent drops of blood.

'Thank you, senhor padre, I'm so grateful you could spare the time to talk,' said Mother Teresa, 'I wished to say something about Dona Elisabete Louçá e Medronho.'

'You certainly have an eminent new congregation member,' Harrington said levelly, determined the Superior should guess nothing at all about what Dona Elisabete might be to him.

'Yes, indeed,' Mother Teresa replied, 'and I know how much good we shall be able to achieve because of her generosity, which is a blessing from the Lord, of that I'm convinced.'

'What do you know about her?' Harrington asked, still doing his utmost to ensure his voice had a professional objectivity about it. Mother Teresa was an even greater lover of gossip than Dona Maria Winter and he was confident that with the right approach, information would be forthcoming.

Mother Teresa beckoned him to take one of the chairs and, rather to his surprise, sat down opposite him. This, he surmised, was to be more than a perfunctory meeting.

The nun tucked the folds of her skirts around her and settled herself on the unyielding chair. *It's all very well for her,* Harrington thought as he shifted uncomfortably on his own unyielding seat, *she's used to going without comforts.*

'I think I may tell you,' she began, 'there's tragedy in Dona Elisabete's life.' She spoke in classical Portuguese, without a trace of a regional accent 'Of course, I realise you'll not know her, but I can tell you she's been most unfortunate.'

'What do you mean, unfortunate?' Harrington asked.

Mother Teresa gave a small and, Harrington thought, surprisingly delicate shrug. 'Her husband, he was one of the Viriatos.'

Harrington recognised the name: Viriato was the legendary leader of the Lusitanian people in heroic combat against the invading Romans more than two thousand years before. His name had been adopted by those Portuguese who had gone with Salazar's blessing to fight for Franco.

'Such a noble calling, defending truth and religious freedom against the lies and oppression of the godless communists,' Mother Teresa declared.

Harrington had been told several of the convents of the Sisters of Divine Mercy in Spain had been pillaged and the nuns raped by Republican forces in the course of the savage civil war. He had also been told of the ferocity of Franco's North African troops and their merciless slaughter of civilians.

'The poor man hasn't come back and the lady, naturally, is suffering in consequence.'

He'd wondered why Dona Elisabete had never mentioned the circumstances of her solitary state, why she didn't wear a wedding ring. Surely she should have been proud of a husband who had only left her to go on a military crusade? She'd never given any sign of distress but the lady was so discreet; if only he had known the circumstances he could have offered some spiritual consolation. Or, if he were to be totally honest with himself, might he have taken the opportunity to... to what?

Flirting was something he associated with his cousin Brigid preening herself for the attention of the young men who had been hanging around the house in Salford the last time he had been in England.

No, flirting was the wrong word to use in connection with Dona Elisabete, though there were times in the conviviality of after-dinner chat at Maria Winter's house when they'd indulged in moments of light-hearted conversation of the kind he imagined Dona Elisabete appreciated. She spoke some English but she was happier in her own tongue and Harrington enjoyed the opportunity to stretch his vocabulary beyond the demands of the usual exchanges with the college servants and the occasional sermon.

Mother Teresa hadn't finished. 'I have a favour to ask,' she said.

Harrington looked at her. There seemed something almost coy about the way her fingers were playing with the fringe of the oilcloth table cover and coyness was an attribute he would never have associated with the strong-willed nun.

'What can I do for you, Mother?' he asked politely. In his experience, favours for nuns rarely came without a burden of some sort and he was ready for a request that would be time-consuming and tedious. English lessons, perhaps; Mother Teresa had once expressed regret that she didn't speak the language, though the way things were going he thought German might be a more useful second tongue.

'It's not for myself,' Mother Teresa said quickly. 'It's for Dona Elisabete.'

'How can I help the lady?' It was all he could do to keep his voice even. Mother Teresa was about to tell him Dona Elisabete was going to join the convent and she was looking for someone to help dispose of all her assets.

'As I say, she's alone in the world. It would be an act of mercy if she had someone to talk to. You have what I would call the listening ear,' Mother Teresa said, 'which is exactly what Dona Elisabete requires.'

Harrington experienced a sudden shortness of breath. 'I'll be happy to give Dona Elisabete whatever support she may need,' he said cautiously. 'But as you know, there are requirements, necessary precautions, when a priest is counselling a lady. If the woman needs to confess there's a time and place, at a publicised hour in a church.'

Saying that made him feel a total hypocrite because he tingled at the thought of sitting down to a heart-to-heart with Dona Elisabete. He knew beyond doubt the first thing he'd want to ask her was to do with the mystery of Senhor Medronho's fate.

'She's a troubled soul,' Mother Teresa told him, 'and it's not all of her own making. It's not confession she's after. I think all she needs is to talk to someone who will listen, someone who isn't involved.'

He could hardly admit he was involved, however innocently. Never having lived in close proximity to a woman apart from his mother, and having undergone an education and training specifically designed to minimise contact with women, Harrington had always been distinctly cautious as far as the fair sex was concerned but he was accepting more and more that Dona Elisabete was very very special to him. She was vivacious, able to hold her own in the conversation around Maria Winter's table, a good person to know better.

He'd listened and watched in admiration every time Dona Elisabete made an apparently innocuous response to one of the more fatuous statements put out by the dinner guests: innocuous that is until he heard the slightly extravagant lift of the voice, noticed the subtle emphasis on certain words and seen the characteristic tilt of the head signalling her true opinion on the matter. She'd even winked at him once across the table, drawing him in as a conspirator in her mild anarchy.

'Reverend Mother,' said Harrington, 'if that's what you wish, I shall of course be happy to offer my services.'

'Thank you, senhor padre. I've been presumptuous enough to tell her you will be available tomorrow afternoon, here in the parlour, at five o'clock.'

Harrington smiled inwardly. He might have known; that was the way nuns worked, all planned and settled beforehand. Mother Teresa had never considered the possibility of a refusal and for once her machinations chimed perfectly with his inclinations.

8

Dona Elisabete was already in the parlour when Harrington arrived to keep the appointment. He found the atmosphere in the cheerless little room stifling; the one window was paint-jammed tight shut and even with the door ajar the air was heavy with Dona Elisabete's perfume. He wondered if the lace mantilla covering her black hair and her shoulders was intended to be in some way a reminder of the solemnity of the occasion, a guarantor of the proprieties. But it left her beautiful face clear so he had open sight of her large brown eyes.

She was still wearing that plain dark grey dress, deliberately designed, so it seemed to Harrington, to accentuate her beauty by setting it in relief. Her full lips seemed too natural to owe anything to lipstick.

'Dona Elisabete, can I ask you something?' he murmured in an attempt to turn his thoughts away from admiration of her beauty.

'By all means,' she said.

'You did tell me you were going to support the Sisters of Divine Mercy, and I know they are immensely grateful for your patronage. But I wonder why you've chosen to come all the way from Lapa to join us here at Mass. Surely there must be churches nearer to your home? I know the Estrela basilica has several Masses every morning.'

'You don't want me to be here in the congregation?' Dona Elisabete asked, a slightly teasing tone in her voice.

'Of course I don't mind you being here. It's your right. I just wasn't expecting to see you, that's all.'

She looked at him intently then suddenly murmured: 'I think it's time I told you more about myself.'

He couldn't help nodding eagerly. 'Yes, please do. I'm completely at your service. So,' he gave a slight shrug, 'how shall we proceed?'

He heard the awkwardness in his question. The truth was, he realised, he didn't really know what to say next or what to do. It was one thing to dream about having Dona Elisabete to himself but, for all the pleasure it gave him, he was discovering being with her in the privacy of the parlour was somehow quite intimidating.

Fortunately, it was Dona Elisabete who broke the silence. 'This place isn't exactly like Dona Maria's dinner table, is it, senhor padre?' she said, with a little smile.

'No, it isn't,' he agreed, 'but on the other hand,' and he was conscious of how daring the next thing he was going to say would be, 'in company we never quite reveal everything of ourselves, do we?'

'Do you mean people generally don't do that, or that you and I don't?' Dona Elisabete asked him intently.

'I mean the latter.' Not sure quite what he meant.

'I agree with you. So, where shall I begin?'

'Wherever you wish.'

'Well,' she said briskly, sitting upright, 'Perhaps I should start by explaining I am an only child.'

'What a coincidence! So am I.'

'Ah, but in Portugal, to have only one child is almost as bad as having no child. We Portuguese like big families.'

'I understand. So do the Irish.'

Dona Elisabete knitted her eyebrows. 'Irish?' she exclaimed. 'I thought you were one of the English Fathers?'

'I am,' Harrington tried to explain as he had to Koenig. 'I was born and bred in England but my parents came from

Ireland. I know my father was ashamed he'd only been able to parent one child.' Harrington didn't add that Dada – his father had always been called that, even by his own wife - had been torn between pride that a son of his had embraced the priesthood and anguish that the calling would mean the ending of his branch of the Harrington line.

'Then we have more in common than I had imagined,' Dona Elisabete said.

Harrington felt a thrill of intense pleasure as he heard her say this. 'And your own childhood?' he enquired, delicately.

'Very ordinary,' Dona Elisabete said. 'A convent school in Evora. All the usual subjects thought suitable for a young lady. Dance, deportment, delicate eating habits, piano playing - I was never very good at that - were all the survival skills I needed. And a smattering of languages, French and English. Utterly useless for any sort of independent existence but then my destiny was always designed to be marriage.'

Harrington couldn't blame her for sounding bitter. And what of his own survival skills? Seminary training: theology, scripture; they wouldn't help him outside the context of the priesthood. He didn't even know how to boil an egg.

'I'm sure your parents loved you,' he said sympathetically.

'Oh, they did. I was their *querida*, their darling, their *anjinha*, their little cherub, but in the end I was most valuable for what my marriage might bring to the state of their finances.'

Harrington was taken aback by such a cynical statement on the lips of this lovely woman and something in his expression must have communicated itself to her.

'I don't mean they were totally mercenary,' she said in their defence, 'but, you know, parents of a certain class in this country always look to what the suitor will bring with him.' She sighed. 'You might say I was *uma patetinha,* a silly little idiot, to go

45

along with their plans for me but girls in this country aren't accustomed to questioning their father's decisions.'

'I'm sure you weren't a silly idiot at all.' Harrington protested loyally.

'Oh, I think I was, though indeed I don't know who was the bigger idiot, my father or myself. Garcia Medronho was supposed to be the perfect catch. He was older than me, thirty years of age to my twenty. He'd never married, as he explained to my father, because he'd devoted all his energies to making a success of the cotton mills he owned up north in Oporto. Of course, when he said that, my father was completely won over. My father was obsessed with money and with recovering the family fortune.'

Dona Elisabete gave Harrington a sad little smile. 'The Louça estate had been in the family for more than three centuries. I believe it extended to over ten thousand hectares at one time, and there was even land in Brazil, but it had all got eaten away over the years. You know what such families are like.'

'Well,' Harrington replied, 'to be honest, no, I don't know much about what rich families are like. I'm from a humble background, Dona Elisabete. I don't think my father ever owned much more than the clothes he stood up in, and they,' he added in deliberate self-deprecation, 'weren't of the smartest.'

'Ah, but you became a priest! That's a special kind of wealth.'

He was rendered momentarily speechless by this unexpected illumination. Was that what his precious vocation had ultimately been about, a flight from the vice-grip of poverty? He'd sometimes vaguely wondered about that, but the question had never before occurred to him with such frightening clarity.

'You believe so?' he asked.

'Certainly I do. Though, of course it does rather limit you in some ways,' she conceded, 'as regards marriage and all that.

Mind you, marriage isn't all it's made out to be. I know that only too well.'

'Do go on, Dona Elisabete,' he murmured, by now utterly intrigued.

Well, as I was saying, about the family estate. Over the centuries it got nibbled away. There were grand schemes that came to nothing and family feuds. You wouldn't believe how vicious such things can be. One way and another there was precious little left by the time Garcia came along. So it was all arranged: Garcia and I would marry, the profits of the mills would restore the house and even perhaps buy back a little of the land, a vineyard or two, a couple of farms.'

'So what went wrong?'

'What went right, would be a more proper question. From the first, Garcia was not what we'd thought him to be. He pretended some initial interest in me but his real nature soon became all too apparent. When things at work didn't go his way he'd take his frustration out on me and sometimes even hit me. But that wasn't the worst by a long way. I thought at first Garcia was simply a playboy but it wasn't long before I discovered the truth was very different. He soon began to bring young men home, quite openly. Father,' she concluded dramatically, 'the man was a *veado* of the worst sort.'

Harrington was shocked to hear the vulgar word for a homosexual on such ladylike lips. 'Oh dear,' he said, at loss for what to say.

Dona Elisabete nodded sadly. What is it you say in English? *You've made your bed and now you must lie on it?* Well, Father,' she went on, 'I might have had to lie on the bed, but I should have had someone to share it with.'

She sat back in her chair and daintily crossed her right leg over her left. Harrington might have been mistaken but he thought she caught his eye as she did so. 'Which is why,' she continued, 'not only am I without a husband but neither do I have a single child to comfort my loneliness. The men, you wouldn't believe, Father, the animals I've had to accept into my house because of that unprincipled creature.'

She leaned forward, touching the left sleeve of his black jacket to emphasise her point. 'We travelled. He claimed he was studying mills in other countries but it was just an excuse for him to sample men who shared his perverted tastes.' She smiled. 'I don't think there are many cotton mills on the Côte d'Azur or in Le Touquet.'

Her trusting gaze as she delivered this intimate portrayal of the spurned marital bed seemed to him highly disturbing.

Oblivious to the effect her recital was having on him, Dona Elisabete continued blithely, 'You can't imagine, Father, the nights I've lain alone, while he, with his....' She reached in her handbag for a little lace handkerchief to dab delicately at her eyes.

'Most distressful,' he murmured, 'but did you have to accompany him on all these excursions?'

'Naturally, my father wanted me to please Garcia,' she carried on bravely. 'It was because of the money, of course, and while he was playing with the little friends he'd found I was at least free to explore the places we visited. I love London. You're so lucky to have such a wonderful capital city.'

Harrington decided not to tell her he'd never actually been there.

'Not as beautiful as Paris, I agree, no,' she went on punctiliously, 'but such an interesting city! Trafalgar Square, the Mall, Buckingham Palace!' Her face suddenly became more doleful. 'So sad, about your lovely king Edward. Why didn't you let him marry according to his heart's desire?'

Harrington gave a brief shrug. Not another one! he thought. 'The British government couldn't countenance the king marrying a woman who'd been divorced not once but twice. And the Church is of the same view.'

'Pouf! If you priests could marry, you'd soon see things differently, I can tell you.'

'Priests marry! Well, that would be something.' He recalled a scandalous case in the Lisbon Archdiocese a year or two earlier. A senior priest on the staff of the cathedral had run off with his housekeeper to where her family had a farm, somewhere in the north near Viseu. News of the affair had been mostly suppressed, as was only proper, but enough had leaked out to cause a fair degree of excitement. Harrington had been taken aback when Maria Winter had asked her dinner guests in her cynical way, 'Why couldn't the silly man have been content with a comfortable domestic arrangement in the lovely little house that went with his post at the cathedral? He's working on a pig farm now, so I hear.'

'Anyway,' Dona Elisabete declared, 'in the end we were all led astray. Garcia's so-called fortune proved to be an illusion.' She sniffed. 'There's another expression I remember you have in English: *led up the garden path*? We all were: Papa had thought the marriage would restore our fortunes. Garcia, on the other hand, was under the impression that the Louça estate would redeem his failing enterprises. Eventually the Oporto mills were repossessed – they'd been mortgaged to the hilt - and what was left of our lovely estate had to be sold for a fraction of its worth. And I'm the last of the line.'

Such intimate revelations left Harrington feeling distinctly uncomfortable. He didn't dare ask what had happened to the man she had so innocently married. Was she divorced? He knew Salazar was working towards the abolition of the law allowing divorce in Portugal but he didn't think the plans had yet been carried through. There had been a legal separation, perhaps?

He didn't know whether Dona Elisabete was finding it uncomfortable to continue with the interview but for him the tension was becoming unbearable and it had nothing to do with the penitentially hard chairs they were sitting on. There were things he wanted to say, gestures he wanted to make. When she reached out again across the table and put her left hand on his left forearm he instinctively covered it briefly with his right hand, drawing it back hurriedly as though he'd been burned.

A shadow flitting across the half-open door, it might have been Mother Teresa on the prowl, made him realise that despite his joy at being with Dona Elisabete, it was time to bring this exciting but uncomfortable audience to an end. 'I really must be going, Dona Elisabete.'

'You've been so kind,' she detained him, her hand still upon his arm. 'There will be another meeting, won't there?' she said anxiously. 'I'm so looking forward to it.' She frowned and looked about her. 'But not here, please. This place is like a dungeon.'

Harrington could not help but agree. The conventional religiosity of the parlour lacked anything that spoke of human warmth. It was all cold relentless piety: the pictures, that crucifix, the chairs; the whole ambience, he thought, might have been planned to subdue any earthly sentiments stirred up in such close proximity to a lovely lady.

'I've a perfectly good apartment in Lapa,' she told him, adding with a smile, 'and there's a live-in maid, Ana Bigode, so the proprieties would be observed. What do you say?'

It was, he recognised, a decisive moment. He should say something, anything, to call an immediate halt to the developing relationship; tell her that his commitments to the college didn't allow him to spend more afternoons with her, that he wasn't the person she needed.

But was she the person he needed? The dreams he'd been having recently, misty scenes of unfocussed delight in feminine encounters, the daytime fantasies that came upon him unexpectedly, the unprompted irregular motions of the flesh as he'd been taught to call the spontaneous urgings of his virile member: perhaps they were all nothing but the produce of primitive physical attraction, what his moral theology text books called proximate occasions of sin, but deep down he was coming to the conclusion the books might be wrong. Yes, there was the attraction of a warm beautiful body, but wasn't his yearning for something a lot more? He sensed that even if Dona Elisabete had not been as beautiful as she certainly was, he would still want to be with her. She wasn't just a beautiful body; she was a beautiful person, with sparkling wit and understanding.

'I would be so grateful if you would come to my place,' she said. 'We would be so much more comfortable *chez moi*.' She smiled broadly. 'French! You see, my convent education wasn't entirely wasted.'

'Very well then,' Harrington said, trying to give the impression he was only agreeing for her sake.

'Rua do Prior,' she told him, 'Number Five, on the right as you come up the street. I'm on the second floor. You'll love the views.'

'The views?' he asked.

She smiled. 'Yes. Of the river. Of course.'

In a moment of sudden silence that seemed to Harrington to last for ages but which probably lasted no more than a second or two, he wondered what to do. He was poignantly aware that what he next said was possibly going to result in his life being changed for ever. 'Next Thursday? It's a free day in college. No lectures. In the morning I've got some preparation work to do, for my lectures.'

'Perfect. Shall we say three o'clock? I believe you can catch a tram in the Chiado that will bring you practically to my door.'

He stood outside on the convent steps. He felt a sudden and urgent need for the smells of the Bairro to return him to reality; grilling sardines, bad drains and the waft of roasting coffee beans from the nearby Cafêteria Angola.

9

Dona Elisabete had exaggerated slightly in saying the tram would take him to her door. He didn't think any tram would have dared show its common yellow snout in Rua do Prior in Lapa, a far cry from the Travessa dos Inglesinhos in the Bairro Alto and only a stone's throw from both the German Legation and the British Embassy.

Everything, the ponderous nineteenth-century style of the architecture, even the cleanliness of the street; all uttered a stern warning to the lower orders not to trespass. High stone walls laden with purple-flowering bougainvillea protected gardens Harrington could only guess at from the sight of the tops of trees. Bearded stone caryatids guarding the doorway to Dona Elisabete's apartment building frowned their disapproval at him as he hesitated before entering, glancing up at the swags of stony floral ornamentation around the heavily barred lower windows of the building. *Money,* the whole street shouted, *and there's lots more where that came from.* He thought about the way Mother Teresa had eulogised the lady's contribution to the Convent funds. Surely, Dona Elisabete's claim that she was more or less penniless was a bit exaggerated if she could afford both to support the Convent of Divine Mercy and live in this sort of place?

He'd passed a flower-seller at the tram stop and on impulse had bought a small bouquet. The colours were pretty and he thought Dona Elisabete might appreciate them. Feeling rather self-conscious to be wearing a clerical suit and carrying a bunch of flowers, he entered the foyer of the apartment building, forgetting that places of this sort had someone on guard against unwelcome visitors.

The man who stopped him in his tracks reminded Harrington of José, the professors' major-domo, except that this man was dressed in a smart dark blue uniform with gilded crossed keys in his lapel button-hole. He greeted the newcomer courteously enough and after enquiring his business invited him to take the lift, adding helpfully, 'The second floor, senhor padre.'

Harrington checked his appearance in the mirror of the elegant little gilded lift as it creaked into life. His black suit and dog collar looked shabby in such elegant surroundings and when he stepped out of the lift he found himself treading on yet more elegance, a deep-pile carpet with a spectacular design in red, green and gold. Although the weather was fine and street outside perfectly clean, he instinctively lifted first one and then the other foot to check he'd not brought in any dirt on his shoes.

The corridor led to Dona Elisabete's door, where he was greeted by a solidly-built woman of uncertain years, dressed in a uniform of grey smock and spotless white apron. Ana Bigode was almost certainly, he supposed, the product of one of the Casas de Santa Zita, the religious houses of formation for domestics. She treated both Harrington and the flowers to a suspicious visual frisking before reluctantly conceding he might go through to the drawing room. She herself retreated down a corridor he presumed led to the kitchen.

Once in the drawing room he had a confused impression of massive dark furniture, floors of highly polished wood, tall windows veiled in dark velvet drapes. There was a chess set, he noticed, set on a rosewood table beneath the window on the far right of the room. The board's squares were black and light grey and gave the impression of being made from hammered leather. The pieces, black and white, had a vaguely oriental look to them.

But it was of course Dona Elisabete who captured his immediate attention. Dressed in a flowing high-necked dress of inoffensive lavender hue, she held up her face for a kiss to both cheeks. It was a customary enough greeting but in the privacy of her apartment, its innocence carried with it, Harrington thought, a subtle promise of something more adventurous.

She admired the flowers and pressed a button set in the wall to call the maid. Harrington heard a bell ring somewhere in the depths of the apartment. When Ana arrived, Dona Elisabete asked her to put the flowers in a vase and bring tea.

As the maid went off to discharge this duty, Dona Elisabete invited Harrington to sit on one of a pair of finely carved chairs with yellow silk seats while she took the other. On the low marble topped table between them he saw a brightly coloured magazine. The French title, *Femmes d'Aujourd'hui,* and the cover drawing of two smartly dressed women gave him the clue to its contents; women's fashions and the international society gossip the ladies loved.

For a few minutes they chatted. He told her something about his lectures but he realised that, although she expressed a polite interest, to her it was all dull stuff. In any case he was distracted. Being tête-à-tête with her in this sumptuous apartment and very conscious of her light flowery perfume, he was alarmed to find himself having difficulty in keeping control of his sang-froid.

The maid Ana's appearance with the tea-tray allowed him to regain some composure but as soon as she had laid the tray on the table she retreated once again. He noticed she hadn't brought the flowers. Perhaps they weren't considered good enough for the drawing room.

'I'm so fond of your English customs,' Dona Elisabete confided as she poured pale amber liquid into delicate china teacups from an elegant silver pot, 'though of course, you know we Portuguese introduced the drink to you.'

She offered him small round almond biscuits, just the kind he liked, and she tinkled with laughter when he expressed doubts about the origin of such an essential ingredient of British daily life.

'But it's true!' she protested. 'Our Princess Catherine of Bragança, when she married your King Charles, she introduced *cha* to the Court, and the habit spread to all levels of society.'

The special blend she poured him was a far cry from the copper-coloured tannic brew he'd been used to drinking in Salford and the tea served in college was hardly any better. But perhaps she was right; more things than tea had undergone a sea-change in passing from one culture to another.

He resigned himself to listening to further outpourings of family woes about the wicked relatives, male and female to the third and fourth degree, who had perpetrated generations of evil-doing upon her branch of the family. Fortunes had been squandered in lawsuits, when not dissipated by extravagant living. 'Some of the extended family have done quite well out of us,' she told him with a note of bitterness in her voice. 'There's my father's cousin who raises the fighting bulls.'

'I remember, that time at Dona Maria's place. They must have known about him and wanted to embarrass you.'

She smiled. 'It was kind of you to come to my rescue on that occasion. I do care so much about the welfare of our animals and I'm afraid I got rather carried away. And then you stepped in.'

'Some of your compatriots are far removed from the Franciscan ideal.'

Dona Elisabete smiled agreement. 'Gaetano, that's my father's cousin's name, seems to be doing well with his fighting bulls and, as I said, there are other members of the clan who have prospered, but as for us, it all went, all lost at the throw of a card.'

She didn't elaborate as to what card and whose hand had thrown it. Dona Elisabete's narrative rather resembled one side of a telephone conversation from which he, Harrington the eavesdropper, had to construct a meaning as Dona Elisabete interspersed her stories with mystifying asides; 'as you know', and 'of course you'll understand', and 'you'll remember.' She took it for granted he had a detailed knowledge not only of the notoriously Byzantine Portuguese political history but also of the machinations of the Portuguese aristocracy, of which he knew a little from his friendship with the Fonsecas.

The dress was proving not quite the demure article he'd first thought it to be; teasing, tantalisingly suggesting what lay beneath the lavender. He couldn't say it was seductively cut but the way her body moved within it lent it a disconcerting allure that wasn't diminished by a glimpse, as she shifted around on her chair, of an oyster-coloured slip. And there was the way she moved her hands to emphasise a point, the coquettish little tilt she gave to her head, her dark brown eyes fixed on him, as she listened to any comment he made, and the habit she had of tucking back an errant lock of her long black hair behind her left ear.

'Dona Elisabete,' he began, hardly knowing what he was going to say next.

'Oh, please! *Dona Elisabete* sounds so formal and I was hoping we could be friends, you and I. Call me Beta, and I'll call you,' she paused for inspiration, '*Mickey!*'

Harrington was suddenly conscious of having a life in which nomenclature played a considerable role in indicating who he was... and who he wasn't. His students called him *sir*, the servants knew him as *senhor padre;* cousin Brigid back in Salford had insisted on ironically calling him *Father Michael,* and his colleagues knew him as plain *Michael:* never anything else.

Mickey. He tasted the name cautiously. Mickey Mouse. A rodent. But wasn't he the irrepressible hero of tens of cartoons, epic encounters Harrington himself had occasionally used as illustrations in his own lectures? *Mickey.* It would do; their private, secret, name, not to be divulged to outsiders. He could live with that, just between the two of them.

He watched the way she leaned forward to replenish his cup, saw again the gentle movement of her body under that deceptive lavender dress. To distract himself he put a question. 'You never told me what became of your husband.'

'Garcia? Did I tell you he was a *viriato*?'

'Mother Teresa mentioned something of the sort.'

She laughed. 'Viriato! Yes, indeed! As well as being a *veado.*' She continued: 'He didn't strike me as the type to risk his life for a noble cause so I can't imagine what possessed him to go off to war. Well, I can, I suppose. Soldiers: young men. Need I say more? They say he took a sniper's bullet outside Toledo. There was no question of bringing his body home, thank goodness, though I've a sneaking suspicion the sniper was nothing more than a convenient fabrication. For all I know he's indulging his perverse desires in some Moroccan backwater under an assumed name. At any rate, I'm well rid of him!'

'But surely there was a death certificate?' Harrington wasn't sure why he'd asked that question.

'The people in the War Ministry have informed me, unofficially, of his decease. Who am I to probe any further? I'm not going to marry again anyway.'

Why did it matter to him so much whether she was a widow or not? Harrington wondered. He couldn't properly identify the emotion her statement aroused in him. In the course of these past few weeks his friendship with Dona Elisabete, no, *Beta*, he must get used to that name, had become akin to one of those whirling, tumbling, amusements his father had put him on when the travelling funfair came to town. The fairground roller-coaster had left him with much the same feeling as he was experiencing now.

'It's so pleasant to spend this time with you, Mickey,' Beta said. 'My life is frequently so very busy and this time with you feels like a quiet retreat.'

Her glance took in him and then went to the table on which the chess set sat. Harrington saw the direction of her gaze.

'Do you play chess?' he asked.

'Yes, a little. At least, I used to. My father taught me.' She laughed. 'It's an inexpensive pastime, so it suited my family well, but I don't get the opportunity to play these days. Do you play yourself?'

Harrington nodded. 'I sometimes play against the lads in college. When I was younger I was a reasonably strong player, but my chess is rusty. Now, I'm not very good.'

'You mean you're not very good at chess?' Dona Elisabete replied immediately, giving him a teasing smile.

He smiled back. 'Yes, not very good at chess.'

'Well, neither am I,' she said. 'So, shall we have a game and see if I can beat you?' She smiled. 'It would feel pleasant, I think, for me to master you.' She took in the surprised expression on his face and giggled. 'On the chessboard, I mean.'

So Harrington went over to the rosewood table, carefully lifted the chessboard and the men and brought it across to the table between himself and Dona Elisabete. The board and the men were heavier than he expected; the leather of the chessboard itself had been nailed into some heavy wood, teak or mahogany he thought.

'The set was a gift to my father from one of his friends who had travelled in India,' Dona Elisabete explained. 'I often used to play with him. He won most of the time though occasionally I managed to win against him and when I did he was very proud of me and seemed more pleased at having lost than if he'd won!'

He gave her the privilege of being white and of thus making the first move. As she picked up the knight on the king's side of the board and moved it two squares forward and one to the left, he thought how strange and also disturbing it was to be contesting on the chessboard with such a beautiful woman. He'd had many fantasies - he suddenly and abruptly admitted it to himself - of being in bed with her and touching her and kissing her, and more. But this game, this contest, this battle of the wills and mind on this exotic and mysterious chess set that had been brought from India - home, he knew, of the *Kama Sutra* - seemed to Harrington in its own way erotic and tantalising, indeed perhaps even more tantalising than when she had, probably completely innocently or unaware, revealed the movement of her body under her dress.

He replied to her first move by pushing the pawn in front of his queen two squares forward.

And so the contest began. He wanted to win but he did not want to do so too quickly, not willing to humiliate this beautiful woman, whom he was only too aware of gradually starting to adore.

But she knew what she was doing and he soon realised she understood the fundamental art of the game, of getting one's pieces into good squares on the board. In fact, he felt she had an advantage as they left the first few moves behind them and he had to think hard and do what he could to avoid being overwhelmed by her forward-thrusting pieces.

'Your father certainly helped make you a good player,' Harrington said to her, feeling both embarrassed and yet also excited in a strange way at how good she was at chess.

'Oh, Mickey, you're too kind. Please don't let me win. I don't want you to let me win. I want you to play as well as you can.'

'I assure you I'm certainly doing that,' he told her, and that was the truth. Playing against the lads in college, none of whom seemed to have much of an understanding of the game, was not like this. But Dona Elisabete, *Beta,* he told himself sternly, was a beautiful woman who was mastering the board as well as his senses. She really did know what she was doing. And as he sat there, playing as best as he could and trying to make his pieces active, he suddenly realised that, despite saying she rarely got the chance to play, she was better than he was at the game, and he really was rusty.

The game lasted for maybe forty minutes - delicious ones to Harrington - and throughout its entire course Harrington was as conscious of her beauty, of her dress, of the slip he had seen beneath it, and her olive-coloured skin, as he was of the exotic black and white pieces they were moving over the board of black and grey beaten leather.

He felt entranced by a whirl of senses he couldn't ever remember experiencing before. Her perfume and her charm mingled inextricably with her skill on the chessboard to make him feel he'd entered another world.

Soon his position on the chessboard lay in ruins. She had won most of his pieces, and his king was naked and exposed. She glanced at him with her big brown eyes and said earnestly: 'Mickey, you must promise me you've not been letting me win.'

'I really haven't, I absolutely have not. You're simply a much better player than I am.'

'I don't think that's the case. I think I've just been lucky. And perhaps you were not completely telling the truth about not letting me win.'

'I am telling you the truth.'

She smiled and lifted the white queen and placed it next to his king. He saw at once he couldn't take the queen because it was guarded by her white-squared bishop.

'I'm sorry Mickey, but I think you'll find that's checkmate.'

Harrington glanced at the board. 'Oh, good gracious. Yes, yes, it is. Well, you've beaten me fair and square. You really have.'

Dona Elisabete smiled. 'It's only a game, Mickey. Not real life.' Suddenly she looked at her wrist watch. 'Goodness,' she exclaimed. 'Is that the time? I'm sorry Mickey, but delightful as this has been, you'll have to excuse me. An errand of mercy. I promised Jacinta Louleira I'd look in on her. She broke her ankle last week and the poor creature can scarcely hobble around.'

They got up together and he was about to offer her a farewell kiss on the cheek when he took the initiative and planted his lips full on hers. It was impulsive, unplanned and hardly lingering. 'Mickey,' she breathed when he released her, and her hand came up to caress his cheek.

He stammered some sort of apology but she brushed his words aside. 'It's I who should apologise for burdening you with my family troubles,' she said and promptly kissed him back even more resolutely. 'And,' she promised, planting another kiss, 'next time, Mickey, we'll touch upon happier matters.'

As the maid showed him out she leaned into him, blocking his exit for a moment. 'You'd do well to remember, senhor padre,' she hissed before she let him go, 'my Dona Elisabete is an honourable lady,'

Lost for a response, he could only nod in agreement.

Still slightly dizzy, he was grateful for the long walk down to the tram stop. Kissing her like that! He didn't know whether to be ashamed or exultant. She might have rebuffed him, told him to behave, but she had reciprocated. It meant she wasn't entirely indifferent.

What had Ana Bigode meant by her parting shot? There were stories he'd heard, from the remoter areas of the Beiras of central Portugal or up beyond civilisation in Trás-os-Montes in the far northern mountains on the Spanish border, of vendettas, blood feuds nurtured over centuries, involving knives and mutilation. He wondered, still slightly delirious, whether Bigode hailed from one of those regions. Perhaps, Harrington wondered, she carried a dagger, sharpened upon the stone steps of the apartment building by the light of the full moon, with which to wreak vengeance on would-be besmirchers of her lady's honour!

10

The Upper House lecture hall was the scene of most of Harrington's labours. The room was in fact the college library, with windows overlooking the garden, the shelves lining the walls filled with thousands of books, some bound in leather or vellum, many dating back hundreds of years. Below the lecturer's pulpit, two long rows of tables accommodated those students who were in their final years of preparation for priestly ordination. The arrangement was identical to what it had been when Harrington had been a student and he suspected it had changed little over the centuries.

With memories of the dry-as-dust performances he had suffered as a student, Harrington had always prided himself on delivering a stimulating discourse, encouraging his students to question and debate. But as he sat in the pulpit that Friday afternoon, the day following his meeting with Beta in Lapa, he was acutely aware his lectures had been going to pot for some weeks.

His habitual careful preparation had become perfunctory and his delivery of the material was wooden and sometimes erratic. That afternoon the students' resentment was almost palpable. The biblical commandment, *Thou shalt not commit adultery,* with all its ramifications, was proving a peculiarly difficult text to interpret because Harrington was struck, not for the first time, of the incongruity of a celibate teaching celibates the moral niceties of the Catholic doctrine about sexual union.

He suddenly felt reckless. He slammed shut the heavy Latin tome in front of him and brushed aside his notes, ignoring a loose page that floated down to the worn floorboards.

'You will have noticed,' he began, 'that our friend Noldin is only interested in the circumstances in which sexual union may be considered lawful by being open to the procreation of offspring. He's got absolutely nothing to say about that union being essentially an expression of warm human love.'

Over the years of lecturing he'd grown used to the mention of any matters sexual producing a studied silence among his students, a heads-down concentration on their notebooks, but today he saw faces turned up towards him – expectant or apprehensive?

'Noldin's only concern.' he continued, 'appears to be that the act of sex should be performed in such a way as not to impede fertilisation of the woman's ovum.'

He paused for a moment aware the silence in the room was almost palpable. 'So very clinical, and so very lacking in any real understanding of humanity. Human beings are made for one another. Doesn't it say so in the Bible? And doesn't it follow that the relations between man and woman must be of heart and mind as well as body? Doesn't this seem to suggest to you that the first purpose of sexual union is to express that heart and mind? And what,' he added recklessly, 'of people past the age for procreation? Are they to abstain because their intimacy can no longer be fruitful?'

No one said a word; there was a scraping sound as someone shifted uneasily in his chair. Harrington was determined to brazen out the silence. It was Fielding who at last raised his hand. 'Do you mean the textbook is wrong?'

'Blinkered, perhaps,' Harrington replied calmly.

Fielding was clearly taken aback. 'But, surely, sir, Noldin's an authority, entirely orthodox?'

Harrington welcomed the whiff of rebellion. 'When you have two opinions, how do you decide which makes the more sense to you?' He could feel something of the struggle in Fielding's mind.

'I suppose,' Fielding answered unsteadily, 'the one that fits in with your...' He hesitated. 'I was going to say, your experience of life,' he finished lamely.

'But, of course,' Harrington responded, 'in this particular area we don't have any experience.' Even from a distance he could see Fielding's face redden.

The fingers on the clock at the far end of the room were approaching the hour, the signal for the lecture's end, but having gone so far it was too late to stop. 'You know,' he added, doing his best to soften his words, 'you've surely come to appreciate the importance of all human relationships in your life. Try to understand that the special relationship we're talking about here is perhaps the most fundamental of all.'

Harrington stopped short there. His students had been dragged away from their families at the age of twelve or thirteen, as he himself had been, at that stage in life when self-awareness was beginning to blossom, to be thrust into an all-male environment where what were circumspectly described as 'particular friendships' were actively discouraged. It had taken his own friendship with Beta to open up for him a vista of what lay on the other side of that narrow horizon. Would such an opportunity ever open to Fielding and his fellow students?

'Just think about it,' Harrington admonished his audience, gathered up his notes and his books, opened the little gate that had closed him in the pulpit and climbed down, confident that what he had said was explosive enough for the moment. He stooped to pick up the stray page of notes and swept from the room.

He knew the classical Christian authors, St Augustine - even Thomas Aquinas - all regarded women as fundamentally inferior beings, representing temptation; unfortunately necessary for the continuation of the human race but otherwise to be held severely at arm's length. No papal pronouncement had ever been issued in praise of women, apart from the unattainable sanctity of the Virgin Mary who had achieved parenthood without recourse to the messy necessities that went with normal conception and birth. As he headed for his own quarters he wondered whether one or other among his students might be emboldened to carry a complaint to the college president that Father Harrington was preaching some sort of heresy.

11

'I've given Ana the day off,' Beta explained as she admitted Harrington into the apartment in Rua do Prior the following Thursday afternoon, 'She's got a sick aunt over the river in Trafaria.'

The kiss seemed quite natural this time and it lasted a good deal longer than before.

Beta was wearing a different dress this time, a flowery pattern and floaty, swirling about her as she walked. She led the way into the living room, chatting gaily about how hot it was but how the fresh breeze off the sea was so welcome. She asked how his journey from the college had been, hoping the tram ride hadn't taken too much out of him. She expected that as a priest he'd be used to rubbing shoulders with the *campónios*, a word Harrington mentally translated as *the great unwashed*.

He answered her questions mechanically as he followed her down the corridor. The apartment seemed suddenly a so much more private environment this afternoon. He supposed that knowing that the maid was lurking in the kitchen had provided some restraint before. Now they had the place to themselves, Harrington felt more vulnerable; which he found both worrisome and exciting.

On his previous visit he'd scarcely been aware of the décor but now he deliberately made a point of looking about. She noticed his interest in the heavily varnished paintings. They're portraits of my ancestors', she carelessly remarked. The highly polished silverware on the burred walnut sideboard, shining testimony to Ana Bigode's industry, were 'just some bits and pieces of my grandmother's.' The chessmen still sat on their leather board and he wondered whether she would offer him a return match.

Standing on an ebony pedestal in one corner of the room was a carved ivory column some three feet tall he hadn't taken in before.

'Do take a look,' she invited, to his acute embarrassment when closer inspection proved the work to consist entirely of exquisitely carved men and women, mostly naked, both sexes bountifully endowed, entwined in unmentionable activities.

'It's been much admired by connoisseurs,' she told him, appearing not to notice his flushed face as he stepped back. 'Eighteenth-century Indian work. A great uncle, who was Viceroy of Goa, procured it.' She giggled. 'He had a terrible reputation. Everyone said he'd married beneath him.'

Many of the ivory women were beneath too, and some on top and some, precariously, on their sides. Was it physically possible, Harrington wondered, for the human body to assume such athletic postures in the performance of sexual union? And, moreover, to judge by their smiling faces, they all seemed to be positively enjoying themselves.

'The ivory. D'you like it?' Beta demanded.

'Well, it's artistic, I suppose,' Harrington replied hesitantly.

She laughed merrily. 'You're blushing, Mickey!' she said. 'It's supposed to have some sort of religious significance in their culture. We have to accept that the natives' ideas about proper behaviour are very different from our own.'

'There is that, I, ah, expect,' he conceded, 'which is why we've a duty to educate.' As Antonio Fonseca might have pointed out. And Harrington wasn't too sure her assertion about different ideas of proper behaviour would bear much scrutiny. He shouldn't be stirred by what he'd seen but he'd be lying if he claimed the carving had left him entirely unmoved.

69

'Oh, yes indeed, you're right,' Beta continued blithely, 'we mustn't ever forget our civilising mission. But come on, we're neglecting our refreshments.'

It was coffee this time, and some of the delicious little confections that answered to the Portuguese appetite for sweetmeats. 'Come and sit down,' she encouraged him, patted the place beside her on the sofa.

The coffee, he supposed she had made it herself, was delicious, as were the cakes. He ate a second one at her insistence It was honeyed, filled with marzipan and dusted with powdered sugar that clung to his fingers.

Beta pushed aside her plate and, as Harrington watched fascinated, licked sugar from her fingers. 'Mickey,' she said, 'I've told you so much about my family misfortunes. I'm sure you've a much happier tale to relate about yourself.'

'You don't want to know,' he mumbled.

'Oh, but I do.' She turned to him. 'You said you came from a humble background.'

'That's about it, really, there's nothing much to tell. We were very poor. My father came from Ireland to escape the hardships there and only found even greater hardship in England.' He tried to explain. 'There's a huge canal, sixty kilometres long, from the sea to the inland city of Salford, though the canal is called the Manchester Ship Canal. Enormous vessels come from all over the world, right into the heart of England. My father worked as a casual labourer on the docks. My mother took in washing to make ends meet.' He looked into her face. 'You must find this all very hard to understand.'

'With you as my teacher?' she breathed. 'Certainly not.'

'I was only a boy when I got a place at the college here in Lisbon. I suppose my parents must have been very proud.' He recalled what she had said earlier about the priesthood being a different sort of riches and his own more recent thoughts about it being an escape route from poverty.

'It's the same thing with us,' Beta said. 'A priest: what a blessing or, if it's a girl, she might become a nun. If we hadn't been in such financial difficulties my parents might have been content to let me take the veil.' She saw his incomprehension. 'It's the dowry, you know. You have to be able to offer something substantial to the community you are going to enter and my father would have been too embarrassed with the pittance he could have afforded.' She smiled. 'You see, the only convent he would have considered suitable for me was very aristocratic.'

'In my case,' Harrington said, 'my bishop saw to the cost of my stay at the college as long as I was a student and when I was ordained the college sent me to Rome to complete my studies.'

'And did you never return to England, you poor thing, Mickey?'

'As a professor, I could go back every year, if I wanted to. But I haven't been back for several years. What's there for me in England?'

'Your parents, surely?'

'My father's dead. My mother? The first time I went back, I seemed like a foreigner to her.' He paused, aware that sounded callous. 'I shouldn't talk like that, I know, but that's what it felt like. I think she went in awe of me because I'd been magically transformed into a priest, and in her book priests were to be put on pedestals, not really human any more. Being a priest, in the end you're always alone,' he added rather forlornly

'But your colleagues in college,' she said, 'you have your friends around you, surely?'

'Oh, we work together, we have meals together, we pray together. And then we go off, each into our own private little cells.'

'Cells?' she exclaimed. 'You make it sound like a prison.'

71

'Rooms can be like prisons,' he replied bitterly. 'If you've no one to share them with.'

'So sad,' Beta whispered.

'For years I've always done what I thought was right, what was called for as a priest. And now it all seems to have been nothing but a waste. I don't know if you can understand, but it's hard to come to the conclusion you've been on the wrong track all this time.'

Somehow, in the course of his story, he discovered she had snuggled up to him. His embrace of her was spontaneous, instinctive, childlike in intensity. 'You must think I'm pathetic,' he managed to say, 'going on like this about myself when you've got your own troubles. I don't know what's come over me all of a sudden.'

'Shush, *querido*, shush. You're distressed,' Beta exclaimed, 'I think I must have upset you somehow.'

'*Não é nada.* It's nothing, nothing at all,' Harrington said, far louder than he'd intended and suddenly aware he was on the verge of tears. 'You haven't upset me. Not you. Oh well, I suppose...'

He was teetering on the rim of a bottomless precipice, on the brink of falling back to the safety of arid ground or letting himself go, to fall into the magical depths. He could smell that tantalising fragrance she used, mixed incongruously with the sweetness of the sugar from the cakes. He touched her hair, wondering what it would look like let down to tumble over bare shoulders. He should leave this minute, make any excuse to get away.

She was doing something to her dress, loosening the straps, fiddling with what lay underneath. So, that was what her hair looked like over bare shoulders, over her naked breasts.

Harrington had seen paintings of female nudes in the Queluz palace art collection and there were plenty of monuments dotted around the city that made much use of the female form. But theirs were breasts of paint and stone and here was the real thing; living flesh, warm dark cream, crowned with dusty pink nipples, moving as she turned, their warmth yielding softly to his touch. Her consoling breasts, Harrington thought as he buried his face in those generous swelling mounds.

'Poor man,' she said softly, her hands gently caressing the back of his head as he pressed into her, 'is life so terrible for you?'

He'd never thought in those terms before. 'If you only knew how often I've longed...'

'I know,' she hushed him, taking his wet cheeks in her her hands. 'I know. We understand each other, you and I.'

Human warmth was what he needed, after years of being cooped up in that barracks in the Bairro. He was parched, he thought, as he responded to her caresses, nothing more than a dry stream.

Here was a real and seductive female body totally open to him and he suddenly realised he didn't know what exactly he was supposed to do. Within moments he found he needn't worry because she was guiding him to caress and play with her. He had liberty, her every action was saying, to do as he pleased to please her. Her skin was warm and silky smooth. He held his breath as he touched her breasts, tentatively at first, then smoothing round the contours, touching her nipples so they grew hard. And she was doing things, loosening his clothing, unbuttoning, opening. He gasped as she took hold of his growing erection and the same time guided his hand down her own belly to the soft folds within their dark nest. He was vaguely aware of murmuring, between words and groans, issuing whimpers of delight and awe in experiencing sensations he'd never in his life felt before.

'You know,' Beta breathed into his ear some time later, 'I think we both needed this, you and I. But, Mickey, we ought to find somewhere more comfortable.'

She eased herself from the sofa and brought him to his feet. She was in charge, in the winning position, just as she had been in the chess game, and he was only too willing to be vanquished once more.

The last time he had been naked in front of anyone was in the course of his medical examination prior to coming to Lisbon. Such had been the discretion in the Harrington household about all things remotely sexual that the first sex information he'd ever received was at school, in mangled form, from children of less fastidious homes. He'd heard there was a seminary somewhere in England where the students were required to wear special gowns in which to take their weekly baths.

And now here he was in a woman's bedroom, unashamedly letting her uncover his secrets, and it was exhilarating, liberating, delightful to be allowed to explore and to be explored, hands free to roam, her skin against his, his hands on her, teasing and being teased. No need to worry about precisely how they would work together, he could be sure she would know how to manage things, and indeed she led all the way, insisting with exquisite delicacy, with him her fumbling pupil, until they both collapsed on the silk sheets in a huddled heap of mutual consummation.

They finally eased themselves apart to lie companionably quiet side by side, only hands touching. After a while she hauled herself onto her right hip and elbow, leaning into him, her dark hair forming a curtain over his head so the world was reduced to their two faces. 'Was it what you expected? Did I make you happy, Mickey?' she whispered into his ear.

Happy wasn't the word. Delirious might have been nearer the mark. Amazed was another word that came to Harrington's mind. He didn't know what he'd expected, only knew now he had never felt so drained and so contented in his life, empty but full, he tried confusedly to explain.

She must have understood something of his inability to articulate because she put a finger on his lips. 'I know, darling. Me too, since I first saw you, I think.'

'I had dreams about you,' he said. 'But I thought that's all they were, dreams.'

'And have the dreams come true?'

'More than true,' he admitted. What she had done, what they had both done, was far beyond the limits of the dream machine.

Beta was suddenly practical. 'We need refreshment!' She swung off the bed and padded naked in the direction of the kitchen, to return a few moments later with a bottle, a corkscrew and two glasses. 'I asked Ana earlier to put this in the fridge,' she said with a naughty smile. 'It would be a shame not to open it.' It was a *vinho verde*, the sparkling light wine of the north. 'This is man's work, really,' she said mischievously, offering him the corkscrew.

It wasn't the wine that made the world wheel drunkenly around him as he walked down the hill towards the tram stop. So that was what it was all about; this glorious delirium the text books coldly called carnal knowledge! Were they all so ignorant, those learned theologians and moralists or were they so terrified by the power of human attraction that they could only claim that sex was the invention of the devil? He didn't care. However they tried to justify what they said, they were wrong.

He was brought back to some semblance of reality by the rattle of the approaching tram. It was the busy time of day and all the seats were taken. He hung on to the hand rail near the driver, but a woman, seeing his dog collar, stood to let him sit in her place.

Could she see? It should be written on his face! And this other woman sitting next to him, wouldn't she smell the love-making on him? It filled his nostrils still: it must be obvious to everyone on the tram. She sniffed, but then produced a handkerchief to dab at a summer cold. All the same, he would have to change the moment he got back to college.

12

Euphoria, Harrington remembered someone once saying, was like a balloon, too easily pricked.

When he turned up as usual at the Convent of Divine Mercy to celebrate the morning Mass, Dona Elisabete was not in her accustomed place in chapel but he didn't dare ask Mother Teresa if there was a reason for her absence. *Beta's avoiding me,* was his first thought, *regretting the way she let herself get carried away.* And then: *Is she ill?* He wondered whether he should telephone her but couldn't summon up the courage.

When she didn't turn up on Saturday serious doubts began to creep in. The ecstasy he'd experienced with Beta, Harrington asked himself, had it after all been a sinful delusion? He'd been taught all his life that the road to hell was broad and fine. Was that the path he'd blithely set foot upon?

For years, ever since he'd returned to Lisbon from his studies in Rome, he had made his fortnightly confession to the Irish Dominican Father Fergal O'Dowd in his snug room on the top floor of the huddle of monastic buildings behind the church of Corpo Santo.

Harrington had always found O'Dowd to be a reassuring presence in his life. The elderly priest, a whippet of a man with a fringe of grey hair around the bald freckled dome of his head, was rarely seen without a cigarette in his mouth, Sweet Afton as often as not, cadged from Irish sailors whose ships had come into harbour. He had lived in Lisbon longer than Harrington had been alive and was a mine of information about the more disreputable portions of the city's history.

Harrington's confessions had always been routine, what he thought of as a sort of spiritual house-cleaning, a kind of keeping of accounts: so many times he'd been distracted in prayer; this often he'd been irritable, been lackadaisical in his lecture preparation; those rare occasions he'd been visited with impure thoughts. O'Dowd would dispense routine words of wisdom, Harrington would make a firm purpose of amendment, receive O'Dowd's words of absolution and be sent on his way after a glass of Irish whiskey.

This was something monumentally different, what O'Dowd would certainly class as a serious moral lapse. According to the theological text books, O'Dowd would be right: a priest having carnal knowledge of a woman was breaking all the rules. Harrington remembered the cathedral priest who had fled up north on discovery of his delinquency and how he himself had shared in the scandalised tut-tutting around Maria Winter's table.

But the dread of being found out wasn't the same as consciousness of doing wrong. There had been times when Harrington had done something he'd afterwards recognised as wrong, usually prejudging someone else's behaviour or making an accusation against a totally innocent person. At those times, Harrington had been pricked by his own conscience until he'd tried to right the wrong he had done by apologising to the person concerned.

What he and Beta had done wasn't at all like that. If he went to O'Dowd, what would he confess? True, he'd broken his solemn promise of celibacy, but had that been a fair demand the Church had made of him in the first place? Again, he'd always believed and taught sex outside marriage was a mortal sin, but the delights of Beta's embraces had taught him a different lesson.

That afternoon, Harrington got as far as putting on his jacket and walking down to the Arches before he stopped. Why waste his time? What could O'Dowd say? That he should pray for forgiveness for being stubbornly in denial about the wrongness of his lapse and never see Dona Elisabete again?

He turned, offering a distracted *good afternoon* to Cordeiro who was sweeping the floor, and returned to his quarters. He shut the door behind him and sat, elbows on the desk top, his chin in his hands, staring aimlessly out of the window. *If you don't want the answer, don't ask the question.* It was one of Martin Blount's favourite dictums.

Harrington had never been quite sure of the precise hidden meaning lying within the saying but he knew he certainly didn't want the advice O'Dowd would surely give him. From now on he would have to work out his own salvation.

13

'D'you think what we're doing is wrong?' Harrington asked Beta the following Thursday. It was the first time he'd conducted a theological seminar lying naked on scented sheets.

'Wrong, *querido* Mickey?' She sounded astonished. 'How wrong?'

'You know. Against the teachings of the Church.'

Beta gave him a lazy smile. 'You're the expert, Mickey, but if you ask me, I'd say, what does the Church know about this? You love me, I love you. I've longed for you since we first met. And I think perhaps you were not so different. And neither of us could bring ourselves to admit it, except in our dreams.' She chuckled. 'Did you dream about me doing this to you?' Her hand moved cunningly on him. 'Or about this?' She readjusted herself on the bed and her head followed her hand.

'Beta!' Harrington gasped, 'That's outrageous.' But he didn't stop her.

It was late in the evening before he slipped out of her door and trod lightly down Rua do Prior, one eye cocked for a returning Ana, Dona Elisabete's live-in maid.

Harrington's life fell into a strangely ordered pattern though it demanded a degree of subterfuge. Thursdays were Beta days, nothing to do with the rest of his existence, and his ingenuity in providing his colleagues with fictional accounts of his activities rather surprised even himself.

Though Harrington had never explicitly given him reason to think so, Martin Blount got it into his head that the Thursday absences had something to do with a mission to bring back to the practice of the faith a young Portuguese gentleman who had become embroiled with the Freemasons and he took the opportunity of Harrington's absence one Thursday lunchtime to urge the other members of staff not to press him on such a delicate matter.

Bob Knox, a comfortable man, well-rounded both physically and intellectually, with years of experience of parish work in London's East End, took Harrington aside the next day after breakfast. 'I just wanted to let you know, now the Old Man's put us in the picture, that you're to be admired. In England we think the Masons are a trifle laughable, with all that funny rigmarole and dressing up. In France and out here in Portugal, these Grand Orient people, the sort you're up against, they're an entirely different breed. I know Salazar's banned them officially, but they're still around and they've still got plenty of influence. I can see the strain it's having on you, trying to get the better of them, and I want you to know we wish you all the best.'

Knox forestalled any attempt of Harrington to reply. 'A burden shared is a burden halved, don't they say?' he said. 'You know, I've always had a high regard for you, Michael, and I hate to see you bowed down under the load. Any time you want to talk about it, just say the word.'

'That's kind of you, Bob.'

'Well, the offer's there, old boy, and don't you forget!'

High regard! It wasn't Harrington's fault if Blount had chosen to elaborate a vague story about giving a helping hand to someone in need into a fanciful tale about Freemasonry. But if he'd poured out the truth, what advice could Knox have offered? The eminently sensible thing to do would be to hand in his notice and return to England. leaving Beta to do without him.

That was something he'd already decided he couldn't do. They loved each other, despite the irregularity of the relationship, and nothing could alter the fact.

And suppose he did make an heroic sacrifice and go back to England to endure existence in a Salford parish, amidst the cold and fog of northern England, what good would that do? He couldn't see himself sharing a damp, soot-encrusted Victorian presbytery in the company of the kind of opinionated clergy he remembered - *cocks o' the walk* his father had called them - whose self-importance grown of years on the mission was only matched by their complete ignorance of a world beyond the confines of the Manchester Ship Canal.

But there was something else, at the back of his mind, a fear he'd rather not dwell upon. Suppose she grew tired of a middle-aged priest with nothing to offer her? She had said most adamantly she would never marry again but the time might come, no, he had to admit it, the time *would* come when a different future opened up for her, and then she wouldn't want to be saddled with someone like him.

Martin Blount's fanciful construct of his imagined efforts with the Masonic gentleman gave Harrington an idea. As long as they confined their activities within the walls of her apartment, it was not much of a problem that the only clothes he had were clerical ones. The man who guarded the entrance to the building, Harrington had discovered his name was Bento Magalhães, had become quite friendly and if he suspected what was going on he never raised the issue But the clerical suit and dog collar that made Harrington instantly recognisable was a serious impediment once they emerged from that shelter of the apartment. It simply wouldn't do for a priest and a single lady to be seen enjoying a meal in a restaurant or sauntering along the seafront in Estoril.

Suppose he let it be known to his colleagues that, in order not to attract attention to himself when visiting his would-be convert, he would be better off without his dog collar? It was a plausible argument. The Masons still exercised considerable influence in the country and Harrington could imagine them being capable of vindictive action against one of their number who was consorting with a priest. What more natural than that he should seek to conceal his priesthood from prying eyes?

He put the question to Blount after lunch one day as they were taking a turn in the garden. 'This matter I'm dealing with. The problem is, if the person in question were seen to be having dealings with a priest, there might be unfortunate repercussions. We've tried to be circumspect but one never knows who's on the look-out.'

Blount was immediately sympathetic. 'I see your dilemma. That's quite a problem.' They were standing under the Judas tree, almost stripped now of the last of its pink petals, occupying the centre of the garden. He mused a moment and then said, 'Civvies. That's what you need. I've seen you, over at Pêra, informal, just shirt and trousers. I don't suppose you could, you know?'

Harrington immediately shook his head. 'Hardly, Martin, not in the city in those clothes, not the thing at all, I'm afraid.' He hesitated expectantly.

'The collar's the real problem, isn't it?' Blount said. 'The suit, well black's not fashionable perhaps, but the collar's the serious obstacle.'

'A tie, then?' Harrington suggested tentatively, 'and a white shirt instead of the black false dickie-front?'

'Would you know how to fasten a tie?' It was asked with a smile but it was a serious question. Neither of them had worn a tie since they had been children. Taking on the college costume at the age of thirteen, they had merely moved up a size as they had grown and, once ordained, had graduated to wearing the uniform of suit and clerical collar.

'It must be like riding a bicycle,' Harrington grinned, knowing he had won his case. 'One never forgets.'

'D'you know, I've never ridden a bicycle,' Blount replied seriously.

'I've still got the scars on my knees from falling off.' Harrington felt he could afford to be flippant; he'd got what he wanted, acceptance from the college president to flout the rules. There would still be restrictions: no question of spending a night or two in a hotel where identity documents would be demanded. Care would be needed in the city but now he and Beta could take the train up the coast without drawing undue attention to themselves and enjoy a meal in one of the many pleasant little restaurants to be found in Estoril or Cascais.

'It wouldn't do for the students to see you in that garb,' Blount admonished with a smile. 'It might give them the wrong idea.'

'I shall be the soul of discretion,' Harrington assured him. For the first time in his life he thought how apt was the name *dog collar* for the strip of celluloid he wore round his neck.

Buying a shirt and tie ought to have been a simple enough procedure. There was a very good general store in the Chiado that would fit him out with whatever he desired but he felt woodenly awkward at the counter and in the end found himself muttering something about purchasing presents for a friend as the assistant showed him a selection of what he claimed was the latest fashion in neck-wear. In the end, despite the young man's disapproving frown, he settled for the least gaudy, a plain grey article, and asked for it to be wrapped up with the shirt.

Tying the damned thing was more difficult than he'd imagined. So much for the bicycle analogy, Harrington ruefully admitted as he studied his first attempt in the mirror.

Beta was quite taken by his attire though she rather thoughtlessly said it reminded her of an undertaker on a day-off. Still, the first time they went into the little bakery hard by the Jerónimos monastery at Belém to sample a couple of the little *pasteis de nata,* the custard creams the place was famous for, Harrington felt for once he wasn't the centre of attention, 'though I do feel a fraud,' as he explained to Beta.

'But why, *querido*? I think you look very nice. The suit, I agree: we definitely need to do something about that.' She wrinkled her nose. 'And as for the tie, I'd like to see something a little more colourful.' She giggled. 'Don't forget, you're not an undertaker.'

'I feel as though I'm a secret agent, going under a false identity.' Which, he supposed was an accurate enough description for a priest in mufti.

'Well, doesn't that make it all the more exciting?' Beta wanted to know. 'Here,' she pushed the plate of custard creams towards him, 'have another, before I eat them all up.'

14

Nearly all of Harrington's acquaintances were convinced war was inevitable; this year, next year, one way or another. He was aware that although there were ardent supporters of the British cause among the upper echelons of Lisbon society, there were others, fervent Salazarists, of whom Fonseca was a prime example, who made no secret of favouring the Germans, perhaps with some reason.

Franco, Harrington knew only too well, had won his war in Spain with German help. The bombing of Guernica by the Condor Legion had demonstrated to the world the power and efficiency of a re-armed Reich in repelling the forces of the Reds. With a divided Britain, and the Americans showing no signs of wanting to be involved in another of Europe's little spats, Harrington had no option but to conclude that strong men were in the ascendancy, in Italy as well as Germany; in Portugal just as much as in Spain.

Strangely, Koenig was one of the few who thought there was still a chance of peace. 'Our beloved Leader already has Austria and Czechoslovakia, plenty of room there for him to wriggle his toes,' he told Harrington when the inevitable subject came up over a beer in the Cervejaria Trindade. 'If you ask me,' he added, 'all this noise about Poland is just a tease, to keep the French and British on edge.'

As for the swastika flag hanging above the Augsburger office doorway, Koenig explained: 'It's window dressing, that's all. I'm keeping my nose clean with the powers that be.'

Harrington supposed Koenig was referring to head office. 'One of my Portuguese friends,' he said, 'claims someone in your Legation told him the Führer really does have plans for the whole of Eastern Europe.'

Koenig shook his head. 'Tell your friend he shouldn't believe all he hears from that source. No, Michael, we all have our own opinions about our dear Leader but he's no fool. He's already getting what he wants by making noises; why should he want to risk everything in outright conflict?'

Harrington accepted what Koenig said, though he wondered quite how much of the apparent cynicism about Hitler was genuine. The São Jorge cinema had long been showing newsreels of the rallies organised by the Nazis, the adoring masses hanging on Hitler's every word, the obvious popularity of the repressive measures against the Jews. It would be hard, he reckoned, for any German to keep himself completely untainted by such infection.

Koenig's office was not the only business in the city to be sporting a swastika and the last time Harrington had been to the British Embassy he'd thought the solitary Union flag fluttering above the roof had a certain air of majestic dignity about it in comparison with the increasingly ostentatious display down the road at the German Legation. He'd had to laugh when Miss Singleton solemnly remarked that the Ambassador, Sir Walford Selby, was thinking of applying to the Foreign Office for a hundred yards of red, white and blue bunting, 'though where we'd hang it all, Lord only knows.'

A few weeks previously, Harrington had been to see the German cruiser, the *Admiral Graf Spee*, in Alcântara dock on what was described in the press as a courtesy visit, her sleek greyhound lines, flamboyant ensign and menacing gun turrets a sobering reminder of what might be unleashed if Koenig's prediction proved wrong.

The visit was widely advertised and hordes of people were taking advantage of the open hospitality on board. Although Harrington hadn't gone on the ship, a few of the students had profited from the invitation and Martin Blount had been obliged to issue an edict forbidding any further fraternisation after one group had returned to college reeking of strong drink.

The arrival, a couple of weeks later, of the elderly V Class destroyer *HMS Valorous,* a relic of what some people were beginning to call the Last War, had been interpreted even by Anglophile Portuguese as a pathetic response to the *Graf Spee's* demonstration of raw power. That didn't stop Arthur Cope, the college bursar, who also held the title of honorary chaplain to the Royal Navy, taking the opportunity to visit *Valorous.* He'd come back with a handy stock of whisky and cigarettes, sufficient to tide the staff over until the next Royal Navy ship came into Lisbon.

With the unseasonal warmth, the fresh breezes in Lapa were all the more welcome and with Ana Bigode out on her by now regular Thursday days off Harrington found himself arriving earlier than ever at Beta's apartment. Their love-making was no longer the desperate coupling of their first encounters, becoming more of a sort of comforting ritual accompaniment to their growing closeness.

There was so much to talk about. She regaled him with accounts of the places she had visited on her travels; she could even begin to make light of the odious Garcia. She was knowledgeable about the cinema world, she had her favourite actors and actresses, was discriminating in her choice of movie and was able to discuss the merits of the various plots.

They went to see *Goodbye Mr Chip*s showing at the São Jorge cinema on the Avenida and he was a bit taken aback when Beta compared him to the eponymous hero, dedicating his life to the cause of education. He'd found the teacher rather a dull character and, though he recognised she was teasing him, it worried him that she saw any point of similarity.

Gone with the Wind was the first film either of them had seen in the spectacular new Technicolor format. Beta was captivated by the story, 'so romantic, so tragic,' she said, though Harrington found it all far too emotional and melodramatic and he wasn't entirely convinced that films in colour were better than the conventional black and white.

Beta was utterly enraptured by the characters played by Clark Gable and Vivien Leigh. 'Their story was so heart-rending,' she declared as they left the cinema, 'unlike so many of the films that say nothing true about love, that are so *trillado, gastardo*. How do you say that in English?'

Hackneyed, Harrington guessed would be about right, 'if you mean the themes are all so similar, so well worn?'

'Exactly! Now, our story,' she added slyly, 'would make a story-line worth watching.'

Even the mere mention of publicity made Harrington immediately nervous. 'What we have, it's just between the two of us, isn't it?' he demanded as they walked along. There was a little restaurant he thought they might try, further down the Avenida from the cinema.

He had insisted they should maintain a little fiction in their visits to the São Jorge, contriving to arrive simultaneously at the ticket office as though by accident. Beta thought the subterfuge was quite silly but delicious, 'like something out of a spy movie.' She'd seen Hitchcock's *The Thirty-Nine Steps* the year before and was disappointed Mickey had missed it. 'I know you would have enjoyed it, Mickey,' she told him. 'All the intrigue, the daring, and the cunning wickedness of the German agents.' She shivered dramatically. 'They really were relentless, those Germans! But they were foiled in the end by that brave Englishman.' She snuggled her free hand into his. 'Now, sweetheart, where's this place you want to take me to?'

15

It was on a Thursday afternoon, a couple of weeks later, as he was searching on her dressing table for the wrist watch he'd removed earlier, that Harrington came across a small enamelled brooch, red, white and black, bearing the same swastika design he had seen bedecking the German Legation building and flying from the superstructure of the *Graf Spee* and dangling over the door of the Augsburger office in the Avenida.

In the dressing table mirror he could see Beta watching him from the bed, propped up on one elbow, her delightful breasts exposed above the fine silk sheet. 'It's just a piece of nonsense,' she said with what seemed to him casual indifference.

He picked up the brooch, suddenly recalling something he'd half-overheard ages ago, at one of Maria Winter's dinners, before Beta had joined Maria's select band of table guests. The table talk had been the inevitably rich compote of gossip, not entirely malicious but always enticing. Someone at the other end of the table had mentioned the name, to the accompaniment of a muffled giggle among the ladies of the company. He'd not paid much attention to this at the time, but from amidst the chatter one phrase returned to him now as he stood with the brooch in his hand. *She's far too cosy with the Legation, if you ask me.* They were talking about the German Legation; not much more than a stone's throw from where he was now standing, and the name of the lady had been Dona Elisabete Louçá e Medronho.

'The badge, it's nothing, darling,' Beta said, 'they give out those favours to everyone.' She adjusted the sheet, artfully contriving to expose more of herself. 'Aren't you going to give a poor woman a proper farewell kiss?'

He looked down at her, the swastika badge still in his hand. 'You visit the German Legation?'

She pouted. 'Am I supposed to stay cooped up here all week? You should come to the Legation yourself some time. They aren't so bad, those diplomats. Some of them are quite agreeable, you know. And the food's delightful, if a little heavy and Germanic for my taste.'

'But,' he began, and then realised that there was nothing for him to say. Beta was a typical Lisbon social butterfly; last week the German Legation, next week the Americans or the French, and if the British Embassy put on something sufficiently entertaining, she would be there too, flirting with the gentlemen and gossiping with the ladies. Half the people he met at Maria Winter's dinner table enjoyed similar trivial diplomatic rounds. It didn't mean anything, here in Lisbon on the edge of the continent, it was just a way of oiling the wheels of society, brightening up the daily round.

'You wouldn't wear it though, would you?' he demanded, holding up the badge.

'Darling, of course not!' She laughed. 'Someone gave it to me the other night. I should have thrown it out.'

'Do a lot of people go to these German parties?'

'Quite a few. Some English actually, and people from the other Embassies. There's a delightful young man,' she said, elaborately casual, 'from the American Embassy. So charming! They say Americans are unsophisticated boors, but it's not true.' She smiled sweetly, deliberately inviting a reaction from him.

Harrington knew better than to be drawn. 'And there are Germans, I suppose.'

'Well,' she drawled, favouring him with an arch smile, 'It is the *German* Legation, after all!' Beta sat up, throwing the silk covering completely aside. 'Darling, do come and give me a kiss.'

He abandoned any attempt to remonstrate. She was Portuguese and the Portuguese had no quarrel with the Germans. He couldn't help thinking it was priggish of him, in this neutral country, to take offence at his lover enjoying the company of nationals with whom the British might soon be at war. And, hadn't she just said, some English people were among the Germans' guests? That blond nephew of Dona Maria, who sometimes came to celebrations at the college, the one who he suspected Maria was trying to marry off to Beta: Andy Winter. He was in export-import, a convenient description, Harrington thought for business activities that were murky at best. He could imagine Winter snuggling up to the emissaries of the Reich, if there was profit in it for him.

She wanted more than a kiss but this time Harrington wasn't in the mood for dalliance and though she pouted beautifully she eventually conceded defeat. 'All right then, you old grouch,' she dismissed him. 'Get back to your beloved college.'

16

'A telephone call for you, *o senhor padre Arrington*.'

'The telephone? For me? Who is it?'

'*Não sei. Alguém*' José Fernandes, the professors' major-domo, shrugged. He didn't know. Someone. It wasn't his job to enquire more closely.

Harrington supposed the man knew where he was with an ox or a donkey, a hoe or an axe, but he probably thought it was against nature to have a voice coming at him out of a little piece of black devilry. Confident of his position in the servant hierarchy, heavy footed and of doleful expression, with dark pouches under his eyes and pock-marked cheeks, José clearly had a deep distrust of an invention smacking of the village witchcraft he'd run away from years before.

The telephone, the only one in the entire establishment, dwelt on a little marble-topped side table beside the door in the professors' dining room. Harrington hurried along the corridor, down the stairs to the ground floor and burst breathlessly through the heavy door, his shoes clipping noisily on the marble floor.

'*Estou.* I'm here.'

'Michael my friend, you're so out of breath!' The concern in the light tenor voice came clearly over the wire.

Heinz Koenig. What the devil did he want? 'I'm all right. The phone's rather a long way from my rooms.'

'Could you make yourself free this afternoon, for a little meeting?'

'This afternoon? That's not possible I'm afraid.' Perhaps the Augsburger salesman didn't have enough work to fill his days

94

whereas Harrington had to pluck spare time from the college schedule when and as he could.

A fractional pause at the other end of the line. Then: 'I think it's important.'

'I'm very busy just at the moment, Heinz. Next weekend, perhaps?' There was a lecture to give, test papers to mark and he was struggling through a theological work by an Austrian author whose opaque Latin, a literal translation from what was probably even more ponderous German, was not offering him any comfort.

'It's important,' Koenig repeated firmly. 'I don't think it's something that can wait.'

'I'm sorry, but I'm really tied up today.' Harrington tried to keep the impatience out of his voice.

'I believe we've a mutual friend.'

'Oh yes?' Who's that? Would Koenig perhaps have met Fonseca at one of the German Legation's receptions?

'A delightful lady.'

A sudden chill gripped his bowels. He said nothing. *Our little secret*, he heard a voice in his head say.

'And I think it might be in both our interests for us to talk.'

Harrington groped for the nearest chair. *Those things she goes to at the German Legation. She's been talking, surely not deliberately, but she's said something that's given us away. Koenig's picked up gossip, he wants to warn me, one friend to another, there's tittle-tattle going around.* 'Where d'you want to meet?' He immediately regretted giving in so easily; it was almost as good as a confession.

'Not the Trindade. Let's say the Estrela Gardens, opposite the basilica. There's a bench in the park, facing the main entrance. At three o'clock.' The line went dead.

'I say! Are you all right? You look frightfully queer.' Arthur Cope had come through from the kitchen and was standing over Harrington as he sat slumped on the hard-backed chair he had dragged from the dining table.

'It's nothing. Just a little turn. I'll be all right in a moment.'

Cope carried too much weight, his brow was beaded with sweat and he gave off a faint whiff of body odour. 'Can I get you something, Michael? A glass of brandy?'

'God, no!' He hadn't meant to snap back like that. 'No, I'll be all right in a moment. It was the telephone, I had to hurry down, I should have taken it more gently. That's all.'

'Nothing unpleasant, I hope?' Cope was studying him, head cocked to one side, his brow furrowed. 'Not the...?' He hitched up his right trouser leg, exposing a length of hairy white calf.

'What? Oh, the Masonic thing. No, no; just someone I met in town. He wanted to know the time of Sunday Mass.'

The spur of the moment lie seemed to satisfy Cope. 'Well,' he said, 'if you're sure. But I hope you're not going down with anything. You certainly look a bit peaky. Why don't you pop across the road to the French Hospital for a check up? What do you say?'

'I'd say that I'd be a damned sight better off if people kept their noses out of my business!' They looked at each other, both aghast. 'I don't know what came over me,' Harrington said by way of apology. 'The truth is, I think I *am* perhaps going down with something. I'm supposed to be giving a lecture this afternoon. I don't suppose you could fill in for me?'

'Delighted, old boy,' Cope replied, anxious to placate his colleague. 'I can entertain them with some of the shadier aspects of commercial life in England.' His family had for generations been iron founders in Wolverhampton and Cope invariably spent some of his annual vacation 'helping out,' as he liked to put it, in the factory's accounts department.

17

'I'm grateful to you, Michael, for agreeing to meet me at such short notice.'

With their backs to the well-tended tree-lined gardens, Harrington and Koenig were sitting on a bench facing the twin bell towers and grey dome of the Estrela basilica. To any passerby, Harrington imagined, they would appear to be two quiet respectable gentlemen, both foreigners and one a priest, come to admire the eighteenth century church built in gratitude for the birth of a son to Queen Maria I. The buzz and racket of passing trams was the accompaniment to the murmur of their conversation.

'What's this all about?' Harrington's throat was dry and he knew his voice sounded choked. *Keep cool*, he told himself, *this might all be something about nothing. Koenig's a friend. He's on your side.*

'It's a delicate matter and I needed to give it some thought before approaching you. There's a lady, a Portuguese lady. I believe you know her quite well.'

It was as he'd thought. Koenig wanted to tip him the wink that people were talking. Well, it was a bit embarrassing, he had to admit, but Harrington was grateful for the warning. 'It just shows how careful you've got to be,' he said, 'as soon as you agree to counsel a woman.'

'I'm sorry?'

'You know, spiritual advice, that sort of thing.' He tried for a light-hearted laugh but it came out as a croak. 'Women, they've always got worries of one kind or another, marital problems as often as not,' Harrington added in what he hoped would seem an attempt to make this seem man-to-man talk about silly females. 'Nothing that couldn't be sorted out if they would only just sit down and discuss things with their husbands.' He was talking too much, too fast, and talking nonsense to boot.

'Oh, I see.' Koenig said and then paused before adding thoughtfully: 'This lady is a slightly different case, I would say.'

There was nothing Harrington could do to stop the nerve in his left leg jumping, and he had to put his hand on his knee in an attempt to steady it. The drumming of his fingers was intended to convey his impatience to be off about more important business.

'Dona Elisabete Louçá e Medronho?'

'Dona Elisabete? Ah yes, we've met.' The drumming became a tattoo.

'More than once,' Koenig said, smiling. 'I believe. I hear she's become quite attached to you.'

'As I said, I've been giving her occasional spiritual counsel.' Harrington could feel cold sweat trickling from his armpits.

Koenig's smile turned into an appreciative laugh. 'Oh, very good.'

Harrington didn't like the tone of that laugh. 'The lady's suffered a good deal,' he said defensively.

'Not at your hands, I trust? You've been gentle with her, I hope?' Koenig interlaced his plump fingers over his rounded belly. 'Let's be frank, Michael. You've been having intimate relations: that's the right expression? Intimate relations? I know my English isn't always perfect.'

The sympathetic smile on Koenig's face had turned quite sinister. 'I don't know where this has come from, but you've got entirely the wrong end of the stick.' Harrington did his desperate best to play the dignified injured party. 'She's a lady I've been trying to advise,' he said, 'and I can't help it if idle gossip's been reading something into that.' An elderly couple on their way to the basilica turned at the sound of the suddenly raised English voice.

Koenig laid a hand on Harrington's forearm. 'Gently, my friend, gently. We don't want to attract attention to our little discussion, do we? Now, all this may be part of your counselling,' he continued in a reasonable, matter-of-fact way. 'I don't know much about these modern techniques: Jung, perhaps, or the admirable Doctor Freud?'

'This is all nonsense,' Harrington blustered, 'and I don't see why I've got to sit here listening to it.' Beta was a woman without guile and the problem with guileless people was they were inclined to talk too much and not wisely. She'd mentioned his name at one of the Legation parties. Koenig was a sharp bird and something about Beta's artless prattle had given the game away.

'I hope we're friends,' Koenig replied. 'That's why I asked you here. It's no concern of mine that you are, as I think our American friends would say, *screwing the dame,* but there's something else to consider.'

'Such as?'

'You're a priest.'

'So?' It was a losing battle and he knew it.

'Forgive me, Father,' Koenig was grinning broadly now, 'but, by sleeping with the lady, haven't you placed yourself in rather a tight corner? If your authorities should come to hear of the liaison?' He leaned back, a man totally at ease, enjoying the afternoon sun, sliding his bottom so near the edge of the seat that it looked as though he might decant himself onto the pavement.

'In the Augsburg Gymnasium,' Koenig continued, 'we studied one of your Shakespeare's plays. *Othello, the Moor of Venice.* I found Iago's character most interesting. You'll probably remember the scene where Iago speaks of reputation.'

He pursed his lips and frowned in concentration. *'Who steals my purse steals trash.'* The carefully quoted words were softly spoken. *'But he that filches from me my good name...'*

'Makes me poor indeed.' Harrington's Lower House students had made a detailed study of the same play the previous year. 'What d'you want, Koenig? Money?' The chill he'd had in his innards ever since that telephone call had now set like concrete. 'If that's what it is, you're barking up the wrong tree. I'm not wealthy. We get sixty pounds a year and our keep.'

Koenig sat up straight. 'Is that all?' he said in astonishment. 'So little for so much work? I reckon they're getting you very cheaply.' He shook his head. 'No, Michael, you mistake me entirely.'

'What then?'

'If the liaison were to become known.' He paused, lips parted as if to deliver a telling blow.

'Get on with it.' It wasn't Shakespeare's Iago who sprang into Harrington's mind but the cheating steward of the gospel parable. *To dig I am unable, to beg I am ashamed.* Koenig was quite right: thrown out of college, if the affair came to public knowledge, would he even have the chance to beg? He'd been dreading the prospect of having to return voluntarily to Salford. Exposure of the kind Koenig was threatening him with would be far worse. And what about poor Beta? Wouldn't her reputation, too, be utterly ruined?

In an abstracted sort of way, Harrington had been watching the progress of a grey-uniformed city policeman, holstered pistol on his belt, strolling up the Calçada de Estrela. As he drew level with them, the policeman dawdled to a halt. Perhaps Dr Salazar had issued a decree that two men weren't allowed to sit side by side on a park bench in front of a sacred building. Perhaps the policeman was merely thinking of taking the weight off his feet for a while. A crazy thought: *Officer, this man's blackmailing me because I've been having dalliance with one of your Portuguese lovelies.* The policeman hitched his belt, thought better of disturbing the foreigners and strolled on to take his rest elsewhere.

'You needn't worry,' Koenig said quietly. 'I don't think anyone else has picked it up. I myself wouldn't have put two and two together if I hadn't recognised who she was talking about. Such a reserved lady usually, and suddenly there she was, like a newly opened blossom. Quite a compliment to you, Michael. Now,' he sat up straight and looked directly at Harrington, 'to be practical. I think there's an opportunity here for both of us,'

'I've told you, I don't have any money.'

'It's not a question of money. Only of,' he paused fractionally, 'shall we say, mutual assistance?' Koenig folded his arms comfortably once more across his belly and looked across at the church as if admiring the architecture. 'The postal service here in Portugal is surprisingly good, I think you'd agree.'

'So? What's that got to do with anything?' Harrington had been impressed at the speed mail was arriving from England now the newly-named British Overseas Airways Corporation had begun the long-awaited regular flights to Lisbon but he didn't see what that had to do with Beta and himself.

'Didn't you tell me once you're in charge of all the post that comes to your college? You're the censor, right?'

'Censor's a bit strong. I don't actually open the letters, I just look at the envelopes. It's nothing more than an old college tradition and I don't know why we keep it up.'

'But of course!' Koenig exclaimed delightedly. 'Without tradition we're cast adrift upon a frightful sea. I forget which of our poets expressed such a thought. It may have been Goethe.' He turned towards Harrington. 'You are familiar with Goethe?'

'I know the name. I don't read German poets.'

Koenig was disappointed. 'Not even in translation?'

'Look, Koenig, never mind Goethe. What's this all about? Whatever you have in mind, get on with it.'

'I'm getting there,' Koenig protested mildly. 'Letters come to the college and you're the first to see them, correct?'

'Of course. After Cordeiro.'

'I think we may discount your admirable porter.' Koenig shifted around, his arm along the bench back, the better to see his companion's face. 'Michael, I have to tell you, I too have a problem.'.

Harrington wasn't interested.

'No, but listen,' Koenig insisted. 'Suppose you were to receive a special letter?'

'A special letter?' Harrington echoed stupidly.

'Indeed. A letter from England, with a special mark on it, a sign you're not to open it but to give it to me. 'Letters, actually. Letters I'd prefer didn't come to the office, that I don't want my secretary Ulrika Uhrig to see. Living over the shop as I do has its inconveniences sometimes. Like your porter Cordeiro, Fraulein Uhrig takes in the post. Unlike your porter, she's a person of some acuity.'

Harrington had met her once and, with a vague memory of a Wagner opera he had attended the previous year, had mentally nicknamed Koenig's buxom blonde secretary *The Valkyrie.*

He suddenly understood what all this was about. Koenig's hinted complaint of being exiled in Portugal: he'd never mentioned a wife and he didn't wear a wedding ring, but that didn't mean he wasn't married. He'd worked for years in London and he'd taken a mistress there. That was the indiscretion his bosses had found out about. German employers were probably very straight-laced, and they'd packed him off to Lisbon to mend his ways. Koenig wanted to keep the liaison going but he had to be careful. Naturally, he didn't want the Valkyrie to know his little game. Now that Koenig had learned about him and Beta, the German felt he could trust a fellow delinquent to act as go-between.

The concrete in his bowels was magically disintegrating. 'What's the mark to be then, Heinz?' Harrington asked, suddenly carefree. 'A heart perhaps?'

'A heart? Koenig asked in surprise.

Harrington could now afford to be amused 'How long did you say you'd lived in London? Pretty, is she?'

'Ah, yes. You're very quick, Michael,' Koenig grinned. 'Why not? Yes, a little heart, opposite the stamp.'

'Well, I just hope she won't be using scented notepaper. Cordeiro might become suspicious and that would never do.'

Koenig nodded. 'I'll make sure to tell her. The letters, they'll not always be from London, by the way. She travels a lot for her work.' He seemed relieved Harrington had latched on to his game so easily.

'And as to delivery? Not to your office, of course.' It was Harrington's turn to play a little.

Koenig held up his hands. 'Certainly not! You'll phone me when a letter comes and we can meet at the café in Campo Grande. It's quieter than the Trindade. '

Harrington nodded. He sometimes took a stroll in the park on the north side of the city.

And, Michael,' Koenig leaned forward towards him confidentially, 'don't worry about Dona Elisabete. She'll remain our secret. No danger to you. You're simply doing a favour for a friend.'

A favour for a friend, Koenig had said. Certainly not a very reputable friend, Harrington thought as he made his way back to the college, and not a reputable favour, but needs must sometimes. He didn't have to approve of what Koenig was up to; complicity was a small price to pay for guarding his own security. There was no need to be too alarmed; Koenig would probably move on to another post before too long and everything would return to normal.

18

Harrington received the first letter on June the twenty-ninth, the feast-day of Saints Peter and Paul, the patrons of the College and a high holiday, with an elaborate four-course lunch, one of the rare occasions when the professors and their guests dined in the students' refectory.

The post arrived as he was getting ready to join the people gathered in the President's Parlour for pre-lunch drinks. Standing at his open door he'd only time for a quick glance at the letters Cordeiro thrust into his hands.

He was about to open the typewritten envelope addressed to him, with a British stamp and a London postmark, until he noticed the neatly pencil-drawn shape in the top left-hand corner of the envelope.

Arthur Cope was standing at the President's Parlour door. 'Come on, Michael!' he shouted across the corridor. 'If you don't hurry up, you'll miss the white port Andy Winter's given us, it's going down fast.' Harrington stuffed the envelope into his cassock pocket and followed obediently.

Winter was one of a handful of visitors crowded into the Parlour. Along with a couple of English businessmen who had done favours for the college, Harrington saw there were three Portuguese he knew, one of them a priest, and standing over by the farthest window was a tall dark-haired man talking to Martin Blount. That would be someone from the Embassy, he guessed. They usually sent along a representative for such occasions as this.

Harrington greatly regretted the college didn't invite ladies to these events. Surely, Miss Singleton would make a much more interesting visitor than the dour-looking character the Embassy had provided. And, although it was no use thinking along those lines, it would have made all the difference in the world if one particular lady were to be in the company.

The Parlour had a comfortable masculine shabbiness about it in contrast to the polished splendour of Beta's apartment. A huge old wireless set, the focus of every evening's after-supper gathering, dominated the far corner. Standing on the worn carpet in the centre of the room was a large round mahogany table on which reposed not only the bottles Andy Winter had brought with him but also a decanter of vintage port, a bottle of brandy and a silver box filled with cigarettes.

From the snatches of conversation Harrington heard as he did the rounds of the crowded room, the talk for once wasn't all about war. Cope had button-holed one of the English businessmen who represented a well-known English electrical firm and was doing his best to negotiate favourable terms for rewiring the entire ground floor of the college. Well, Harrington thought as he moved on, that's what bursars do.

The Portuguese priest, whose English struck him as surprisingly good, was interested in the history of the college. It was a subject dear to Harrington's heart and he was just getting into his stride when Martin Blount tapped the side of his glass to attract everyone's attention. 'We should be going down to lunch now, gentlemen.' They all trooped obediently after the college president as he led the way downstairs to the students' refectory.

Even as a student, Harrington had always reckoned the refectory to be an austerely elegant room with its vaulted ceiling and three large high windows overlooking the garden. The tables were arranged around three walls, the seating provided by benches that formed an integral part of the wainscoting. At the far end of the room the entire wall above the top table was filled with the only decoration, a detailed rendering of the Last Supper worked in the traditional Portuguese blue and white *azulejo* tiles.

Harrington had mixed feelings about the seating arrangements on these occasions. Today, as luck would have it, he found himself with Peter Fielding on his left and Andy Winter on his right. Winter was overweight, with a substantial paunch and fading blond hair, and his flushed complexion wasn't helped by his fondness for the bottle. With a few drinks in him, he was soon loudly expansive over the hors d'oeuvre, slices of *presunto* - cured ham - and assorted pickled vegetables. 'You wouldn't believe the amount of stuff Salazar's sending out to Hamburg,' he barked at Harrington. 'Everything from wolfram to tins of sardines. I thought the Krauts went in for soused herrings, not sardines in olive oil.'

In a suddenly mischievous spirit Harrington interrupted him. 'D'you ever get to visit the German Legation, Andy?'

He was treated to a momentary suspicious glare. 'What if I do?' he snapped. 'Business is business, whatever the politicians get up to.'

Only half listening, Harrington let him rattle on as the main course came around. It was veal, a rare delicacy which he knew Cope had gone to great trouble and expense to procure for the occasion.

Harrington suddenly pricked up his ears as Winter turned his attention to the future. 'If we only had the guts to fight on Hitler's side, we could finish Russia for a hundred years. Adolf's sorted out the Commies in Germany and put the Yids in their proper place. They're at the back of it all, you know, Father, the Yids. If they had their way they'd be running the world right now. Not far off it already.'

Harrington tried to hide his irritation at the tirade. 'You think the Jews will be made the villains if things get as far as

107

war?' he asked evenly. 'I thought that in Germany at least, they already are the victims. Last year, what did they call it in the paper when all the Jewish shops were attacked? *Kristallnacht*.' He was very aware that Fielding, sitting on his left, could hear everything Andy Winter was spouting.

'That was a popular demonstration against the Yids' outrageous prices,' Winter retorted. 'And why do you say, *will be made the villains*, Father? They already are. It stands to reason, doesn't it? Who holds the purse-strings in the States? Who made a killing out of the Depression?' Winter was making no effort to lower his voice and Harrington could see Blount looking anxiously in their direction. 'I don't pretend to be one of your pansy intellectuals, Father,' he continued loudly. 'I'm a man of business, and I know enough of the world of commerce and banking to know who's pulling the strings.'

Fielding suddenly leaned boldly across Harrington, offering Winter the platter of meat. 'Would you care for another helping of the veal, sir? It's really very good.'

Disorientated for an instant, Winter took the proffered dish. 'Thanks. Not a bad spread you've managed to put on today, Father. I had the most god-awful piece of steak I've ever tried to eat the last time I was here. If you people would only be prepared to pay decent wages, I could find you a chef who'd do you proud every day of the week.'

Harrington gave Fielding an appreciative smile. Embarrassed, the young man ducked his head and concentrated on his plate.

19

The offer of the meat platter had been an instinctive gesture of support on Fielding's part. He had a lot of respect for his moral theology professor. Unlike most of the other members of staff, Father Harrington made his lectures lively, he invited comments and could deal with objections. There were times when he seemed to verge on being revolutionary in his approach to his subject but he was always careful to distinguish between his personal opinions and orthodox doctrine. All in all, Fielding thought, he was a priest worth emulating.

With only another year to go before ordination to the priesthood, Fielding was looking forward to returning to England and getting involved in parish work but he knew his fellow students thought of him as something of an egg-head. 'They'll be sending you off to Rome for further studies as soon as you're ordained,' Charlie Russell had said to him only the other day, 'and then you'll come back here to teach. You'll end up just like Harrington.'

It had been meant as a friendly gibe but, Fielding wondered, would that be such a bad thing? There could be a worse life than giving back something to the college that had given him his education, had been his guardian all these years. He loved Portugal, the people and its fascinating history. He spoke Portuguese well enough to be sometimes taken for a native.

As for his family back in England, he would be able to visit them during the summer vacation and spend a few weeks travelling around to renew old acquaintances, meet with former colleagues at the annual reunion of alumni.

All this talk of war was worrying, of course, but politicians were always posturing, war-talk, peace-talk; honey and the stick, as he remembered Father Harrington saying recently in an aside about the possibility of war, during the course of a lecture about the Commandment, *Thou shalt not kill.*

Fielding couldn't understand how Father Harrington had tolerated that odious creature who had been at table with them. He didn't know his name - students weren't introduced to the guests - but he could tell that Father Harrington had been unhappy with the bilge the man had been spouting. The Jews had been persecuted left right and centre throughout the ages, and now Hitler was going for them in a vicious crusade. To think that a fat-faced blond anti-Jewish entrepreneur was a welcome guest at their table offended Fielding's sense of propriety as much, he guessed, as it did Father Harrington's.

Fielding's father had been in the Great War but that hadn't meant much to a little boy. It was only since, prompted by Father Harrington's enthusiasm for the poems of Wilfred Owen, he'd started reading about the atrocities, the mud and the gas, the futility of trench warfare, that he'd begun to understand what his father must have been through and why he didn't want to talk about any of it. It was dreadful to think it might all start over again and that disgusting man he'd sat next to might profit from it.

20

Once the meal was over and the guests had made their farewells, the college sank into the somnolence of a belated siesta. Back in his quarters, Harrington pulled the by-now badly creased envelope from his cassock pocket. He couldn't resist lifting it to his nose and sniffing. Not a hint of perfume: Koenig must have warned her to be careful.

Turning it over, he saw the gummed-down flap bore the initials SWALK. He'd seen that once before, on a letter addressed to one of the Lower House boys. Curious as to what it might mean, he'd summoned the lad. '*Sealed With A Loving Kiss*, sir,' the lad explaining, wriggling with embarrassment. 'It's my sister, sir, she's stupid like that. I'll tell her, sir, not ever again.'

*So, Koenig's young lady doesn't stint on affectionate little touche*s, Harrington thought with amusement,

He hung his cassock on the back of his bedroom door and shrugged on a lightweight jacket, carefully putting the envelope into the inside pocket. The clock outside in the corridor sounded the hour; three o'clock.

He went quietly downstairs and pushed open the door to the professors' dining room. There wasn't a sound coming from the other side of the green baize door leading to the kitchen. Satisfied he wouldn't be disturbed, he picked up the telephone handset and dialled the number Koenig had given him. The Valkyrie picked up the call after the second ring and told him abruptly to hold the line.

'I'll see you in Campo Grande in an hour.' Koenig's voice sounded strained. Well, naturally, Harrington thought, as he headed down the corridor to the Arches, he would be under stress, anticipating the first communication from his loved one.

'*Boa tarde, o senhor padre Arrington!*'

God! He'd forgotten about Cordeiro. The porter beamed up at him from behind the desk in his cubbyhole.

'And good afternoon to you, Manuel,' Harrington replied.

Damn! Cordeiro was sharp enough in his own way and probably knew more about the comings and goings of staff and students than anyone else in college. Not that it really mattered. Harrington was perfectly entitled to go out as and when he pleased and Cordeiro was not to know there was a naughty letter hiding in *padre Arrington's* pocket.

'It's a hot day for being out and about.' The elderly porter was just being chummy.

'I thought I'd take a stroll, get some fresh air.' Harrington knew it was a mistake as soon as the words were out. To judge by the look he received, something like *mad dogs and Englishmen* was clearly in Cordeiro's mind. It might not be midday sun but it would still be stinking hot when he got out into the street and the air would be anything but fresh. He offered a curt goodbye and marched determinedly down the steps, feeling the porter's quizzical eyes on him all the way to the street door.

Koenig was already seated with a bottle and a couple of glasses at a table in the shade of the tall plane trees by the time Harrington arrived at the open-air café in Campo Grande. 'I've discovered this rather interesting white wine,' the German said after they had shaken hands. 'I rather think you'll like it.'

Harrington made to take the envelope from his jacket pocket but Koenig restrained him. 'There's no hurry.' He waved to the vacant chair opposite him and poured the straw-coloured wine. 'He,' with a nod to the café door where the proprietor lounged, reading a sporting paper, 'tells me the wine is from his village near Penela. They're pathetically loyal to their origins, the Portuguese, don't you think? A small-minded attitude if you like, but attractive in its way.'

The cool wine was fragrant, dry but with a hint of honey somewhere in the finish.

'So,' Koenig smiled benignly across the table, 'today's your college's special day, isn't it? I trust it's been enjoyable?'

'Yes, thank you,' Harrington replied. 'And it's a good job your letter arrived today, otherwise I'd have been elsewhere and you'd have had to wait for it.' *It's Thursday. If it hadn't been for the college feast,* Harrington thought, *'I'd have been with Beta.*

'It wouldn't have mattered,' Koenig replied nonchalantly.

'All the same,' Harrington said, anxious to get rid of his burden, 'you really ought to have it now.'

'As you wish.' Koenig scarcely glanced at the envelope before stuffing it in his own pocket.

'I'm sorry it's crumpled and a bit damp. The heat, you know. And,' he added, 'that thing, SWALK, on the back. Can you tell her it won't do, Koenig? After all, the letter's addressed to me and if someone else saw it, they might misinterpret.'

Koenig laughed apologetically after Harrington had explained the meaning of the acronym. 'She's a romantic little soul, you've got to understand. But I'll tell her and I'm grateful you've been so kind as to help me.'

Hardly kind. The other day Koenig had spoken of Shakespeare's play and Harrington remembered another line: *Othello's reputation's gone.* Well, he wasn't going to be another Othello.

A sudden thought struck him, about something Winter had said. 'You're a scientific sort of chap, Heinz. D'you know what wolfram is?'

The other looked at him sharply. 'It's a metal ore. Why do you ask?'

'Someone mentioned it, at table today, and I didn't like to show my ignorance. What's it used for? Portugal's exporting it to Germany.'

'It's also known as tungsten. You've seen it without knowing, in the filaments in light bulbs.'

'So Hitler needs a bit more illumination, does he?' Harrington asked light-heartedly.

Koenig didn't smile. 'It's also used to harden artillery shells.' He poured the last of the wine into their glasses. 'Drink up, Michael, it's time I was going back to the office.'

Cordeiro was still at his post when he returned. 'A good walk, *senhor padre?*' he asked as Harrington reached the top of the steps.

'Lovely, thank you Manuel. I feel all the better for it.'

He returned to his rooms, thinking of Koenig's delight at being at last able to read his lover's letter after so long a separation.

What would it be like, he wondered, to be deprived of Beta's company for a fraction of that time? He thought of the previous night's dream, the clearest he'd ever had. There had been the same sunlit woodland glade as in previous dreams, the same delicate swirling dress, tantalisingly transparent when she stood backlit in a beam of light. But then she'd fled, giggling, with him in pursuit. He distinctly remembered how he'd stretched his arms in a vain attempt to catch her. Then he'd tripped over something, a branch perhaps or a stone, and in his imagination he could still hear her peal of laughter at his plight. Just remembering the startling clarity of the dream was enough to arouse him.

In an attempt to distract himself, Harrington thought he'd read a couple of chapters of *The Fashion in Shrouds,* a recent Margery Allingham novel he'd bought at the Livraria Bertrand in the Chiado. He was usually fascinated by the doings of Allingham's hero, Albert Campion, but today he couldn't concentrate. The dream had left him unsettled and besides, he felt something wasn't quite right.

He was surprised he hadn't thought of it before. Koenig must have already been sending letters to his lady love; so how was it only now the German needed his services as go-between? Perhaps he'd had another contact in the city who had gone away, obliging the salesman to look for another postman?

He shrugged off the useless speculation. The important thing was that his cooperation ensured both Beta and he were protected at very little cost. Koenig had never said explicitly where he'd got his information about them but Harrington reminded himself to warn gently Beta against letting slip any more indiscretions when she was visiting the German Legation.

21

Harrington continued to receive a string of the special letters. He was surprised how extensively the lady travelled. To judge by the post marks, her journeys took her around southern England, though it seemed she also had business in Birmingham and Liverpool. One letter had been posted in Coventry another in Manchester and one in Leicester. Sometimes the address was typed, sometimes written in a neat feminine hand, but always with the simple heart shape in the top left hand corner. Thankfully, there were no more envelopes sealed with loving kisses.

They would sit at one of the open-air tables in Campo Grande if the weather was fine. On the occasional wet day Harrington and Koenig took shelter in the stuffy café interior with the coffee machine belching away in the corner behind the bar. There were rarely many other customers in either case and the owner had grown accustomed to having a bottle and glasses ready.

Beta's sumptuous apartment in Lapa had become Harrington's regular Thursday home. Though making love was still important to them both there were times when all they wanted to do was to chat companionably.

Sometimes the chess set came into use again. Harrington tried much harder when he played her now and honours were about evenly matched, though he had to admit Beta's game occasionally had an unexpected edge, producing inspired moves that left him floundering. She claimed she'd never had formal tuition in the game so he could only conclude that her feminine mind made imaginative leaps his methodical approach failed to anticipate. She modestly claimed her successes were down to mere luck and even accused him once or twice of letting her win. Secretly, her innocent pleasure on these triumphant occasions gave him a piercing and disturbing delight.

It was mid-July now and the end of term marked the time for the college to migrate across the river to the house at Pêra. In Harrington's opinion the primitive accommodation wasn't much changed from the time in the eighteenth century when an exiled English gentlemen had bequeathed the property to the college as a holiday house. Harrington had enjoyed the place as a student but with advancing years he found Pêra held less and less attraction for him and in any case he had other plans.

It would have been easy enough for him to slip away back across the river and see Beta as often as he wished but he had to let her know he'd promised Fonseca to act as chaplain at the Quinta de Laranjeiras until the last week in August. In an ideal world Beta would have been able come with him; he was sure she'd have got on well with Carmelita and the children. But they had to face reality. Beta let him go resignedly, telling him that a period of being apart would make their reunion all the sweeter.

Koenig was less obliging. 'We had an agreement, you and I,' he said when Harrington told him he would be away for several weeks. 'My friend is going to be very disappointed.'

'Surely she'd understand, if you let her know the circumstances? And there'll be all her letters waiting for you when I get back.'

'It's all right for you,' Koenig sounded more angry than disappointed. 'you've got your lady-love around the corner, you can see her any time you want.'

22

Fonseca met him at the railway station in Sintra with the Hispano Suiza. 'I'm glad you could come just now,' he said as they drove out of the station forecourt, scattering a couple of stray dogs who had been snoozing on the warm cobblestones. 'Today's Saint Monica's day.'

'I thought her feast day was at the end of August? The twenty-seventh, if I remember rightly. That's nearly a month away,' Harrington said, desperately clutching the leather strap attached to the door. Fonseca's driving seemed more erratic than ever.

'This is Saint Monica Vergonhosa,' Fonseca told him, 'not Saint Monica the mother of Saint Augustine. Quite a different lady.'

'I've never heard of her.'

'I doubt many people have. She's our own village's patron saint. In fact,' Fonseca said with a smile, 'I'm not sure she's a real saint at all, but the villagers love her all the same.'

Carmelita was her usual charming self when she greeted his arrival and the boys were a little bolder than the last time Harrington had met them. Carlos wanted to show him a model aircraft someone had brought him as a present. The Dornier 17, painted in Luftwaffe colours, with a swastika on the tailplane, was frighteningly realistic, even down to the bomb doors that could be opened to show the loaded racks within. 'It can blow up whole houses,' Carlos told him, proud to show off his knowledge.

Harrington preferred the kite Daniel wanted him to launch in the park beyond the formal gardens behind the house.

Though they bore a strong physical resemblance to each other, the twins were not identical and were quite different in their temperaments. Harrington could already see characteristics in Carlos that would make him one day like his father. Daniel, he thought, showed signs of taking after his mother.

Harrington was used to the extravagance of Portuguese religious festivals but he could see this one was clearly going to be exceptional. The villagers had been busy about the streets all morning, Fonseca told him, decking doorways with green branches, hanging colourful bedspreads from balconies. 'We'll have just a light lunch,' he explained, 'something to be going on with. This evening's feast is the main menu today.'

Though Harrington had been told the procession through the village was scheduled to begin at six o'clock, the church bell had struck the half-hour before they moved off, headed by the band's discordant hooting of brass and banging of drums.

Behind the band were the villagers, men, women and children, singing hymns whose tunes seemed to bear little relation to the blaring noise in front. Finally, behind the village priest padre Jerónimo, the Fonsecas and Harrington, came six strong young men carrying a flower-decked platform on which was secured a highly coloured nearly life-size statue of a woman dressed in a simple white shift and surrounded by lurid leaping plaster flames.

Earlier in the afternoon, padre Jerónimo, a tubby bald-headed man, who'd served thirty years in the parish as he proudly told Harrington, had explained that Santa Monica Vergonhosa had been burned to death in an *auto-da-fé* in Rossio square in Lisbon in 1536 after claiming to have had visions of high-ranking clerics, including the Cardinal Patriarch, being thrust down to Hell by the Archangel Michael. The priest was more than a little vague regarding the circumstances of her subsequent rehabilitation and he was utterly indifferent to Harrington's squeamishness about the holy woman's sufferings. 'She was a *santinha*, a little saint!' the priest reminded him. 'What are flames to the blessed?' Such opaque logic was beyond reasoning.

As they walked along in the procession, Fonseca offered Harrington a silver hip flask engraved with the family coat of arms. 'Cognac,' he muttered by way of apology. Apparently, the traditional tipple on this occasion was *aguardente*, rough grape spirit. 'The story goes,' Fonseca explained, 'that holy Monica's detractors claimed her visions were the result of her drinking too much of the liquor her father distilled from the grape harvest.'

Harrington had seen leather bottles being passed among the villagers and guessed that the increasingly alarming things now happening to the volume and harmony of the singing indicated that everyone in the procession was sharing in the inspiration of the same spirit. It was all very jolly, he reflected gloomily, or would have been with Beta beside him.

Late in evening the banquet in the lamp-lit square got under way. The whole village was there, Harrington saw, ranked in order of importance with padre Jerónimo as the guest of honour.

'These folk, they're the salt of the earth,' the priest told him as they ate. 'I know them all and all their little ways, and they know me, and what I say is good enough for them.' He reached his fork for another morsel of the excellent Alentejo pig that had been spit-roasted over hot coals at the other side of the square.

There was nothing restrained about the abundance on the tables. The roast pig was accompanied by mountains of *presunto,* deep bowls of shellfish with rice, baskets of enormous early season figs and demi-johns of potent red wine from last year's vintage. There were baskets of bread rolls to soak up the juices and not a vegetable in sight.

Harrington had drunk a drop too much of the wine to be entirely diplomatic. He'd seen a handsome well-dressed woman fussing around the parish priest after the procession and there she was again, holding court among a flock of other women at the table opposite but clearly with half an eye on what was going on at the top table.

'The clergy round here,' Harrington said, refilling Jerónimo's glass from the nearest wicker-bound flagon, 'I suppose they all have housekeepers?' Seeing the woman had made him think of Beta. He'd known he would miss her but hadn't imagined how much her absence would upset him.

'You don't expect a priest to do his own cooking, do you?' Jerónimo gave a knowing smile, 'his own laundry, dusting and polishing? That's the trouble with you seminary professors, if you don't mind me saying so, with your books and your learned discussions. You're out of touch with the real world. Me, I haven't looked at a book in thirty years, and I don't need to. It's all in here.' He tapped the side of his head. 'Life's that counts, not books, my friend.

'You ask about *governantas*,' he went on, 'and I know what you mean. Well, what I always maintain is, a man is a man, and a man has needs, whatever Holy Mother Church may say.' He looked at his plate, trying to decide whether it too had needs. He glanced up. 'Providing a man's discreet of course, you understand.'

Harrington understood.

He watched the villagers file away home some time after midnight, children carried on shoulders, dogs at heel. Dona Carmelita had retired some time earlier, pleading a headache, and the twins had only been allowed to have a taste of the feast before being carted off by their nanny. Padre Jerónimo was among the last to abandon the table, making his unsteady exit with assurances to his host that he knew the way home perfectly well, 'as so I should, after thirty years.' The woman had lingered after her companions had departed but now followed closely in Jerónimo's footsteps.

'They're good-hearted people,' Fonseca declared when he and Harrington were at last alone. Antonio had liberated a bottle of fine Armagnac from a sack he'd kept under the table. 'My family's been here for centuries, and they've been here with us. That's the way it is and that's the way it will always be, if Botas has anything to do with it.'

'*Botas*? Boots?' Harrington asked.

Fonseca grinned like a naughty schoolboy. 'A term of affection. Dr Salazar is partial to wearing elastic-sided boots.'

'He seems remarkably indulgent about wayward clergy.'

'Who? Salazar?' Fonseca asked with a frown.

'Padre Jerónimo.'

'Well, it depends what you mean by wayward.'

'I was asking about the priests hereabouts. He interpreted *housekeeper* quite broadly.'

'I imagine he had reason to,' Fonseca replied nonchalantly. 'What was it your Queen Elizabeth once said?' He concentrated for a moment. 'Ah, yes! *I would not make windows into a man's soul.* Isn't that right?'

'It didn't stop her executing Catholic priests.'

'Perhaps not.' Fonseca was not really interested in the ancient rights and wrongs of a far-off country, 'but that was politics. Our village clergy now, they lead lonely lives. It's hardly surprising some of them look for consolation wherever it may present itself.'

'So, you condone priests maintaining mistresses?' Harrington asked as casually as he was able.

Fonseca favoured him with a knowing smile. 'There's much to be said for a discreet arrangement with a trustworthy woman.'

'And if the trustworthy woman produces a child?' It wasn't an entirely academic question. The risk had crossed Harrington's mind more than once, though Beta had assured him that side of things was all taken care of; quite how, he'd never cared to enquire. He'd never taken any precautions on his own account. Even if he'd had the nerve to ask for them, the sale of rubber goods had been altogether banned by Salazar.

'There are orphanages,' Fonseca said, 'and there are barren women crying out for *um recem nascido*, a new-born, to coo over.' He selected a fig from the basket on the table, took a knife and neatly opened up the fruit to reveal its sweet glossy seed-laden interior. 'The fig's the emblem of our fertility, don't you think? Its shape, so suggestive of,' he gestured towards his groin. He picked up the halved fig and sucked the contents noisily into his mouth.

Jerónimo's comment about books stuck in Harrington's mind. Wasn't it the experience of life itself, not theories, that dictated how life's problems were to be worked out? The solution the parish priest of Laranjeiras had provided seemed to satisfy him and, as the day's celebrations had shown, his parishioners obviously doted on him.

Harrington wondered whether this pragmatic approach wasn't much different from the way his own life was evolving. He did all the work required of him in college; Beta apart, he attended to all his religious duties. Was keeping a mistress – he enjoyed a frisson at the use of the word – such an evil thing? Even the censorious Maria Winter had only condemned that priest on the cathedral staff for running away up north. He'd been a fool, she'd said, to relinquish his comfortable house in Lisbon.

Suppose, Harrington wondered, he wasn't tied to the college? Fonseca had, perhaps jokingly, once suggested he could become the permanent chaplain at Laranjeiras. He allowed himself to speculate: the duties would be light, the company delightful. He could lend a hand to padre Jerónimo occasionally. *Who knows,* he told himself, *one day I could take Jerónimo's place, with Beta as my governanta.*

Governanta: what an intriguing word, he thought. The Portuguese expression merely meant housekeeper but, for an English speaker, there was the tantalising suggestion of being ruled. Beta didn't exactly dominate him but it was she who led the way in their love-making, just as she sometimes managed to do in their games of chess, and he had no difficulty with either.

23

Dona Elisabete was experiencing the delicious pain of separation from the one she loved. People who didn't really know him might think of Mickey as a sad lonely case and more than once she'd heard snide comments around Maria Winter's table, patronising remarks about an 'innocent old sober-sides.' But from the outset she'd seen something different in him, a timid shy creature she was thrilled to have led to emerge from under cover.

It was a pity they weren't able to parade their love more openly but she knew enough of the censorious attitude of the Church to appreciate Mickey's fears on that score and her fertile brain was already casting about for lasting solutions to their problem.

She hadn't mentioned anything to him of course, but she'd been toying with a plan of emigrating to Brazil or to Angola, where he could join her and where they'd be able to begin a fresh life together. The Lapa apartment would fetch a good price and living costs would be so much cheaper in South America or Africa than they were in Lisbon. He spoke very good Portuguese and in the free-for-all she understood both those places to be she was sure that, with her help, he'd be able to find a suitable niche.

That was long-term planning; for the moment, however, she had somehow to fill her days in Mickey's absence and she was happy to receive an invitation to an informal soirée at the German Legation. This time it was to be an evening of Bavarian food and drink.

The Legation was crowded and she was delighted to see quite a few familiar faces, friends she could chat to. It was such an attractive ambience, and the attendants, muscular young men with close-cropped blond hair and clad in immaculate close-fitting suits, were obsequiously polite even if none of them spoke more than a few words of Portuguese. She noticed they all wore the same badge in their lapels. The double zig-zag sign, she supposed, was the mark of their calling. Most of the Legation staff were in civilian clothes, as were the guests, but of those in uniform she thought the most dashing by far were the Germans.

The food was tastefully arranged on silver platters laid on damask-covered tables beneath the crystal chandeliers in the big first floor reception hall. Long banners covered the walls with dramatic splashes of red, white and black, the silky material shifting lazily in the slight currents of air coming from the windows that opened out onto little balconies with views of the garden below. A four-piece band at the far end of the hall provided a subdued leitmotif to the hum of conversation and laughter.

Dona Elisabete waved to that nice man Abe Eldridge from the American Embassy.

'Hi, honey,' he called to her, breaking off his conversation with one of the German diplomats for a moment, 'don't forget now, what I've told you.' He was flirting with her as usual. 'A visa for the States, any time you want it, at the drop of a hat.'

As she moved on she had to giggle at the way he'd expressed his assurance. *At the drop of a hat.'* English had such strange expressions. Dona Elisabete had an image of Mickey – come to think of it, she'd never seen him wearing a hat – throwing his headgear on to the floor as a starting signal for their love-making.

She politely avoided the array of sausages, cured meats and pumpernickel, in favour of a few nibbles of strudel - she loved the flaky filo pastry and the sweet apple fillings - and tried a mouthful of something she was told was called *Gugelhupf.* An impossible name - German was such a strange gruff language she always thought - but the product was delicious: doughy cake stuffed with raisins, almonds and soaked in cherry brandy. There was Sekt to drink, not on a par with the Moët et Chandon that had been her dear father's favourite, but good enough all the same.

'*Guten Abend, liebe Dame Elisabete!*'

She turned, pleased to find Heinz Koenig at her elbow. '*Boa tarde, senhor Heinzi,*' she responded brightly.

Since discovering quite by chance that they had a mutual acquaintance in padre Harrington she was always pleased to see Heinzi at these Legation parties. Not a looker, she had to admit, but he was pleasant and so attentive, never presuming too much familiarity. He was gossipy, but then so was she, and he always had some amusing story to tell about the people he met in his course of business. This evening it was a complicated tale about a client in Olivais, on the other side of the city. The man had come to the attention of the PVDE for printing some rather seditious stuff.

She knew the *Polícia de Vigilância e de Defesa do Estado,* the national security police, didn't have a good reputation in some quarters. One heard stories about goings-on in their prison at Caxias but clearly it was the man's own stupidity that had landed him in his predicament.

'He claimed innocence,' Heinzi told her with a chuckle, 'on the grounds that it wasn't his job to read the things he printed.' He showed his teeth in a sympathetic grin. 'And now he's cooling his heels, courtesy of the PVDE.'

'They have a duty to keep us safe,' she told Heinzi who agreed with her entirely.

'And our friend, I trust he's well?' he asked politely.

'Mickey?' The name slipped out unintentionally, probably because of the silly picture of the hat she'd just had in her mind. She was halfway through her third large glass of Sekt and the bubbles of the sparkling wine were having a not unpleasant effect on her concentration. 'He's well,' she told him, 'but I haven't seen him for a while. He's been invited to stay with the Fonseca family over on the other side of Sintra.'

'Ah yes,' Heinzi said, nodding, as though the name Fonseca was familiar to him. 'Padre Harrington's a man much in demand.' He paused and raised quizzical eyebrows. 'Mickey?'

'It's what I call him,' Dona Elisabete said unsteadily. Her secret name for him, just as Beta was his name for her. But Heinzi was their friend, wasn't he? It wouldn't go any further. 'My private name, you understand, just between the two of us.'

'Of course.' Heinzi, ever the soul of discretion, understood immediately. 'In confidence, *natürlich*. I'm delighted to have met you again, Dona Elisabete,' he said, 'but you must excuse me. I see our Commercial Attaché, has need of me.' She watched as he bustled off to the corner where she could see Abe Eldridge still in conversation with his German friend.

24

On Monday in the last week of August, Harrington was back in Lisbon, heading for Cais de Sodré to cross the river en route to his responsibilities at Pêra. Although there was a small foot-passenger ferry from Black Horse Square, Harrington much preferred the big boat that took lorries and cars. He always enjoyed listening to the drivers as they gathered in the bar for the fifteen minute crossing to smoke and chat about their work and fuel up with *bicas,* tiny cups of black coffee, and *aguardente.*

Disembarking on the other side and all ready for the long walk up to Pêra, he was delighted to find their tenant farmer, unloading a cartload of vegetables on to the crowded quayside. 'For the Lisbon market,' the grizzled old man explained. 'I'm going back empty if you want a lift.'

'That's a fine mule you have there,' Harrington said as he climbed up on to the driving bench.

'Eh, you have to pay the best if you want to get the best,' the man commented as he flicked his whip over the animal's ears without touching the beast.

Soft-hearted Beta would like that little consideration, Harrington thought, as the mule's hooves struggled to find a grip on the smooth cobbles and the cart lurched into motion.

Thoughts of Beta immediately made him feel guilty. He ought to have gone to see her on his way back from Laranjeiras but he simply didn't want to face Ana at the apartment. and in any case the maid's presence would have meant that he and Beta would have had to be on their best behaviour. Far better, he'd thought, to wait until he was back in the city when they could be alone for a long and delightful Thursday reunion.

He found Bob Knox sitting in the shade side of the Pêra courtyard, wearing a big straw hat and reading what looked like a paperback Western. 'They're all out, thank goodness,' he said to Harrington as he struggled to get out of the creaking wicker chair he must have dragged from the common room.

'They're a lively bunch, a bit too lively for my liking,' he said in answer to Harrington's question of how he'd been getting on. 'Over-excited, you might say. I'll be glad of a few days of peace and quiet back in the city.'

'It's not surprising they're a bit on edge,' Harrington said, 'with all the talk about war.' Blount had encouraged the staff to adopt the line that even at this late hour, as long as Chamberlain and Herr Hitler were still talking, reason might still prevail; advice that had been cynically interpreted by Tom Pargeter as *heads in the sand, boys.*

Harrington went up to leave his baggage to his room at the end of the first floor corridor. José had made up his bed, he was glad to see, and he checked his lamp had oil in it. He might once have thought of staying at the Pêra house as an adventure free from the usual constraints of college life. Now, as a member of staff, he was only too aware of the disadvantages of living in a barn of a place without electricity or running water.

He supposed he ought to be thankful he wasn't required to share the infamous long-drops used by the students. A lavatory, a sort of garderobe, had been installed for the exclusive use of the staff on what had been a balcony, with a cistern filled by one of the servants who lugged up pails full of water from the well in the yard.

His mattress, he reassured himself by bouncing up and down on the bed, had springs rather than the straw he'd had to make do with as a student. Ah well, he thought, a week of rough comforts wouldn't be too bad so long as none of the young men he had charge of didn't break a leg or go down with some dreadful disease.

In the event, Harrington was thankful the week passed without any incident worse than mild sunburn. The younger ones made daily treks to the long beach at Caparica or played rounders on the field below the house. Older and more adventurous students planned walks along the coast to what they called Salt Lakes and some made an arduous climb over the Arrabida mountain range to visit one of the little hidden south-facing beaches on the far side.

Among the tattered stock of novels that had accumulated in the staff common room Harrington found one of C. S. Lewis' novels, *The Beast Must Die*, written under his pen name of Nicholas Blake. He wondered if Martin Blount had contributed it; the old man had a curiously wide taste in reading material.

The pot-boiler, for that was Harrington's opinion of the book, didn't keep his mind from wandering. It had been really stupid of him not to have called in on Beta before coming to Pêra. Surely, she could have found an excuse to get the maid out of the way for an hour or two?

The recognition of his lapse set off fresh anxieties. Hadn't Beta been just a bit too easily resigned to losing him for a month? She was a very attractive woman, a good ten years younger than himself. What if, he couldn't stop himself wondering, there was someone else in the background, someone more eligible than himself?

He remembered how, talking about the odious Garcia, she'd dismissed the idea of ever marrying again, but he was powerless to stop his imagination from running riot. He pictured Beta strolling along the promenade in Estoril on the arm of a charming younger man – Harrington could see him clearly

- about Beta's own age, slim, fashionably dressed, amusing, wealthy, everything in fact that he wasn't.

Driven frantic with such thoughts, Harrington tried making a long solitary walk to Trafaria and back. That might have been a mistake for it simply gave his imagination space to work on. Suppose he'd decided to brave the maid's dour presence and had dropped in on Beta unexpectedly on his way back from Laranjeiras? Might he have found her entertaining a gentleman friend?

Sexual jealousy was a new experience for him. Once seeded, the noxious weed grew rampant however much he tried to suppress it no matter how often he told himself it was all the more ridiculous for having no evidence to back it up.

He recalled the first time he'd visited Rua do Prior; what had Ana said when she stopped him on his way out? Something about her lady's honour. Why would she have menaced him in that way if she didn't think he was the latest in a line of suitors for her lady's hand?

25

On the last night of their stay at Pêra, Harrington found it a welcome distraction to be persuaded by some of the senior students to show off his knowledge of the stars after supper. It had been Father Blacklow, the college president of his own student days, who had introduced Harrington to some of the basics of astronomy. He'd never followed up that initial instruction but neither had he forgotten the general outline of the night sky.

They gathered in the courtyard where Harrington thought he'd start by pointing out the obvious. 'That band of light above us. You can see why the Greeks called it the Milky Way. And there's Orion and his belt, and that's the Plough. It's sometimes called the Saucepan. And over there you can see Cassiopeia and that cluster is the Pleiades. That,' he added, pointing lower on the eastern horizon, 'is Mars.'

'The war, sir,' Fielding intruded an unwelcome reminder of how things were in the world beyond Pêra, 'it's really going to come any time now, isn't it?'

'What makes you think that?'

'Hitler always wants more,' Fielding said. 'He's always taking something. First it was Austria, then the Sudetenland and then the rest of Czechoslovakia. So far he's got away with it. Now it looks as if it's Poland's turn.'

'I had a letter the other day,' Thompson butted in. 'My mother says they've sandbagged all the ground floor windows in Blackburn Town Hall.'

'And they've dug trenches in Regent's Park to stop gliders landing,' someone else added.

'Where my folks live,' Charlie Russell said, 'they've collected all the iron railings and pots and pans. For the war effort, they say. I don't know what they think they're going to do with them. The aluminium perhaps, but you can't make planes out of cast-iron, can you?'

It was at moments like this Harrington wished he retained the powers of censorship of the mail his predecessors had enjoyed. 'The government has to cover all eventualities,' he told them, 'it doesn't mean war's inevitable.'

He wished he believed that. He'd recently received a letter from his mother, telling him she'd decided to go and live with relatives in Ireland. *With your Dada dead I've nothing to keep me here*, she'd written. '*so I might as well go where I'm wanted and at least I'll be out of the way of the bombs.* There was a great-niece in Ballyduff, Maureen Prendergast, with a brood of children to fuss over and her man away with the British Army.

So, Harrington thought, she was returning to her own roots in Wexford. He knew she'd visited the place once since his father had died but he wondered how she'd adapt to living permanently in the Free State. Better than the Salford back-to-back at any rate, and as she said, she'd be safe from the bombs that were sure to rain down on the docks and the neighbouring factories.

'War. It's all pointing that way, and soon, isn't it?' Fielding insisted.

'That's as maybe,' Harrington countered, 'Our job here is to keep the faith and soldier on.'

'Soldier on,' Fielding echoed. 'They had conscription, in the last war, didn't they?'

'Towards the end. They relied on volunteers in the early years.'

'Did you get your call-up papers? Russell asked.

'Out here? I'm not sure I'd have been old enough,' Harrington replied, 'and in any case there was exemption for clerical students.' He paused a moment. 'Some students did leave though. Aidan Durkin. I remember he was the first. One day he just told everyone he was off back to Blighty and he'd found a berth on a Booth Line ship bound for Liverpool.' Harrington sighed. 'It was pointless, really, one more body for the Flanders' mud.'

'They called it the war to end all wars,' Thompson said. 'How wrong can they be?' He'd brought out his guitar and was strumming it softly, searching for the chords to support a song they all knew by heart. In a few moments the courtyard echoed to a ragged rendition of *Pack up your Troubles*.

There were a few more songs before Harrington shooed the party off to their beds.

Fielding lingered by the house door.

'Did you want something?' Discipline might be more relaxed at Pêra than in college but it was way past lights-out time.

'What you mentioned earlier, about soldiering on.'

Harrington could sense Fielding was troubled. 'Don't you worry your head about that,' he said.

'But it *is* going to happen, isn't it?' Fielding insisted. 'The war, I mean?'

'I suppose you're worried about your family. And you've a younger brother, I remember you telling me once.'

Fielding smiled. 'Edwin, sir. It was a bit of a shock when they told me I'd got a little brother. Then, when I went on home leave in '35, there he was, wanting attention like a little puppy. He's nine now, doing well at school and mad keen on stamp collecting.'

Harrington smiled. 'He sounds to be quite advanced for his age.'

'I wondered,' Fielding continued, 'what you said, about that one who left the college in the war. What happened to him?'

'Durkin? We were told he was killed the first day he went up to the front.' Harrington shook his head. 'He thought he was answering his country's call but there was a higher calling he should have responded to.'

'By becoming a priest?'

'Of course!

'But in time of war - couldn't you say there was a greater need?'

'In time of war,' Harrington admonished, 'people need spiritual comfort more than ever and they aren't going to get that if the priests have all joined the armed forces.'

He was sorry he'd mentioned Durkin. 'Now off you go. It's late and I don't want you setting a bad example to the younger ones. We've got to go back to Lisbon tomorrow.

Harrington thought he could see the way Fielding's mind was working. And if he went, others would follow. It had been the same in the last war: Durkin's departure had triggered an exodus and by the end of the war another dozen students had gone. This time, there might only be a rump of seniors left and a gaggle of mere children. The college wouldn't survive. Ironic, that their star student might set an example that might bring down the whole establishment.

Harrington wondered. He'd told Fielding that Durkin – he had been from a coal-mining community in South Wales - should have pursued a higher calling and perhaps, for some, the priesthood was a higher calling. He'd certainly thought so on the day of his own ordination. Now he was no longer sure. Priesthood was one thing; celibacy was quite another. If celibacy wasn't inextricably linked to priesthood he, Harrington, could be exercising his holy orders with Beta openly at his side instead of skulking in the undergrowth, pretending to be something he wasn't.

He lingered in the courtyard for a while. Strange, he thought, the odd things one remembered: Durkin had kept a pet canary in his room and sometimes the pair of them could be heard performing as if in a duet, the human voice lamenting some by-gone pit disaster, the avian music trilling and soaring in counterpoint. Durkin had been the first to go, and the first but not the last to die.

26

Back in college, on the third of September, Harrington sat in the President's Parlour with the rest of the staff clustered around the wireless set, listening to the short-wave recording of Chamberlain's solemn announcement: *This country is at war with Germany.* The wail and crackle of the atmospherics provided a weirdly appropriate background to the declaration.

Harrington wondered how the war might change their lives. In a way, he supposed, it changed everything, presenting Europe with the prospect of the century's second descent into hell, if the worst predictions were proved true.

On the other hand, here in Portugal, what change would there be? If the last conflict was anything to go by - he remembered a few shortages, minor inconveniences - life would continue much as before. Salazar, intent on protecting his precious New State, would do everything in his power to remain on the sidelines.

Martin Blount switched off the wireless. 'Gentlemen, I believe we have to be prepared for a long haul.'

Harrington thought the college President's little rimless glasses and generous mop of snowy hair, giving him the appearance of a benign slightly absent-minded elderly uncle, contrasted starkly with the solemn measure of his words.

'It's happening all over again,' Cope said morosely, 'just like last time.'

Harrington turned to him. 'Not quite. You and I were here in Lisbon but Martin was already in Rome, at the Gregorian University, and you, Tom,' he looked across at Pargeter, 'you only arrived long after it was all over. In 1924 wasn't it?' He glanced at Knox. 'You'd gone back to England before war broke out, hadn't you?'

Bob Knox was puffing at his pipe. 'That's right. I'd just taken up my first curacy in the East End when the war broke out. It was dire in London, I can tell you. There was bombing; first the Zeppelins and then, towards the end of the war, those ruddy great Gotha bomber aeroplanes. A lot of people were killed and everyone was terrified. And there were food shortages until they brought in rationing. That wasn't much better.'

He laughed. 'The stuff they called raspberry jam, we reckoned it was really made out of beetroot. But we survived. Why should it be any different now? The Boche are still the Boche and our people will sort them out, as before.'

Harrington listened as Knox's assertion lit a train of argument between his colleagues: Blount was reminding them that the last war had been won by the entry of the Americans, while Cope asserted the Yanks wouldn't want to get involved again on the far side of the Pond.

'It will be different, this time,' Blount said, 'even here in Portugal. Franco has won his victory in Spain with the help he got from Hitler and Mussolini. Our Dr Salazar's instincts have always been for self-preservation, and he must know the Germans would make a much better ally than a foe.'

Harrington agreed with that. It was a line of reasoning he'd heard more than once at Laranjeiras.

'Portugal only joined in the war last time under pressure from Britain.' Knox said.

'It wasn't quite like that, Bob,' Harrington put in. 'Germany actually declared war on Portugal because she'd sequestered German shipping at Britain's demand. The Portuguese sent troops to the front in 1916 and they got laughed at for their pains because they'd brought their umbrellas with them. Anyway,' he added, as much to convince himself as to persuade the others, 'this declaration of war, it's nothing more than an invitation to bring Hitler to his senses.'

They turned to him. 'That's my opinion anyway,' he muttered. At the very worst, Fonseca had said, there'd be a few brief skirmishes before a patching up of differences, some adjustments of territory - the French will have to give up Alsace again - and then there'd be a united front against the Soviets. He had it on good authority, he'd assured Harrington, from his friends at the German Legation.

'And Poland?' Blount wondered. 'Isn't that why we've gone to war?'

He got no immediate reply. Cope was toying with his glass. 'That bombing in Spain,' he murmured absently, 'the Germans learned some valuable lessons there. As for Poland, that's Hitler's first step to sorting out Russia.'

'It was the Reds who were responsible for the war in Spain,' Harrington said. He reached forward and helped himself to a cigarette from the box on the table. 'Where are the matches?' He'd only recently started smoking again and he knew Beta didn't approve. The only time he'd ever lit up in the apartment she'd warned him that Ana would spend the next day sniffing the air and opening all the windows.

'Sorry. Here.' Knox threw him the matches. 'Both sides in Spain had a lot to answer for, Michael,' he said, 'but don't forget it was Franco who started the war and he's gone about things pretty savagely since it ended. I was talking to a fellow, a Spaniard, the other day, in the Suiça café. From what he said, I gathered that now the Generalissimo has won he's embarking on a plan to completely wipe out the opposition: prison, mass executions. This chap was lucky to get out and he's making sure he keeps his nose clean here in Portugal while he's waiting for a boat to South America. Spain's like a prison camp now, he says.'

Harrington was no longer really interested. They could argue as much as they liked; it wasn't going to change anything. His eye was caught by the faded tapestry hanging on the wall opposite the wireless set. It was a familiar piece but he'd never studied it before in any detail. The work depicted the biblical Jewish heroine Judith beheading Holofernes, commander of the Assyrian army. The figure of Judith loomed over the sleeping Holofernes, with an expression of grim determination, while a more shadowy female figure in the background held a large cloth in which to catch the severed head. It seemed a strange choice of subject for an academic institution dedicated to the education of clergy but perhaps, Harrington thought, there was an allegoric significance that escaped him.

'What do you reckon then, Michael?' he heard Pargeter demanding.

'I'm sorry?' Harrington saw that they were all staring at him. 'I thought... oh, the war?'

'You dozed off,' Arthur Cope laughed. 'That Freemasonry chap must be wearing you out.'

'I didn't, I wasn't,' he stammered, trying to re-orient himself, wondering for a wild moment whether there was a double meaning to Cope's jibe. 'We're safe enough here in Portugal, I suppose, come what may.'

'We weren't talking about Portugal being invaded,' Blount pointed out, 'and anyway, weren't you telling us just now that this war business is only posturing?'

'And if it isn't,' Tom Pargeter put in, 'we'll have to give Hitler a bloody nose.'

'We?' Harrington asked.

'You know what I mean. In any case, we're safe enough out here, as long as Portugal stays neutral.'

'I've papers to mark,' Blount declared as he got out of his chair. It was the signal for the soirée to break up.

Harrington thought he'd take a walk up on the Observatory roof and Pargeter said he'd join him.

Ahead of them as they walked down the dimly lit top floor corridor a light was suddenly extinguished in one of the student's rooms. There was electricity in the corridor but the students only had oil lamps and they should have been put out half an hour earlier.

'How old were you when the war ended?' Harrington asked. 'Eleven?'

'Nearly ten,' Pargeter said.

'I don't suppose you remember much about it.'

'I remember the Zeppelin raids Bob was talking about. One came over Kelvedon Common, not far from where we lived, and got hit. It went up like a Roman candle. We thought it was very exciting.'

They'd reached the door to Pargeter's room and the steps up to the Observatory lay just ahead. 'D'you ever have doubts, Tom?' Harrington asked suddenly.

'Doubts? What about?'

'About what we're doing here.'

Pargeter laughed uneasily. 'About my lectures? Frequently! But I don't think they're any worse than the ones I had to sit through when I was a student.'

'I'm serious, Tom. Doubts. Real doubts.'

'I suppose, before I was ordained. Whether I was worthy, that sort of thing. That's only to be expected.'

'What I mean is, d'you think we're doing any good here?' Harrington realised Pargeter was embarrassed but though he regretted starting this line of questioning he couldn't stop himself.

'Doing good?' Pargeter replied. 'Well, I think we're doing the best we can. I'm sure our students are getting as good an education here as they would elsewhere.'

'I didn't mean good in that sense,' Harrington replied. 'It's about the whole way of life thing we're passing on. Celibacy, the demands of the priesthood. We take it all for granted, it's become part of us, the way we act, the way we think. Suppose we're on the wrong tack altogether?' Suppose we shouldn't be channelling young lives into the same rut we're stuck in?'

'Big questions, Michael!' Pargeter exclaimed. 'Too big for me at this time of night. I won't go upon the roof with you. It's well past my bedtime so I think I'll turn in!' He couldn't move fast enough to get on the other side of his door.

He thinks I'm losing my grip, Harrington told himself, *and perhaps he's right.*

The Observatory steps were narrow and he had to go carefully. Once on the flat roof, he walked to the parapet and gazed out over a city threaded with lights. Over to the east he saw the bulk of St. George's castle crowning the hill that contained the ancient districts of Lisbon, the old Moorish quarter of the Mouraria, and the cathedral. *If this were England,* he thought, *the whole scene would be in total darkness.*

Turning in the other direction, he could see the dome of the Estrela basilica outlined against the western horizon. A luminous chain marked the southern shore of the wide river. It was a world away from war.

Someone down in Rua Nova do Loureiro, a more accomplished player than young Thompson, was strumming a guitar; there was a snatch of song, a burst of laughter. Down there, Harrington mused, people were living, eating, drinking, singing, fornicating for all he knew- though they'd call it making love - truly living, with all the sweaty faults that made life real.

He looked over the parapet. It was a long way down to the ground. *Put out the light: and then put out the light.* Melodramatic nonsense, he told himself, standing back from the edge.

27

The next morning Harrington, with a calm and determined resolve, telephoned the Augsburger Druckmaschinen A.G. office. 'We've got to put a stop to our arrangement,' he announced abruptly as soon as Koenig came on the line.

'But why ever should that be?' The familiar voice was unctuously friendly.

'You know perfectly well. Now our two countries are at war it wouldn't be right.'

Harrington cocked an anxious eye at the swing doors leading to the kitchen. José was in and out of the dining room, clearing the breakfast dishes. He was harmless as he didn't understand English, but there was always a chance that someone - Arthur Cope most probably - might burst in unexpectedly. 'I'm sorry, Koenig, but there it is. In any case, as the lady's English, I can't imagine she'll wish to continue her friendship with an enemy alien.'

He heard Koenig chuckle. 'Love knows no boundaries, my friend.'

'All the same, I'm sorry, but I must insist. No more letters.'

'Just one moment, Michael, please. We had an agreement, if I understand correctly, you and I. You to do something for me, I to refrain from doing something about you.'

'Yes, well, now I'm saying that the agreement simply can't continue.'

'You mean, I'm free now to speak to your college president about your relationship with the delightful Dona Elisabete?'

'You wouldn't do that!'

'Oh, but I think I would be obliged to do so,' came Koenig's silky reply.

'I can't believe you'd do that, after all I've done for you!' Harrington almost screamed down the line.

'But, my friend, we have to be even-handed, haven't we? Our agreement was what I think could be described as a verbal contract. And I'm sure you know a contract may only be terminated by mutual agreement. The breaking of the contract by either party releases the other party from all contractual obligations hitherto entered into.'

Harrington had to concede it was a text-book definition. 'You spent your time in England well,' he retorted sarcastically. 'Such perfect English.'

'You're too kind,' Koenig replied. 'But I think I'm right in my understanding.'

'You wanted to keep your flirtation secret. I was prepared to help you. Perhaps I shouldn't have co-operated but I suppose, given the circumstances, I wasn't in a position to refuse,'

'Indeed not,' Koenig murmured.

'But now, the war; that changes everything. It's a sort of...' Harrington searched for the right expression, '*force majeure*, annulling normal contractual obligations.'

'If you like,' came the silky response, 'so long as you understand the consequences.' There was a click and purr as the line went dead.

Harrington knew he was trapped. He saw there was nothing for it but to carry on and he could only console himself with the thought that passing on love-letters was hardly a hanging matter. The alternative, playing the patriot, would certainly mean disgrace and an ignominious return to England and no more Beta. If Koenig's lady friend could square her conscience in carrying on a friendship with a German, Harrington decided he could put up with being a go-between.

Beta was indifferent to the news that Britain was at war with Germany. 'It's nothing to do with us, darling,' she declared, the first time they met after the declaration, when Harrington reminded her that Portugal was England's oldest ally. 'A quarrel between two other nations isn't our affair. Embarrassing, I agree. It's like when old friends fall out and you're left wondering how you should go on being nice to them both.'

Harrington's wild doubts about Beta had evaporated the first time they'd met after he'd come back to the city but he felt a twinge of alarm when she said she saw no reason why she should give up the occasional evening at the German Legation.

'If your Embassy invited me to something I'd certainly go,' she said, smiling beguilingly, and kissed his cheek. 'Maybe you could arrange an invitation?'

The college did receive invitations – the King's Birthday, one or two garden parties – but he could hardly turn up at the Embassy with a lady on his arm and in any case, even if Beta could get an invitation on her own account, they'd only be able to converse over the canapés as casual acquaintances.

28

By the end of the year the war had become not so much a phoney war - *uma guerra de mentira,* a war of lies, as the Portuguese press were calling this strange stalemate - as it was a phoney peace, Yes, the BBC Overseas Service reported the occasional bombing raid, and there had been naval skirmishes - the Germans had lost the *Graf Spee* off Montevideo - but on mainland Europe nothing was moving. And so may it long continue, Harrington thought.

At Christmas he endured a merciless ragging by some of Upper House at the traditional Common Room concert party. In front of all the students and the staff, Peter Fielding, kitted out in a colourful approximation of full academic costume and in front of a half dozen unruly students, delivered a pastiche of the moral dilemmas Harrington had used in his classes during the previous twelve months.

There was a reference to Irish roots and an immediate ribald response of, 'Would that be potatoes, yer honour?' from one of the disruptive class. And there were numerous references to Honestus and Perfidius and an unfortunate young man called Maledictus who managed to get into the most extraordinary scrapes. It was good fun and Harrington laughed as heartily as anyone else as Fielding declaimed at the improvised lectern.

It was very cleverly done, he had to admit. Fielding looked nothing like him, but there were recognisable mannerisms that had been well caught. There was that habit he knew he had of hesitantly running his tongue over his upper lip before making a major statement, and that thing he did, scraping his finger tips across the right side of his head just above the ear when he was searching for a word. The voice too, according to Cope who sat beside Harrington in the audience, was uncannily accurate. Fielding was a born mimic.

New Year brought one important change to the pace of life as far as Harrington was concerned. He felt obliged to inform Mother Teresa that he would no longer be able to continue as their chaplain, giving pressure of work as his excuse, though in truth he was finding it impossible to continue balancing his solemn ministration at the altar in Beta's presence with the sharing of the more earthly delights on offer in her apartment. 'You'll be more than happy with padre Pargeter,' he told Mother Teresa when she expressed her disappointment at the change.

Explaining it to Beta was more difficult. 'But why, darling?' she demanded. 'The only reason I keep coming all the way from Lapa to the convent is for the pleasure of seeing you.' She couldn't understand his discomfort. 'Don't you like to see me every day? Knowing we share a little secret?'

When he told her that was just the point, she shrugged and said she thought he must be a little *maluco,* crazy, but she loved him just the same and, with a sweet kiss, perhaps even just a little bit more because of it.

Their relationship, with its regular love-making and intimate conversations in the beautiful Lapa apartment, had become such a physical and emotional necessity to him that Harrington couldn't bear the idea of being deprived of it.

Late one January evening, Harrington went down to the riverside Santa Apolonia railway station with Cope to welcome the arrival of a small group of first-year boys whose journey to Lisbon by ship the previous September had been cancelled because of the declaration of war and the fear of an imminent outbreak of hostilities.

Their three-day train journey via Paris and war-ravaged Spain had left the boys cold, hungry, tired and confused but Harrington was amused to hear their chaperon, a former student, cheerfully warning them that the hardships they had suffered was all good training for what they were going to encounter during their time in college.

He continued to hand over the letters to Koenig. The best of enemies, they shared the inevitable bottle of wine at the Campo Grande café and chatted about anything but the war. Some people, Harrington reflected, might have been affronted by his behaviour but he'd grown to think of Koenig and himself as more like fellow conspirators than enemies, each guarding the other's secret.

Harrington's civilian wardrobe had by now been augmented by a tasteful suit in charcoal grey and several shirts and ties, all selected by Beta. 'You haven't the experience, darling,' she'd told him. 'Let me decide for you.'

He was happy to let her take charge. The shirts were uniform white but the ties were of subtly distinctive patterns, nothing he'd have bought for himself. He had to acknowledge that in matters of taste, Beta was the expert.

Disguised in his civilian attire Harrington felt more confident about being out and about in town with Beta, only to be met with a smiling reproof when he wondered out loud whether he could leave some of his things in the Lapa apartment. 'Whatever would Ana say? Do you want to quite destroy my reputation, my precious?' Beta asked him.

'I just had the idea that if I could get changed here,' he said, feeling foolish, 'it might be easier than always trying to sneak out of college in my civvies.'

'You'll manage, I'm sure. And don't forget, Ana attends to all my things,' Beta kindly explained. 'Everything. So what would she say if she found some gentleman's garments hanging next to my dresses?'

'No,' he admitted, 'that wouldn't do at all.'

He didn't like to admit that despite his efforts at disguise he'd attracted some strange looks from the college servants who had caught sight of him in what he thought of as his Beta outfit. José - he probably considered himself especially licensed because of his standing as the professors' major-domo - had gone so far as to remark that *padre Arrington* looked quite *na moda* in his civvy get-up. Being described as 'in the fashion' was a novelty as far as Harrington was concerned and the next time they met he made a joke of telling Beta that José approved of her choice of tie.

29

On the Sunday after the college had returned to the Bairro Alto from the Easter break at Pêra Harrington and Koenig were in the Campo Grande café, enjoying a glass of the Penela wine, when a single word destroyed all Harrington's peace of mind. *Mickey.* Koenig used the name twice in the course of conversation, eyeing him speculatively over the rim of his glass, smiling at him across the table as if to taunt him.

Harrington had never in all his life been anything else than Michael, never a Mike nor a Mick. *I shall call you Mickey,* she'd said. It was to be her private name for him and now Koenig was using it, quite deliberately.

Seemingly oblivious to the silent distress he had caused, Koenig was babbling on; something about the difficulties of getting spare parts for the machinery he was selling. He gave the impression of being slightly aggrieved when Harrington abruptly got up from the table, knocking over his chair in the process. 'I've had enough,' he snarled as he turned away.

'Don't be in such a hurry, Mickey!' Koenig called after him and made as if to set the chair to rights.

Harrington was sure he heard a faint chuckle from behind him as he marched away, his shoes crunching on the gravel path.

His heart was thumping, all the old suspicious imaginings coming roaring back in his mind with a new focus of attention. It was just over a year since Harrington's first meeting with the German and he could still vividly recall that morning, with the smell of the wood smoke, the clip-clop of the ill-treated mule, the crack of the driver's whip, and the plump little man in the doorway of the printer's workshop. *He was lying in wait for me even then*, he thought. That explained all the innocent questions, the artful intimation of loneliness and the invitation to share a drink. Koenig had been planning mischief from the first.

Heinz Koenig, salesman for the Augsburger Druckmaschinen A.G. in Lisbon: Beta must have met him at one of those ghastly German Legation parties she was so fond of. Was it possible that as far back as last year, Koenig had singled him out to be his dupe? She'd told him about the nice innocent English priest she'd met at Maria Winter's parties, the priest who trotted off daily to the Convent of Divine Mercy. Koenig had seen an opportunity, had scouted out the route between college and convent and simply hung about until he could engineer a 'chance' meeting.

It all fitted neatly, like a well-designed jigsaw puzzle. But to what end? Too well-designed, one might say; too complicated a plot to cook up purely so the German could have a courier for his love-letters. But try as he might, Harrington couldn't imagine what else Koenig could possibly have had in mind.

That swastika badge he'd found on Beta's dressing table: Koenig must have given it to her. Harrington remembered the way she'd tried to distract him with the teasing mention of an American she'd rather fancied. He thought about those times when they'd been in bed together, all the cunning tricks she used to arouse him; she hadn't learned those in her convent school and certainly not from the *veado* Garcia.

He thought wildly of Beta and Koenig together, having an affair. Koenig and Beta, in her luxurious bed, sharing a joke about plodding old *Mickey*. Beta, busily wrecking everything he'd thought was so important to them both.

There it was: he'd been trapped into something that he couldn't see his way out of and, what was worst of all, he'd been tricked into committing himself heart and soul to what he'd thought was a deep relationship with a woman who loved him. That was what really made him bitter.

Harrington gave his lectures mechanically. It was easier to dictate sheaves of notes than to enter into any debate, easier to plough on regardless of the restive stirrings on the benches before him.

He set his Lower House Latin class to translating sight unseen a couple of chapters of Caesar's *Gallic Wars*. 'Use your imagination,' was the only curt advice he offered when someone asked him to explain a difficult word.

If his colleagues noticed his more than usual silence at meals they were tactful enough not to remark on it.

30

There was nothing for it; in the end he had to confront her. The following Thursday he nursed his outrage all the way to to Rua do Prior. As usual, Beta must have been waiting behind the door, for it opened as soon as he touched the bell.

'Mickey!' she cried exuberantly, throwing her arms around him, like a noose about his neck. She planted a wet smacking kiss on his mouth, her tongue probing between his teeth.

Didn't she notice his refusal to respond wholeheartedly to her fervent embrace, his wooden stubbornness? Apparently not. She took his hand to lead him down the corridor, chattering gaily about how lovely it was to see him and wasn't it rather too warm for the beginning of June.

She only began to sense his mood when they arrived in the living room. She seized his free hand and turned him about. 'What's wrong, darling?' she said, anxiously searching his stony face. 'What's the matter? Are you ill, my precious? You look awful.'

'Sick, maybe.' he said. He couldn't continue for a moment.

She was immediately all concern. 'Dr Pereira, just down the road, he's my doctor and he's very good. Sit down while I phone to make an appointment for you.' She turned to the little side-table where she kept the old-fashioned black candlestick telephone.

He caught her arm to stop her. 'Don't bother,' he said, 'I don't need a doctor.' He slumped down on the sofa.

'Whatever you say, my dear,' she soothed, 'but you must tell me what's the matter. I've never see you like this before.' She sat beside him, her familiar perfume suddenly sickening him.

Terrified she was about to embrace him again, he edged further along the seat.

'What do you want me to say?' Harrington thought he had prepared himself for this scene but now she was beside him he found his righteous anger had all flown, leaving a heaviness that made words come thick and sluggish.

'Is it a fever?' She made to reach out her hand to his forehead.

'No! Don't do that.' Seeing her recoil as if he'd slapped her face should have given him some small satisfaction. It only made him feel worse.

'Mickey, my love, you've got to tell me what's wrong. Bad news? Is someone ill? It's your mother, isn't it? You've had news she's poorly.' Beta was searching for clues in his face. 'Oh no!' she clapped her hand to her mouth. 'Don't tell me she's dead!'

'Bad news,' he managed to squeeze out the words, 'yes, you might say that. Not my mother though.'

She frowned. 'What then? A relative? A friend? Mickey, you're frightening me. You've got to tell me what it is.' She was touching him again, her hand on his upper arm, stroking him as if he were a dog that needed to be calmed.

He flinched from her, withdrew further down the sofa. He couldn't look at her; facing him across the room, he saw that awful ivory carving and concentrated instead on the window she must have opened before his arrival. 'I've found out,' he said, his voice stupid, 'about you and Koenig. You've gone behind my back, haven't you?' There, it was lying between them, solid as a boulder too huge to climb over. He risked a glance at her.

'What do you mean, darling?' She was frowning, a picture of dismayed confusion. 'What's Heinzi got to do with this?'

'So it's *Heinzi* is it?'

She should have been on the stage, he thought, with that caricature of bewilderment painted on her face. '*Heinzi*. That's what you call him, is it? Your pet name for him? Just like the one you gave to me?'

'Everyone calls him Heinzi,' she said, on the defensive now. 'Everyone, not just me. But what's that got to do with you being unwell?' She attempted to reach for him again, and again he pushed her roughly away.

'Did he seduce you or did you make a play for him?'

'This is a game, isn't it?' she said unsteadily. 'But I don't think I like it.'

'I didn't like it either, when I found out.' He kept a tight rein on his anger by turning it into sarcasm. 'I suppose you thought I was too besotted to realise what was going on. Well, you did quite well. I've only just caught on.'

'Really, Mickey, you're talking nonsense.'

But she moved away, to the other end of the sofa, not quite meeting his eyes. There'd been a college servant who he'd once accused of stealing. He'd had the same shifty look as he'd sworn his innocence.

'Nonsense? You don't deny it was you who told him?'

Beta frowned. 'Told him what?'

'The name. *Mickey*. You told him, didn't you?'

'I don't know what you're talking about.' Her face cleared. 'Oh, yes! Mickey, I'm so sorry. I remember now. There was a party at the Legation. But that was ages ago, last summer when you were away with your rich friends. I think I may have said something, you know, about what a good man you are; nothing bad, truly. You know how it is, darling, at parties. One chats, one has a little drink. And someone says something, and someone else says something else. Chatter, nothing more. The name must have just slipped out.'

It was all too pat, he thought. Perhaps she thought it was amusing to have led him on all these months, drawing him deeper into her clutches, egged on by the German.

157

'So there's nothing going on between you?'

She laughed at that, too loudly. 'Mickey, you're so funny sometimes. Don't tell me you're jealous! Heinzi and me; the idea of it! Heinzi's got a girlfriend in the city. She's Dutch, or Belgian. I can't remember which. Astrid something-or-other. He's always talking about her. He's brought her to a couple of evenings at the Legation. He's a randy little man but I doubt even Heinzi could keep two women satisfied at the same time.'

He'd expected her to burst into tears or issue downright indignant denials but this light-hearted treatment only served to confirm his suspicions. 'Well,' he said heavily,'if you think it's funny, there's nothing more I can say.'

She looked confused. 'Mickey, I don't know what it is you *are* saying. Are you cross because I'm friendly with Heinz Koenig? I thought he was your friend as well. You aren't making any sense at all.'

'You and... and,' the name wouldn't emerge, 'that man.'

'Koenig?'

'Him, yes. You've been conspiring behind my back.'

She must have seen the determination in his face and was beginning to take him seriously at last. 'Mickey, I've explained how it happened. I talk too much, that's all, when I've had a glass or two. It doesn't mean anything. I'm sorry, Mickey, if it's upset you. Will you forgive me?' she appealed.

'I blame myself,' he said bitterly, standing up. 'All this I thought we had. It was too good to be true. I should have known better.'

She looked up at him. 'For God's sake, it's only a name, Mickey. Don't you think you're making rather a fuss about it?'

'It's not the name,' he said, 'at least not just the name. I thought it was private but then I find Koenig using it, mocking me with it.'

158

'Sit down again, Mickey,' she told him. 'I've said I'm sorry. I'll explain to him.'

'When you're in bed with him?' He refused to sit.

'Mickey!'

The outrage was well-crafted, he had to admit, but then she'd had months to cultivate her image. 'Don't bother to deny it.'

'You're serious, aren't you?' she said, wide-eyed and staring straight into his face. 'You really think I've been sleeping with Heinz Koenig? I've no idea where you've got all this from. I've never given you any cause...'

'You told that man about us,' he cut in furiously. 'You can't deny that.'

'I've told you,' she insisted, 'it was a mistake. It just slipped out.'

'And that brooch thing. Have you still got it?'

'Oh, that. They were giving those things out like sweets to children on Saint Anthony's Day.' She sighed in exasperation. 'Mickey, is that all?'

He hesitated. 'Straws in the wind,' he faltered, 'lots of little things that all point the same way.'

'Such as?' She faced him squarely.

There was no answer to that. He just knew he was right.

'I can't believe you really mean it. It's disgusting!' Her face was set deadly pale.

'That's right, it is disgusting. It's disgusting you've been playing with me, the pair of you.'

'I don't know how you can even think such a thing, let alone stand there and accuse me...' She shook her head. 'Totally absurd,' she said, almost to herself.

Harrington heard an unexpected hint of steel in her voice. 'What's absurd is that I should have ever been so naïve,' he said, 'me a middle-aged priest, with a beautiful young woman.' He sighed heavily. 'I don't know why you've done this to me, unless it was some sort of cruel joke.'

'If anyone is playing a joke it's you,' she said icily, 'but if you really think... if you honestly believe I'd do such a thing... I don't know how this has all got into your head and perhaps you really are sick, but if you truly have such a low opinion of me, then best to end things now.' She turned her head away, refusing to look at him any more.

Harrington didn't notice it was raining as he walked down Rua do Prior. He trudged blindly along, his bitterness turned on himself. *No good will come of it,* he recalled his mother saying it when he'd profited from something she didn't approve of – winning a playground fight, once pocketing a half-crown found coin in the street - *The Lord will find you out.* Well, this was the Lord's way of finding him out. It wasn't right to be living a charade; he should have broken off the relationship long before, should never have got involved with her in the first place. The wetness on his cheeks wasn't all raindrops, and damn it all, he'd come out without a handkerchief.

31

Harrington spent the next weekend as the guest of the Fonsecas at the Quinta de Laranjeiras, a long-standing arrangement, knowing he was miserable company but unable to shake off his despondency despite all Carmelita's efforts to lift him out of the anguish she saw in him but couldn't understand.

He overheard Daniel asking his mother, 'Mama, why is that old priest so sad?' Her gentle reply: 'Priests have many heavy burdens to carry that we don't always know about,' did nothing to ease him and he returned to the city as bereft of comfort as he'd left it. *Old*, the child had called him, and for the first time in his life, Harrington felt every year of his age twice over.

Part of his misery was his confused state of mind. What if he'd been wrong? What if he'd ruined everything because of his nasty suspicious mind? Where was the evidence, his normally analytic mind kicked in to question, too late. *Mickey*. What if Koenig had used that name quite by chance? It was all very well to complain that he'd never been called that but it wasn't such an uncommon abbreviation for his full name. Suppose Beta hadn't been putting on a front, suppose her response to his accusations, all that confusion, all that hurt dignity, had been just that; confusion and hurt at the abuse he hurled at her?

He'd made a total mess of things and it was too late to put matters right; Beta wouldn't want to have anything more to do with someone who had treated her so shamefully. What a fool he'd been!

Despite his misery something Beta had said in the course of that disastrous confrontation, it hadn't registered at the time, stuck in his mind; Koenig had a girlfriend here in the city, she'd said. So why was he conducting a long-distance and surely very unsatisfactory affair with a woman in England?

It was while he was preparing a lecture on the commandment, '*Thou shalt not steal*', that Harrington came up with the clue to what the so-called love letters might really be all about. Looking at his previous year's notes, he saw he'd put a note in the margin: *Stealing ideas? Explain patents and copyright.*

He started to sketch another of his conundrums to illustrate the point. *Acquisitus, the wealthy owner of many vehicles for the transport of all manner of goods around the country, discovers that a poor neighbour has invented an ingenious new type of axle for his solitary vehicle, allowing it to run at lower cost. In dead of night Acquisitus goes to his neighbour's yard....*

He got so far and halted. Follow the logic. Koenig had more or less admitted he'd been exiled to this Portuguese backwater and he must surely want to get back into the firm's good books. So, how was he going to do that? Successful businesses only kept their heads above water by constantly improving their products. Koenig must have contacts in England, contacts who could keep him abreast of developments in the printing industry. The 'love letters' in fact contained information about what various English printing machinery firms were up to. Koenig was stealing knowledge, information he could pass on to his bosses in Germany. That would explain why the letters came from so many different places and why they sometimes seemed far too bulky to be simply written declarations of passionate longings. There would be drawings, diagrams.

'My dear friend,' Koenig advanced on him with open arms when Harrington arrived at the Augsburger office, 'what a pleasant surprise! How kind of you to visit. To what do I owe the pleasure?' The welcoming tone was laden with an implicit rebuke of Harrington's presumption in arriving uninvited.

'I've found out your little game,' Harrington said quietly. The Valkyrie was busily attacking the typewriter keys without showing any sign of interest in the conversation but he was aware that many Germans spoke English.

'My game?' Koenig affected an air of mild amusement. 'Look at me, I'm not the athletic type.'

'The letters. I know what you're really up to.'

'Not here,' Koenig said, taking him by the arm. 'Let's walk.' He spoke briefly in German to his secretary; Harrington guessed she was being told to mind the shop for a while.

As they walked in brilliant sunshine down the Avenida towards Restauradores, they had to dodge people crowding the pavement. Lisbon was always full of people rushing about like ants in a disturbed nest; darting in and out of offices, delivering parcels, stopping for a chat under the shade of the trees that lined the Avenida's central reservation.

Down in Alcântara the other day - deprived of Beta's company he'd taken to aimless wandering about the city - he'd seen a different sort of chaos; huddled crowds clogging the doors of the shipping agents, wandering along the pavements or simply standing staring vacantly into space. For the most part poorly dressed, they were refugees he'd been told, looking to escape the pollution of devastated Europe, dreaming of life in the USA or one of the South American countries. As he watched them he'd thought, with a touch of self pity for his own predicament, how dreadful it was to be rootless, utterly at the mercy of the vagaries of fortune.

'Tell me,' Koenig asked as they walked along in the bright sunlight, 'what's the problem?'

'There's no use you pretending any more.'

'I'm sorry, Mickey, what d'you mean?' Koenig asked.

'The letters.'

'Yes. The letters. What of them?'

'All this nonsense about a girlfriend in England,' Harrington said. 'You've taken me for a complete fool!'

'Not true, Mickey, and I'd remind you of our contract.'

'Bugger the contract!' It was time to drop his bombshell: 'It's something to do with your position here, isn't it?'

'You think so?'

'Of course it is!' Harrington said. 'You're a bloody spy! What if I told you I know what's in those letters?'

Koenig didn't break his pace. 'You do?' He sounded remarkably calm.

'They aren't love notes.'

'Oh? Is that so?'

'It was that last one gave the game away,' Harrington said, 'the one I had to pay excess on.' It had been more of a parcel than a letter. 'It must have been stuffed with detailed technical drawings.'

'Really?' Koenig continued walking, a little faster, so that Harrington despite his height advantage had difficulty keeping up with him.

'You can't deny it! You're stealing details to hand on to your bosses in Germany.'

'Have you shared this insight with anyone?' Koenig was marching soldierly on speaking quietly, eyes directed straight ahead, something in his gait warning on-comers to step aside.

'Not yet, but I'm thinking about it,' Harrington said as he trotted after his enemy.

Koenig came to a halt at one of the pavement kiosks selling newspapers, tobacco and lottery tickets. Harrington could see the corner of of that day's *Diário,* wedged between a football paper and a copy of the issue of *Time* magazine he'd picked up at Maria Winter's house the previous week. The *Diário's* headline blazoned the continued triumph of Nazi forces through Belgium and into France. He'd read the *Time* report of further Japanese atrocities in mainland China. The heroic struggles of Chiang Kai-Shek were being supported by communist forces under the leadership of a shadowy communist character called Mao Tse-Tung, though the *Time* columnist expressed doubts about the ultimate success of a union between two such diametrically opposed ideologies.

'The Chinese would be better advised to make their peace with the Japanese Emperor's armies,' Koenig observed, pointing to the magazine's cover picture of poorly clad soldiers marching in column, laden with weaponry.

'I suppose you think your precious Herr Hitler will find common cause with the Japs before too long?'

'With the Japanese?' Koenig barked a laugh. 'What do your newspapers call them, the Yellow Peril? I can't imagine the Leader wasting much time on Asiatics.' He shrugged. 'On the other hand, there's that saying you English have: *Needs must when the devil drives.*'

He took Harrington's arm, gently propelling him to resume their walk. 'Now, my friend, this matter of the letters. Tell me precisely what you've found out.'

'It's espionage. You're trying to get into your bosses' good books.'

Koenig's pace scarcely missed a beat but his grip on Harrington's arm tightened and it was a moment or two before he found his voice. 'And how exactly am I doing this? Have you opened one of the letters?'

That was all the confirmation Harrington wanted. 'I haven't needed to. You've taken advantage of my unfortunate predicament, used me to help you steal secrets from companies in England and America so that your people in Augsburg can

165

improve their machinery and you can be taken back into the fold. Well, what do you say to that?'

There was a long moment's silence before Koenig gave a rueful laugh. 'Mickey, truly I'd never have thought you capable of working this out.' He glanced at his watch. 'Shall we go back now?' he enquired with a smile. 'I've business to attend to.' He set off back up the Avenida at a brisk pace.

Harrington had to admit the man was a cool character. There was nothing for it but to chase after him.

Koenig arrived at his office door and waited for Harrington to catch up.

'Have you got nothing more to say?' Harrington demanded as he drew level.

'What else is there? You've caught me red-handed.' Koenig still had that damned smile on his face.

'So that's the end of it? I've got your word?'

'Come in. We shouldn't be discussing this in the street.'

Confused by the man's apparent lack of concern, Harrington reluctantly followed Koenig under the swastika flag stirring in the afternoon breeze, ignoring the Valkyrie's greeting as they went up the stairs to Koenig's bachelor accommodation.

The apartment was furnished in a starkly modern fashion, the furniture all pale wood and stainless steel. Harrington's eye was immediately drawn to the coloured portrait of the Leader staring prophetically into a mythical Germanic future.

Koenig made a mock salute in front of it. 'Mickey, sit, please. A drink. Schnapps?'

'Brandy, if you have any.' Koenig seemed far too relaxed for Harrington's liking.

'But of course! Courvoisier. Only the best. It won't be long now before we're in Paris. France, you know, is going to be our area of détente.'

'You'll be lucky,' Harrington replied, knowing perfectly well the German advance appeared to be unstoppable.

'Listen, my friend,' Koenig said as he poured a generous measure of the cognac into balloon glasses, 'I'm willing to bet that within a week or so I'll be able to ask one of my friends to send me crates of Courvoisier direct from the French capital.' He smiled as he handed Harrington his glass and settled down in a chair opposite with his own.

'*Prost!*' He raised his own glass in a toast. 'I really do admire your powers of deduction, Mickey.' He took a healthy swig of the cognac and ran it round his mouth. 'Ah, beautiful! The nectar of the gods.'

He took another, tiny this time, sip. 'Now, I think it's the moment to lay cards on the table. You're correct about all this being to do with secret information.' Perhaps he saw the glint of triumph in Harrington's eyes. 'Correct, that's to say, up to a point. To begin with, I went along with your romantic notion about the love letters because I saw it pleased you to think I too had a weakness for the opposite sex.' He gave a little smile. 'However, I fear you're quite wrong in believing all this to be about secrets of the kind you imagined. My company doesn't need to copy lesser manufacturers in England; the Wharfedale, the Crabtree and suchlike. I admit they're good but we've nothing to learn from them. Rather, it's the reverse. Our techniques are widely copied.'

Koenig squared himself in his chair, holding his glass in both hands. 'These are difficult times, Mickey, and we've all got to do whatever we can. We're in the same boat, you and I.'

'That we're not! You're a German and your country's at war with mine.'

'I thought Ireland had declared her neutrality?' Koenig smiled

'Ireland? What's Ireland got to do with it?' Harrington demanded.

'Your roots, my friend, remember your roots.'

'I've come to realise that your roots are where you put them down, Koenig, and mine were put down in England. I don't want to see Hitler riding down the Mall, and for that matter I don't believe that jackboots in Dublin would make Ireland a better place.'

'You'd prefer Soviet tanks in Unter den Linden, would you? And after Berlin, London? It'll come to that, you know, if Churchill doesn't see sense. The Red Army in Windsor Castle? And, finally, the Soviet star on top of the Pillar in O'Connell Street? That, surely, would be a strange feather in Admiral Nelson's hat.' He grinned at his own witticism.

Harrington thought privately that there were plenty of people in Dublin who would like to see the English Admiral toppled from his perch high above the city's most elegant street. 'Of course I don't want any of that!' he said. 'But what's this got to do with the letters?'

'Germany has suffered a lot over the years,' Koenig said. 'She's caused suffering too, I know, but we were brought low after the last war and now we're finding salvation through strength.' He laughed. 'That sounds like something our Leader might say on the Nuremberg podium! But it's true. You don't have to worship the man to know that there's sense in what he says. We stand firm against the humiliation of the Fatherland! The Leader's words again.' He sat back and grinned. 'So much for the propaganda hors d'oeuvre! Now for the meat course.'

Koenig rolled the last drops of the brandy round his glass and tipped them into his mouth. 'Knowledge,' he said, 'is power, Mickey. Knowing the dispositions of your adversary, knowing about troop movements, where new airfields are being built, old ones refurbished, the location of ammunition dumps, shipping arrangements. That's all vital stuff. And you're doing your bit.'

'What do you mean, doing my bit?' Harrington demanded unhappily.

'People supply information. Thanks to your efficient British postal service, they only need to write a letter addressed to you. Well, they can hardly address their letters from England to the Lisbon representative of the Augsburger printing machine company, can they? Me, an enemy alien? Whereas a highly respectable and learned priest in the English College is beyond suspicion. And you pass them to me and I in my turn relay the good news to my superiors in the Abwehr.' He saw Harrington frown and explained, 'German Army Intelligence, that is.'

'I'm working with bloody German spies!' Harrington exclaimed.

'Not actually. Well, a couple are. The rest are concerned English people who've watched the way things are going. People who want to bring this present misunderstanding to an end as soon as possible, who think we should be fighting the Reds together.'

Harrington shook his head. 'Let's get this straight. You're saying that by passing these letters on to you I'm helping to save Britain from being overrun by the Bolshies?'

'I'm told that communist elements in the British Trade Unions are urging workers to withhold labour essential to the war effort. Undermining you from within.'

'They want better pay. That's greed, not politics!'

Koenig shrugged. 'Call it what you will, the effect's the same.'

'You've made me a bloody stool-pigeon!'

'Carrier pigeon, I think, rather,' Koenig said. 'Quite a charming and useful little bird.'

'I ought to inform on you.'

That really amused Koenig. 'Inform who, exactly?'

Harrington faltered. 'Our Ambassador.'

'Sir Walford Selby? He's returning to Britain soon, or perhaps you didn't know. I understand there's to be a little party to mark the occasion. Something informal, a quiet dinner somewhere out of town, just Sir Selby and Oswald von Hoyningen-Huene, our Head of Mission.'

'Ridiculous! And he's Sir Walford, not Sir Selby.'

'My apologies. Your aristocratic system is beyond us foreigners. But, as for the dinner, not at all ridiculous. The civilities have to be observed, especially in a neutral country. There are mutual interests, Mickey, you've got to remember, even if our countries are at war.'

'I don't believe it!'

Koenig shrugged. 'What d'you think they're doing, these diplomats, when they attend functions? The Americans have a party. They invite the British and there's no reason why they shouldn't invite the Italians and the Germans as well. A word's passed here, an exchange of views in a quiet corner. It's all diplomacy, carried on by the back stairs.'

'If I went to our Embassy and told them what you're up to, they'd soon do something,' Harrington blustered.

No they wouldn't, he thought. There was nothing the British could do about a German spy working in Portugal. For all he knew the British were playing the same sort of game as Koenig and his Abwehr. It was quite possible that more than one of the expatriates he came across was engaged in undercover work of some kind or other.

'That's your privilege, Mickey,' Koenig said. 'But there's still Dona Elisabete to consider.'

'That's finished,' Harrington said. 'Over and done with. You've seen to that. You used her, you bastard, just as you've used me.' At last he could give vent to his feelings in front of Koenig.

'I don't know what you mean.'

'You set the whole thing up from the beginning! You put that woman on to me.'

Koenig laughed. 'You really think I planned you should fall for Dona Elisabete?'

'You were waiting for me, that day, outside the printers' workshop.'

'You stepped on me because you weren't watching where you were going.'

'That was no accident. You were on the look-out for me.'

'Mickey! Grow up for God's sake. This is paranoia. Look, I'd been to see the Isidore brothers. They'd bought a flat-bed press and I was checking that everything was working properly. That's my job.' He grinned like a naughty school boy, 'my *other* job.'

Harrington opened his mouth but Koenig was still ahead of him. 'Mickey, in a few months Churchill will have made peace with the Führer and your charming Duke of Windsor will be back on his throne in Buckingham Palace. What you're doing, it's only part of a necessary means to a satisfactory end.'

'That's...' Harrington didn't know how to continue: this time last year all this might have been made into an intricate piece of casuistry for the entertainment of his students. 'Dona Elisabete told you,' he managed to say, 'about us. When you were sleeping with her.'

Koenig burst out laughing. 'Now I know you're crazy! Me, sleeping with Dona Elisabete? I've got a delightful girlfriend here in Lisbon.'

'So I've heard. A Dutch woman.'

'Astrid's Danish, actually,' Koenig gently corrected him.

'Dutch, Danish, whatever. All the more shame on you for consorting with Dona Elisabete as well.'

Koenig couldn't contain himself. Still shaking with laughter, he reached out to refill his own glass and then waved the bottle in Harrington's direction. 'What do you take me for, Mickey? Some sort of latter-day Don Juan? First you thought I had a girlfriend in London, and then you put Dona Elisabete in bed with me and now you're telling me off for having another woman on the side! Dona Elisabete, she talks, Mickey, that's all. She talks to anyone, whether they listen or not. She's not malicious. She's said a lot of nice things about you.'

He took a look at Harrington's face. 'All right, I took advantage of her. No,' he corrected himself, 'that means something different in English, doesn't it? I used the information I got out of her, just as I'm using the information you're supplying through those letters.' He raised his hand, 'Scout's Honour, Mickey, believe me! That's all there is to it.'

'For God's sake! Stop calling me that!'

'Stop what, Mickey?'

The bastard was enjoying himself. 'My name's Michael, as you well know,' Harrington snapped.

'But, I thought,' Koenig looked bewildered 'Between friends, the familiarity was all right. There was someone in London who asked me to call him that.'

If Harrington hadn't known what Koenig was up to he might have thought the smug little face was showing genuine concern. 'No, it bloody well isn't all right! And just forget this rubbish about being friends.'

'Mickey,' Koenig held up his hands to ward off Harrington's fury, 'I apologise, Michael. Please believe me.' He stood up, ready to see Harrington out of the apartment. 'Just one more thing before you go. You can bring the letters straight here in future. No need for you to trek all the way to Campo Grande.'

The knowledge that he had been, however unwittingly, working for German Intelligence might have been sickening if it hadn't been that thoughts of Beta were uppermost in his mind. She hadn't denied she'd let slip the nickname at one of those Legation parties, and that was all he'd need as foundation to build a house of horrors on. It was true, Beta did talk too much, she couldn't let the least detail go by. He remembered how Dona Louleira's broken ankle had become a source of endless speculation and minute clinical detail about the agony it was causing the dear lady. Beta couldn't pass by a milliners' shop without offering a detailed comment about how the hats on offer would suit such and such a person of her acquaintance. It was a foible he'd always thought endearingly feminine.

They were showing *Charlie Chan in Panama* at the São Jorge, Harrington noted, as the tram eased into Restauradores, with Sidney Toler and Jean Rogers. Beta would enjoy seeing that; a mystery film with a happy ending for the hero.

32

Peter Fielding stood at Harrington's open door with a sheaf of letters in his hand. 'Manuel Cordeiro asked me to bring these up, sir.'

Harrington stared at the letters. 'He'd no right,' he snapped, 'no right at all. That's his job, not yours. Here, give them to me.' He reached clumsily for the bundle and they all fell to the floor.

Fielding crouched to retrieve them. 'I only bumped into Manuel by accident in the Arches,' he said looking up at Harrington, 'and I thought I'd save him a journey. These two are for you, sir,' he added, looking at the envelopes as he straightened up. 'I say, that's an American stamp, isn't it? It's cheeky of me, but if you wouldn't mind. My kid brother Edwin's always on at me to send him stuff. An American stamp, he'd love that. When you've finished with the envelope, that is.'

Harrington frowned, stretching out his hand.

Fielding handed the letters over. 'I'm sorry,' Fielding said, 'I shouldn't have asked.'

'What?' Harrington said distractedly as he riffled through the pile, keeping separate the two Fielding had picked out. He handed over the rest. "Here, take these. You can go and give them out. And tell Cordeiro it's his job to bring them up to me, not yours.'

'And the American stamp, sir?' Fielding asked.

'We'll see,' Harrington replied, turning to go back into his room. He saw Fielding was still standing in the corridor. 'Did you want something else?'

'There was something else, actually. You remember what we talked about back at Pêra?'

Harrington frowned. 'About the war?'

'About joining up.'

'I told you about Durkin.'

'Yes. Well,' Fielding replied, 'I thought you'd want to know. I'm thinking of joining up myself.'

'Joining up?' Harrington said. 'Why on earth would you want to do that? This is all going to be over in a few months, mark my words.' He had no doubt Fielding, like everyone else, had been following the *Diário* and the other Portuguese papers. The Wermacht's lightning progress through Belgium and France, the route of the British Expeditionary Force, had put paid to any notion of stalemate. Only the heroic evacuation from Dunkirk had allowed the British to award themselves some glory in defeat.

'Look,' Harrington said, 'I'm sure you're worried about your people at home, about all the dangers they might be running, but you won't do them any good by running off to join the army and getting yourself killed. Come in and talk about it if you want.' He stood back to let Fielding into his sitting room.

'I've already decided to speak to Father Blount,' Fielding said as he entered.

'That's as maybe, but it won't do any harm to chat things over before you do,' Harrington replied as he went to sit at his desk, inviting Fielding to take the armchair facing him. 'Have a cigarette.' He gestured to the packet on his desk. 'They're Navy issue Woodbines,' he explained, 'off *HMS Jersey.*' The previous month the destroyer, en route to Malta, had taken advantage of the twenty-four hour neutral territories rule to call into Lisbon and she'd no sooner docked than Cope had gone on board to stock up with supplies – a few cartons of cigarettes and a couple of bottles of whisky.

Fielding shook his head. 'I don't smoke, sir.'

Harrington helped himself to a cigarette and lit up. 'I thought I'd given up for good until recently.' He inhaled deeply and sat back in his chair. 'Now about this idea of yours. You don't want to do something you'd regret later on. I have it on good authority, it's all going to be over soon.'

'There's no way of knowing that for sure, is there though?' Fielding said. 'It was a letter from my dad that decided me about joining up. He's not much of a one for writing as a rule, not like my mother, but he wanted to tell me about my cousin Robin who joined the Navy last September, he volunteered the day war was declared. Dad was so proud of him.'

'And how's your cousin getting on?' Harrington asked cautiously, having noted the use of the past tense.

'He's missing in action,' Fielding replied bleakly. 'His ship was attacked and sunk by German dive-bombers during the Dunkirk evacuation. Other boats picked up some survivors. My dad says that things are so confused just now that there's always hope.'

'Was he close to you?' Harrington asked.

'Close? Not really. The family live up in Sheffield. We live in Worcester.'

'But you want to take his place?'

'Not take his place,' Fielding said. 'I just thought, if Robin was prepared to fight for freedom, so should I be too.'

'Well,' Harrington replied, 'if that's how you feel. But think carefully.'

'I have thought about it, sir,' Fielding said, 'and I've prayed.'

'Oh, prayer; that's all very well but you've got to live with what you've decided. You know what they say about spilt milk.'

Fielding responded with a faint smile. 'You can't put it back in the jug once it's all over the floor. You just have to mop up the mess.'

'Well, it's the same with your life. You, for instance. You think you want to go to war.'

'Not *want* to, sir. Need to.'

'Need, want; sometimes they're much the same thing. Who knows; in six months, a year's time, you might look back and think, *what if I'd stayed on my first path?*'

'The priesthood?' Fielding said. 'Oh, that's not going to be a problem. I'm strictly hostilities only. I'll be back as soon as we've put paid to Hitler. I'm going to be a bishop before I die.'

Harrington smiled. 'Now that's not something you should be ambitious for, Mr Fielding. No, but seriously, there's always the *what if* factor.'

'You mean, what if I get killed? It's war. I realise that's a possibility.'

Harrington wondered how the prospect of getting killed could possibly be real to someone like Fielding. 'Well, there is that to consider, of course. But that's not what I was thinking of. You might get a taste for the military life. Or,' he added deliberately, 'you might meet someone.'

'A woman?' Fielding shook his head. 'I've always wanted to be a priest, sir. Can't see me changing my mind now.' He paused. 'Did you ever think of another way of life?'

The boldness of the question startled Harrington. 'Me? I've never given it much thought. I suppose, if my father hadn't left Ireland to go to England I'd probably be cutting turf in a Kerry bog now. If I hadn't got my scholarship to come to college here as a student, I might be on Salford docks, heaving sacks of Canadian wheat or sugar from the Caribbean. If I hadn't been taken on as a professor I'd most likely be visiting the sick in Ancoats hospital. I might even,' he added with a smile, 'be hearing the last confession of a murderer in Strangeways Gaol in Manchester.' He saw he was confusing Fielding. 'Take no notice of me. Make up your mind what to do and stick to it. But be prepared for unforeseen consequences.'

As the door closed behind Fielding Harrington experienced a greater-than-ever tug of the by now hauntingly familiar dilemma. He'd been brought up according to a strict moral code that defined right and wrong or more strictly, he supposed, grace and sin, with emphasis on the sin. It was quite simple really: keep the rules and you'd get to heaven. The alternative didn't bear thinking about but there had been a get-out clause: by repenting and confessing your sins you could wipe the slate clean and make a fresh start, as often as you still had life in you, which had made sense until the day he'd decided confession to Fergal O'Dowd would be futile. In the eyes of people like O'Dowd, Harrington knew, he was living a life of sin. In his own eyes he was doing his best to cope with a situation that didn't seem to admit of any perfect solution. He supposed padre Jerónimo must have been placed in a similar quandary and his answer had been pragmatic. Perhaps there was something to be said for abandoning one's books.

The two cases weren't the same, Harrington knew, but in a way both he and Fielding were struggling with the same problem; how to face life outside the familiar guidelines. Fielding's solution seemed clear-cut, however risky, but he felt that he was still very far from finding his own answer.

33

Harrington had been surprised to see the familiar heart scrawled on an American letter. What information useful to the enemy could be coming from the States? he wondered. But, more important was the other envelope, with the Portuguese stamp and the local postmark, the address written in a neat convent-educated script.

The pain of the rupture had grown more, not less, agonising as time went on. In the days following the showdown with Koenig he'd found it progressively easier to admit that he'd been wrong, an admission which finally resulted in a letter, awkwardly penned in Portuguese. Harrington considered himself at home in the spoken language and being in love with Beta had added extensively to his vocabulary, but he discovered that his grasp of the written language was scarcely adequate for the finer points of writing about affairs of the heart.

He'd laboured over every detail of their break-up, admitting how wrong he'd been, begging her forgiveness for the horrible things he'd said. He was too ready to think the worst of other people; his behaviour, he admitted, had been odious. He'd accused her on the flimsiest of evidence, on no evidence at all, and that made him the lowest of the low.

It took him three attempts before he was reasonably satisfied that the letter more or less expressed all he wanted to convey. Perhaps, he thought, even the clumsiness of some of his phrasing might convey to her the sincerity of his contrition.

He had put the final edition together the previous Sunday afternoon and slipped out by the kitchen yard door to post it in the box by the corner of the entrance to the French Hospital across the street. He'd reckoned she would certainly open the envelope because she wouldn't recognise his handwriting, but how much of the letter would she would read before tearing it to shreds?

He eased the letter out of its envelope, a single sheet of heavy cream-laid paper, and began to read. Beta confessed she too had been *estúpida,* a much stronger word in Portuguese than in English. She did indeed talk too much, especially after a nice little glass of something, but when she spoke about him it was only because she could never stop thinking of her Mickey. *That Heinzi,* she wrote, *is too clever and I am too easily led on to babble about what is in my heart.* She resolved never again to go near the German Legation and she would expect him at the usual time on Thursday.

What was he going to say? Should he take flowers? He'd thought all women liked flowers but he remembered how his previous offering had been taken away by Ana, never to return, and he now realised he'd never seen vases of flowers in Beta's apartment. A box of chocolates perhaps? That seemed pathetically inadequate. Perhaps the safest thing would be to simply present his contrite self.

When he rang the bell at the door to her apartment there was an agonising few seconds of delay before Beta responded. *She's decided not to carry this through,* he thought, almost ready to turn back the way he'd come.

Then the door opened and Beta stood there, one hand on the door frame, the other loosely by her side, her face expressionless. She was wearing the same lavender dress she'd worn the first time he'd come to the apartment.

Lost for anything to say, Harrington stood facing her silently for a moment. Then: 'Beta, I...' he began.

He didn't get any further because she flung herself at him, arms round his neck, lips limpet-like on his mouth, smothering whatever it was he'd been preparing to say. Still glued together, she dragged him over the threshold, their feet so entangled they were in danger of collapsing breathless in the corridor.

'Darling!' she gasped when at last she took her mouth away from his, and promptly started to cry. Then, with tears falling freely, she was pummelling his chest with her fists. 'Don't you ever, ever again, ever,' she cried, before wrapping her arms around him again, her mouth fastened to his, practically hugging the breath out of him.

Harrington could feel her warmth through the cloth of his jacket and it was obvious she wasn't wearing much beneath that lavender dress. 'I'm sorry,' he managed to say, but she hushed him and, grabbing both his hands, she led him to the bedroom.

Their love-making was tender and leisurely, each exploring the other almost as though for the first time but with the advantage of knowing the places to visit, until he entered deeply into her and heard her little cry of ecstasy.

Harrington felt rejuvenated. Even Blount noticed the difference, attributing it to an entirely different cause. 'Finished with that little problem at last?' he remarked one afternoon when he found Harrington taking a stroll around the college garden in the shade of the palm trees.

It took a moment or two for him to realise what the college President was talking about. 'Oh, yes. The Masonic thing. Nearly all resolved, I think,' he said, 'thank goodness.'

'You're looking a lot better, Michael, if you don't mind me saying so. It must be a weight off your mind.'

How true, Harrington had thought. And if only he could get Koenig off his back, life might, despite the war, return to something like a reasonable existence.

34

'Take a look at this.' Arthur Cope pushed a copy of *The Times* newspaper across the breakfast table at Harrington. 'My brother sent it to me,' he explained. 'He thought I might be interested in the stories about the Dunkirk evacuation. And then I saw this.' Cope had folded the paper to the second page. 'It's unbelievable what they get up to. We let them come into our country out of the goodness of our hearts and that's what they do in return. He should have been shot in public by firing squad!'

Not understanding what had got Cope so excited, Harrington took the proffered newspaper.

Traitor pays the penalty was the strap-line. Walter Veermerche, a Belgian national resident in London, had been convicted under the Treachery Act that had been given the Royal Assent in May. The article helpfully recited the first clause of the Act: *If, with intent to help the enemy, any person does or attempts or conspires with any other person to do any act which is designed or likely to give assistance to the naval military or air operations of the enemy to impede such operations of His Majesty's forces or to endanger life, he shall be guilty of felony and shall on conviction suffer death.*

Veermerche had been caught sending letters containing information about the construction of a new RAF airfield somewhere on the south coast to an address in Sweden. Other than stating that it was the result of efficient intelligence gathering on the part of the proper authorities the article was silent on the circumstances of his unmasking. Veermerche hadn't been shot as Cope would have preferred; he'd been hanged in Wandsworth prison.

Harrington handed back the newspaper without a word.

'Speechless?' Cope said. 'I'm not surprised.'

'As you say, unbelievable,' Harrington mumbled. He struggled to his feet and managed to get as far as the professors' lavatory before vomiting his breakfast down the pan.

'But, my friend, there's no need for you to be anxious,' Koenig assured him as they sat in the flat above the Augsburger office. 'You're quite safe here in Portugal.' He smiled as he poured more Courvoisier into Harrington's glass. 'Quite safe, as long as we stick to our little arrangement. Of course,' he added with a mischievous grin, 'I wouldn't advise you to go back to England and tell anyone what you've been up to.'

It was completely bizarre that he should be running to the German for reassurance, thought Harrington, sitting under the portrait of that damned Leader. Koenig was the author of his misfortune, who'd effectively, if metaphorically, put the hangman's noose around his neck. Yet here he was, a substitute father confessor, soothing his penitent's fears.

'It's all very well for you to say that, Koenig. It's not your life that's on the line,' Harrington said.

'You think not, my friend?' The smile was more of a grimace than a sign of amusement. 'My masters have a reputation for being unforgiving in certain matters.' He shrugged. 'The Führer has declared that the Reich shall endure for a thousand years but I know that if I don't deliver the goods I won't be part of the scene for very long.' Koenig drained his glass and reached again for the bottle. 'Top you up?'

Harrington held out his glass. 'Just a drop.' He knew he was drinking more than he should. Like the smoking, the alcohol was serving him as a crutch.

'Now don't you worry, Michael. The ones who are writing the letters are the ones who run the risk, not you.'

'I'm not outside the scope of the Act.'

'His Britannic Majesty's writ doesn't run in this country. I doubt if Mr Churchill is in a position to request Dr Salazar to put a stop to our activities.' He gave Harrington a broad grin. 'We're all at it, Michael. If Lisbon were a bee hive the whole city would be buzzing.'

35

Harrington had heard that the former King Edward, now Duke of Windsor, had arrived in Portugal from Spain in early July and was staying with his wife at the Casa de Santa Maria, a sea-front mansion in Cascais belonging to Ricardo Espírito Santo, a member of the prominent Portuguese banking family, an ardent supporter of Dr Salazar's New State, and a particularly enthusiastic admirer of Hitler's Third Reich.

The announcement in the *Diário de Notícias* had been brief but Maria Winter, as ever, filled in the gaps as only she knew how. 'The bounder's on the run,' she declared in the course of a little Sunday supper party Harrington and Knox attended on the weekend after the Duke's arrival in Portugal. 'He quit his Paris house when the Germans invaded and made it in double quick time to his property on the Riviera. Then, when the Italians joined the Nazi bandwagon last month, he legged it into Spain, and now he's cosying up to our lord and master here in Portugal. They say,' she didn't specify who was her informant, 'he's been offered the job of Governor of the Bahamas to keep him out of mischief.'

It was titillating stuff but hardly relevant to them, Knox observed as he and Harrington made their way back to the college.

A few days later Harrington was no less astonished than the rest of the staff when Blount made an announcement. 'We've been requested, I think it would be more accurate to say *ordered*, to receive a visit from the Duke of Windsor.'

'The Embassy wants us to entertain him?' Harrington demanded in astonishment. 'Here in the college? With that woman?'

'Not the Embassy. The summons came from one of his aides. The Duke wishes to dine with us. I had to explain that the college wasn't in the habit of entertaining ladies. Fortunately that was quite understood.'

'What's he after?' Cope grumbled. 'I can tell you, it's going to set us back quite a bit. He'll expect decent wine, good food.'

'No fuss, no ceremony, that's what I was told,' Blount sought to reassure him.

'That's all very well. What's simple and plain to him will be pure luxury for us.'

'But why here?' Like Cope, Harrington was struggling to make sense of the news. 'Why come to the college?'

'The gentleman who made the arrangement said that his Royal Highness understood that ours is the oldest British establishment in the country,' Blount explained.

'English, not British,' Harrington commented pedantically. 'We were founded a century before the Acts of Union. The Irish Dominicans were here in Lisbon before us,' he added grudgingly, 'but only by a few years."

'Be that as it may, gentleman,' Blount said, clearly having no desire to enter into pedantic historical details so beloved of Michael Harrington, 'we've been called upon and we must rise to the occasion.'

Savouring the irony, Harrington stood with his colleagues at the foot of the college steps, an enemy agent awaiting the arrival of a Royal personage. After the first flood of terror upon reading that article in the *Time*s and his conversation with Koenig, he'd more or less succeeded in rationalising his predicament.

If Koenig could operate as a German agent in neutral Portugal, there was no reason why he too shouldn't be safe and, if bad came to the worst and he had to return to England, what likelihood was there that he could be prosecuted, if indeed anything ever came to light, for activities undertaken on Portuguese soil? As Koenig had pointed out, the real crime was being committed in England; he wasn't more than the postman and so, no more than any postman, was he liable for the contents of the mail he handled. It was a thin argument, Harrington recognised, but it served in some degree to quieten his conscience.

The Duke arrived in an unmarked black Mercedes with two other men but only the driver alighted to open the door for the royal guest who, smoking a cigarette, casually acknowledged the staff's respectful salutations and fairly sprinted up the steps to the Arches, while the Mercedes slid away in the direction of the Largo Trindade Coelho.

Drinks in the President's Parlour passed off easily enough. Harrington watched as José, in a crisp new white jacket over his dark trousers, served the Dry Martinis Cope had trained him to make with the help of the ice obtained from the French Hospital across the street.

The Duke, quite affable, shook their hands in turn and made fatuous remarks about needing to behave himself in the company of so many clerics, but something about the royal demeanour indicated to Harrington that their guest had steadied himself with a few drinks before his arrival.

Why on earth had he come? What was he after? Harrington mentally echoed Cope's question. Before the Duke's arrival Blount had reminded them that his grandfather, King Edward VII, after whom the gardens at the top of the Avenida da Liberdade were named, had visited the college in 1903 when he had granted them the right to fly the White Ensign whenever the Royal Navy came to visit Lisbon. But Harrington doubted the Duke would be in a position to offer them any new privileges.

Cope had done them proud, he thought, during the meal in the professors' dining room. Some vinho verde for the fillets of sole, and a very decent red Dão to go with the main course, succulent steaks in a creamy mushroom sauce. He noticed that their visitor only picked at his steak but worked his way steadily through the wine, holding up his frequently emptied glass for José to replenish.

Harrington listened as Blount regaled the Duke with the story of his grandfather's visit to the college. 'He came to Portugal twice, as you may know. The first time as Prince of Wales, some time in the '70s, on board the Royal Yacht.'

'Ah, the old *Vic and Al*, as we used to call her,' the Duke reminisced. 'Not in Papa's hearing though. He was very strict about observing the proprieties.'

'And then he came again, when he was king,' Blount continued. 'That's when he visited the college. I remember it well. We students had all gathered in the garden and then he walked out to us, smoking a cigar. We were awestruck: our King and Emperor standing there in front of us! I was twenty-three and I should have had my wits about me but,' Blount chuckled, 'the only thing I recall is thinking how enormously fat his majesty was, not a word about what he said to us.' He glanced at the Duke, suddenly anxious lest he'd committed a solecism.

'He was monstrous, wasn't he?' the Duke agreed equably. 'Do you still fly the flag as he directed?'

Cope answered in his capacity as honorary chaplain to the Fleet. 'Indeed, sir, and I rather think we should have been flying the White Ensign today in honour of your visit.'

Harrington nearly interrupted at that point. The Duke of Windsor was Army, not Navy, and he'd come overland from Spain rather than in one of His Majesty's warships. 'I trust you're comfortable in the Casa de Santa Maria, sir,' he said instead.

It was probably out of place to enquire after the comfort of a royal personage, Harrington thought, but if the Duke wanted to be so informal as to come to supper without even an equerry at his side then he'd have to put up with commoners daring to ask impertinent questions.

The Duke swivelled round in his chair. 'Harrington, isn't it?' he said, with half-closed eyes, as if trying to recall the introductions in the President's Parlour. 'The Casa de Santa Maria? An excellent little billet. Not up to my place in Paris, but snug enough for the moment.' He turned to Blount. 'You were saying, about grand-papa's visit here. That wasn't long before poor old Manuel got deposed in 1910.'

'Your grandfather sent the Royal yacht to rescue him,' Blount said.

'God, yes. I nearly came out on board her myself that time. Grand-papa thought it would be good for my development and a salutary lesson on the perils of monarchy. Only Dartmouth said I wasn't ready.' He saw their puzzled faces. 'The Royal Naval College,' he explained. 'I might have made a career in the Navy if Uncle Albert hadn't turned up his toes. That put Papa in line for the throne and made me next so it wasn't thought wise to let me continue.' He held up his glass for José to top up again. 'As it was, I only got three months as a midshipman on board the *Hindustan*. A fearful old battleship.'

As the dinner progressed the Duke became embarrassingly frank. Churchill was a fool if he thought Britain could confront Germany's armed might, and there could be an altogether rosier future if Britain united with the Führer against the Communist menace. As for Britain itself, 'There's a firm hand needed at the helm,' the Duke declared. 'When Moseley got his seat in the Commons I thought he might have fitted the bill but now the poor blighter's interned and with Ratbag in charge...' He offered an eloquent shrug.

Oswald Moseley, leader of the fascist black shirts: Harrington was surprised a prince of the realm would have anything to do with such a scoundrel. From what he'd heard at Maria Winter's table, Churchill had at one time been quite amenable to the king entering into a morganatic marriage with the American divorcée but as increasingly lurid stories had emerged about her dubious sexual career the grand old man of British politics had hardened his attitude. Mrs Simpson simply wouldn't do as a royal consort.

The Duke's rant hadn't finished. 'We should round up all the Bolshies and the Awkward Squad. I went round one of those concentration camp places when I was in Germany and I tell you, I thought we could do worse than follow their example.'

The uncomfortable silence round the table was broken clumsily by Blount. 'King Manuel saw out his life in exile in Twickenham. Did you attend his funeral, sir?'

'Indeed I did,' the Duke said, 'we all went. Don't hold with all your Roman rigmarole as a rule but it was a damned fine send-off.'

As the cheese and port was passed round the table, the conversation devolved into a discussion of how the Portuguese aristocracy had survived the proclamation of the republic. 'They've had their ups and downs,' Harrington told the Duke, 'but Salazar recognises the aristocracy have a part to play in the New State.' That was something he'd learned from Fonseca who had once modestly admitted that his family appeared three times in the Almanac de Gotha.

They said their farewells in the Arches. The Duke shook hands with each of them but when he came to Harrington he leaned towards him and said in a loud whisper, 'I take you for a shrewd observer, Father Harrington. You know the lay of the land and all that. Got a few things to discuss. Make yourself available. My chap will be in touch.'

That's the last we'll see of him, Harrington thought as he watched Blount assist the Duke down the steps to where the car was waiting, *I'd be amazed if he remembers my name when he sobers up tomorrow.*

36

Harrington was wrong. The same black Mercedes came for him a couple of days later which, being Thursday, meant he had to cancel his visit to Lapa, having just the time for a guarded telephone conversation to Beta before being whisked off down the narrow streets to the waterfront and along the coast past Jerónimos monastery in the direction of Cascais.

The gates to the Casa de Santa Maria opened as if by magic on the car's approach, revealing a beautiful example of ornate black and white tessellated pavement leading between immaculate English-style lawns, shade trees and beds of brightly coloured flowers. Harrington could see the tip of the Cascais harbour lighthouse peeping above the trees beside the house and wondered if its light disturbed the distinguished guests at night.

At the pillared portico he was greeted by an oriental butler in a formal black frock coat who politely asked, in English, permission to pat him down before he went any further.

The Duke appeared at that moment. 'It's all right Suzaki, I can vouch for Father Harrington.' The butler stepped back respectfully.

'Efficient sort of chappie, for a Nip,' the Duke commented. 'Ricardo Espírito Santo provided him, along with the house. About the security thing. Someone got into the grounds last night, throwing stones at the windows. I've told Ricardo we should have dogs to guard the place. Come this way.' The butler stood impassively to attention at one side, seemingly deaf to the Duke's remarks.

In the centre of the imposing marble-floored entrance hall Harrington admired a Rococo table on which stood an ornate silver bowl filled with a gigantic bouquet of flowers. He wondered whether it was coincidental that the colours of the blooms should be red, white and blue.

The Duke led the way through the house. 'The stone-throwing thing last night,' he continued as they walked along, 'it's happened before. They're thugs, paid by the Embassy, trying to frighten us. They'll have to do better than that, I can tell you. Care for a smoke?' He offered a gold cigarette case.

It seemed rude to refuse.

The duchess was the sole ornament on the terrace, sprawled on a canvas sun lounger and wearing a very plunging vivid green bathing suit. She was smoking too, using a long ivory cigarette holder.

'This is the chap I was telling you about, Wally,' the Duke said by way of introduction. The duchess raised a limp hand, as if too fatigued to utter. 'I thought we might go down to that summer-house place for a chat, if that's all right with you, sweetie.'

'Whatever you please, David.' She uncrossed her legs and used a forefinger to adjust the hem of her bathing suit where a wisp of dark curl was revealed. Harrington saw the hint of a sly smile on the brilliantly red lips as she looked up and caught the direction of his eyes.

Harrington recalled Maria Winter saying that in China Wallis had been bedded by Count Ciano, Mussolini's son-in-law. And, again according to Maria, there'd been a string of other affairs, as well as a rumour of an abortion. If only half of what Maria Winter asserted was true – she also claimed that before the war Wallis Simpson had a fling with von Ribbentrop, the German Ambassador in London - Harrington reckoned the lady in the green bathing suit knew exactly how to play with a fellow's attentions.

The summer-house was a thatch-roofed timber affair, not far from the water's edge, nothing more than a shelter for a bar and half a dozen seats. 'Do sit yourself down, Father,' the Duke invited though he remained standing. 'The Embassy are playing Churchill's game,' he said, 'to get me back to England, but I'm damned if I'm going to walk into that trap.' He paced restlessly around in front of the bar before turning abruptly on Harrington. 'What are they saying about me, eh?'

'Saying, sir?'

'Here, in Portugal.'

'The *Diário,* that's our most authoritative newspaper, recently mentioned your arrival, sir. *Another distinguished visitor for our beloved country* is what the editorial said, if my memory serves me right.'

'Is that all?' the Duke responded moodily. He studied the bottles lined up on the shelves behind the bar and glanced at his watch as if debating whether it was perhaps a trifle too early, and continued his pacing. 'Found yourself a pleasant little hidey-hole here, haven't you, Harrington?'

'Your Highness?' He'd never thought of the Bairro Alto as any sort of hidey-hole.

'Portugal,' the Duke elucidated, 'Land flowing with milk and honey.' He waved his hand in the general direction of the immaculately tended garden. 'You should see what it's like in Spain. I tell you, those Bolshie mountebanks brought that country to its knees and Franco's going to have his work cut out to get it into working order again.'

The Duke turned and gazed up the garden to where his wife still sunned herself. 'They want me to go back there, would you believe?' he said, his back still turned to Harrington. 'To Spain. Got a château or whatever they call it over there, that I could use.' He gave a hoarse croak that passed for a laugh. 'A castle in Spain! I've got a damned fine place in Paris, thank you very much. Suchet's a charming house, and they've promised to look after it until I can get back. And then there's La Croë, down on the Riviera, a lovely little retreat. Mind you, I'm not sure I trust the Italians to take the same care there.'

The Duke turned back to face Harrington. 'I know what you're thinking. Well, it might surprise you to know those people in Paris respect my authority a damned sight more than that crew in London and I've had their word about the house.'

Those people in Paris, He's talking about the Germans, Harrington thought. The Duke had an arrangement with the occupying power to safeguard his property. Of course, he was half German himself, as Maria Winter had said. Some of the top brass of the military in Paris might be related to him and understanding between families would naturally overcome any temporary military embarrassment. Perhaps his friend Hitler had given specific orders about protecting the Duke's house.

'We had the devil of a job getting down to the Riviera from Paris,' the Duke told him bitterly, 'and an even worse mess of it coming over here from Spain. Nobody knows what it was like, no bugger cares. I'm a major general in the British Army and I'm being hounded worse than a fucking private. Do you know Churchill's threatened me with court martial because I'm not prepared to go back to England to be his bloody lackey?'

He stepped back, decided it was after all the acceptable hour and dived around the bar to reach for a bottle. He was in the act of pouring himself a large helping of the Glenlivet before he resumed, 'And I wouldn't put anything past that bitch Cookie. She's got my brother under her thumb. I told Bertie, when he asked for my advice: "If you marry her," I said, "it's good-bye to your independence".'

Cookie, Bertie. Harrington was becoming adept at deciphering the royal cypher book. Bertie was King George VI, currently reigning in place of his brother. Which meant that Cookie had to be Queen Elizabeth. But why *Cookie*? He knew it was an American expression meaning biscuit. Wallis was American and the nickname clearly wasn't a compliment. Perhaps it was the way the stick-thin Wallis was getting her own back against her comfortably rounded sister-in-law.

The Duke took a mouthful of the whisky and some of the tension went out of his shoulders. 'Churchill expects me to shuffle off to be Governor of the Bahamas, of all places! Bahamas! That would be a fate worse than death.' He gave a mirthless grin. 'They're saying there's a plot to have me killed when I get to there, would you believe?' He didn't elaborate as to who *they* might be. 'Anything's possible with that crew in power.'

So Maria Winter was right once again, Harrington thought, at least about the governorship.

'You want a snifter?' the Duke enquired, remembering his duty as host.

Harrington declined. The cigarette he'd accepted had left him unpleasantly light-headed. A tumbler of single malt at eleven in the morning wouldn't make things any better. He wasn't sure he wanted to know any more, wasn't at all sure he'd wanted to hear as much as he already had. 'Sir,' he said hesitantly, 'I appreciate the honour of you calling for me but I don't know how I can be of assistance to you.'

The Duke was comforting himself with another mouthful of Scotch mist. 'Your name's been mentioned. And the other night, when I came to your place, I could tell, straight away. I said to Wallis afterwards, that man knows his way round these Portuguese. You know what's what, I could see that. Not much passes me by, I can tell you. I knew I could pick your brains.'

Harrington thought wildly. His name had been mentioned - by whom? 'Surely, sir, the Ambassador would be better placed to advise you?'

The Duke glared at him. 'Selby? I won't tell you what that pretentious little prick had the impudence to say to me when I arrived. No,' he broke off to light another cigarette, juggling the case, the lighter and his drink, 'what I'm after is word from the grass roots.' He favoured Harrington with a long and penetrating stare. 'How far can they be trusted, these Portuguese? I mean, is it safe here?'

'I'm sorry?'

'This country. Is it safe?' the Duke repeated irritably. 'You've spent most of your life here, you should know. Is it safe, man? I've a reason for asking.'

'There was an attempt on Dr Salazar's life some while ago,' Harrington said. 'It was the work of communists, so they say.'

That was dismissed with a shrug. 'I had a man pull a gun on me once in the Strand. He was a mental case and the gun wasn't loaded. But,' he wheeled round and pointed his cigarette at Harrington, 'is this a safe place to be?' He put his empty glass down on the bar and eyed the whisky bottle speculatively, made up his mind and poured himself another snifter. He didn't bother this time to enquire if his guest wished to indulge.

Harrington thought he'd caught the drift of where this was going. It was all very well for the Duke of Windsor to boast of being a high-ranking army officer, but he'd fled the fighting in the north, first to safety in Biarritz, and then on the fall of France, into Spain; and now here he was in Portugal looking for asylum.

'I've never felt threatened,' he said cautiously, searching for the words he guessed the Duke wanted to hear, 'but then I'm no one important. Your Highness must have influential friends.' *One of whom has mentioned my name to you,* he added mentally, *though God knows why.*

The Duke was off at a tangent. 'This whole bloody war is a disaster that should never have happened. I've talked to Herr Hitler. He's done a lot for his country, reorganised it from top to bottom. We should have taken a leaf from his book.' He took another pull of his whisky.

'I'll tell you something, Harrington,' he continued. 'If *I* were still King we wouldn't be fighting Hitler. What do they say? A country doesn't have friends; it has interests. Well, my country has interests. You don't have to agree with everything the man does to see that he's right about the Soviets for all his temporary treaty with them. You mark my words, when the time comes old Adolf's going to see off Stalin, and we should be in there with him.'

That sounded all too like the sentiments Andy Winter had expressed. Harrington wondered what the Duke thought about Jews. It was difficult to know how to reply. The Duke's face was flushed and he had resumed his pacing back and forth, pulling deeply on his cigarette as if he wanted to swallow the glowing tip. Harrington wished now that he'd accepted the earlier offer of a drink.

'This is my idea,' the Duke threw away the cigarette and immediately fumbled for another, 'I know which way the wind's blowing, as if that wasn't bloody obvious. And then who will they turn to, eh? Answer me that!' He didn't expect a reply. 'And Portugal's a damned sight nearer to home than the Bahamas. I know where my duty lies, and I'm ready to take over when the time comes. Cookie can take Bertie off to Canada if she wants. New Zealand, for all I care. As far away as possible.' He grinned. 'I might let him govern the Bahamas!'

Harrington was both horrified and fascinated by such intimate exposure to the inner workings of a royal mind. The

Duke took his silence for disapproval and glared at him. 'I'm sorry if some people are getting hurt, but they ought to know who's to blame. Churchill. You know, Harrington, I thought that man was my friend once. Just goes to show you can't trust anyone. All this trumpeting about Hitler! Churchill sees this as his moment of glory and he's going to seize it whatever the cost to my country.' He made an effort to take control of himself. 'Now then, what if I stayed put here? What's the sentiment in the country here? Safe haven or what?'

Harrington didn't know how best to reply, but as the silence dragged on the Duke was clearly becoming impatient. 'I'm sure that if it were your decision to stay in Portugal your wishes would be respected, sir. Salazar's a realist. This is a poor country. It may appear picturesque to the casual observer but...'

'Better than Spain at any rate,' the Duke butted in. 'I take your point. You're saying I'd be safe enough here, if need be. Thing is, there's a chap, Fonseca's his name. He's got a bit of property the other side of that place, what d'you call it? Sintra. He sounds to be an interesting chap and he's got the right idea about the Bolshies, so I'm told.'

He might have known: Fonseca, whose 'bit of property' covered a significant proportion of the country, was somewhere behind all this. The Duke's visit the other day had nothing to do with the English College being the oldest British establishment in Portugal, nor about grand-papa's visit or traditions about flag-flying. Someone wanted to use him, a simple English priest, an innocent seminary professor who could be relied on to support a scheme cooked up by Fonseca or, more likely, by someone using Fonseca.

Harrington had a mental picture of Antonio and Carmelita entertaining the Duke of Windsor and Wallis as their house guests at Laranjeiras. Would there be room for their trusty English priest as well?

'You still haven't answered my question.' the Duke was close enough for Harrington to smell the whisky and tobacco on his breath. 'You priests, you're in touch with the people. So, what do you say? Is this a good place to wait for the call?'

'I understand senhor Fonseca's a gentleman of influence, well spoken of.' He meant Fonseca knew the right people and was a supporter of Salazar's New State just like Ricardo Espírito Santo, but the Duke interpreted the remark as an endorsement of the safe haven proposition. He extended his hand. 'Grateful for your counsel, Harrington, good of you to come. My driver will take you back to Lisbon. I might want to speak with you again sometime.'

Wallis was no longer on the terrace and it was clear that a place had not been set for him at the royal table. By the time he got back it would be too late for lunch at the college.

37

The driver was as taciturn on the return trip as he'd been outward bound, which gave Harrington plenty of time to ponder. Windsor, Fonseca, Koenig; each in their own way seemed to be singing a similar tune, but each with his own hymn book. The Duke of Windsor still had his eye on the throne he considered was his natural birthright, stolen from him by the machinations of narrow-minded bigots. Koenig, for all his flippant remarks about Hitler, was dedicated to the cause of German triumph. As for Fonseca, Harrington thought that gentleman might be echoing the inclinations of his political master.

He could forgive Fonseca's attitude; a small country like Portugal couldn't afford to antagonise what was bidding to be one of the world's great powers. Koenig was doing what he thought was his patriotic duty. But the Duke of Windsor, beneath all his bluster was only interested in his own aggrandisement and that of the woman he called his wife.

Harrington knew Beta would be anxious to hear every detail of what had gone on at the Casa de Santa Maria. 'Drop me off here, will you?' he called out to the driver as they approached the Avenida Infante Santo.' Better to walk up to Rua do Prior than have the driver see where he was going.

Beta was delighted to see him. 'I thought I'd have to do without you today. Now,' she said, 'I want to hear all about it.'

But Harrington's immediate mind was on food. 'It isn't too late for lunch,' he told her. 'If we hurried we could go to that little restaurant in Rua das Janelas Verdes. I'm told they've got a tank of live lobsters and the one you pick they'll cook for you on the spot.'

'I know that place!' she exclaimed in disgust. 'Shame on you, Mickey, for even thinking of such a thing!' At least, at the bullfight, she reproached him, the animal had a chance to show his vigour, 'but as for the poor creatures in that tank,' she shuddered. 'I should have thought better of you, my darling.'

Harrington felt that for the sake of harmony it would be better to settle for the cold collation Ana had left out. 'She told me she'd prepared plenty, in case a friend came to join me,' Beta explained with a giggle.

'She knows, doesn't she?' Harrington asked anxiously, 'About us, about me?' as Beta busied herself setting out plates and cutlery, playing the housemaid for the day, as she laughingly described the chore.

'She isn't paid to know anything more than how to keep this place clean and what to do in the kitchen,' Beta responded loftily. 'Here, open this bottle.' It was Colares white. 'It's none of her business what I do with my life.' All the same, there was something in her tone of voice that suggested otherwise.

Over the slices of *presunto*, soft ewe's-milk mountain cheese, corn bread and the tiny seafood quiches that were Ana's speciality, she wanted to know all about Mickey's meeting. What did the Duke look like? What was he wearing?

She was disappointed when Harrington couldn't supply all the details she was thirsting for. 'He's quite small,' he managed to remember. As short as your friend Heinz Koenig, he was tempted to add. 'And he wore a blazer. It had a sort of stripe in it. He smoked a lot, and drank a lot of whisky.'

'Men,' she sighed theatrically, 'you're hopeless when it comes to important things. "A sort of stripe". Really!' She was inclined to forgive the drink. Royalty, she decided, had their own rules. As for the smoking: 'Ah, a cigar,' she said, reminiscing, 'my father was fond of a cigar in the evening. He always smoked Monte Cristos.'

'The Duke was smoking cigarettes, actually.'

'Oh well,' she generously conceded the point, 'I expect they were of a very expensive brand.'

He wasn't able to help her there. The cigarette he'd been given had left him quite dizzy even without the addition of having to listen to the Duke's fantasies.

'He doesn't want to go back to England.'

'You mean, he's going to stay here in Portugal?' Beta asked excitedly. 'Isn't that marvellous! Think of it, Mickey, a king living here. There will be parties, balls, grand receptions!'

'He's not a king,' Harrington reminded her, 'and he's got responsibilities as an officer in the British Army.' He decided not to tell her about the Duke's ambition to regain the throne. 'Anyway, it won't come to anything, Beta,' he said. 'He'll be gone soon. I don't think there's going to be any invitations to balls and garden parties.'

Beta did her best to overcome her disappointment by demanding details of her Royal Highness. 'That's who I really want to know about. How I would have loved to have been there! If I'd been with you I wouldn't have missed a thing.'

'We didn't talk,' Harrington said. 'We just said hello. Not even that really. She was sunbathing.'

Beta eyed him speculatively. 'What was she wearing?'

'A bathing-suit, of course.'

'Of course. But what was it like? Was it something that would have suited me?'

'It was bright green,' Harrington struggled with the description, 'and rather skimpy. It showed a lot of her bust,' he demonstrated against his own chest.

Beta laughed. 'I hope you didn't ogle her Royal Highness!' she said, giving him a sly glance.

Harrington thought he wouldn't mention the provocative thing Wallis had done. 'She isn't a royal highness, any more than he's a king,' he said instead. 'The Duke called her that but I understand the title's been refused her. She was smoking, too.'

'Now that I don't approve of,' Beta retorted, 'ladies smoking. Though,' she added by way of concession, 'she *is* American and it *was* in private. I suppose that makes a difference.'

Curiously, at least to Harrington, Beta didn't seem particularly interested in anything the Duke had said. She was much more interested in basking in the reflected glory of having a lover who consorted with royalty. She gave Harrington a lingering kiss. 'But I'm so proud of you, being so important!'

38

Harrington received an invitation to the Quinta de Laranjeiras a few days later. *It's Carmelita's birthday on Sunday. We are having a few friends to celebrate with us. Let us know what time you will be arriving in Sintra and a car will pick you up.*

The car Harrington found waiting for him outside Sintra station was an elderly Renault. 'The boss doesn't let anyone else drive the Hispano,' the young lad wearing a chauffeur's cap a size too big for him, told Harrington by way of apology.

But the car was comfortable enough, the driver a good deal more considerate than Antonio, and he kept up a cheerful stream of chat. Harrington gathered preparations for St Monica's day were almost complete. The previous Sunday, padre Jerónimo had preached a fierce sermon warning the villagers not to put their trust in book learning. The young chauffeur chuckled. 'Half of the village can't read but it's the sermon he always gives about this time of year. We take bets on how long he's going to take.'

On arrival at the Quinta, Harrington was dismayed to discover what Fonseca understood by 'a few friends.' The courtyard at the front of the house was packed with vehicles and when the footman introduced him to the magnificent mirror-lined ballroom, walls and woodwork decorated in cream and eau-de-nil, he found at least fifty men and women, all strangers to him.

Servants moved discreetly around with canapés and trays of drinks. The children were nowhere in sight. Carmelita, in a beautifully-cut creation of blue and white, saw him enter. She came across to him and graciously accepted his congratulations. His gift, a little box of Scottish shortbreads he'd bought on impulse from a shop in the Chiado specialising in luxury foreign goods, seemed ridiculously inadequate in such obviously affluent company.

He felt awkward and out of place, knowing his black clerical suit, made for him by a tailor in Rua do Loreto, didn't bear comparison with the expensive outfits these men and women were wearing. Why on earth had he been invited to this sort of gathering? He would have much preferred to have been summoned for another St Monica's feast day.

Carmelita excused herself to greet the arrival of yet more guests, leaving Harrington standing alone, glass in hand, until Fonseca came to his rescue. 'I'm neglecting you,' he exclaimed. 'There's someone here who wants to meet you. Come outside.'

He led the way on to the terrace where the previous year they had lunched in the spring sunshine. On the far side, standing by the balustrade overlooking the formal garden, Harrington saw a small group of men in quiet conversation but Fonseca drew him away to the other end of the terrace. 'I understand you've been talking to the Duke of Windsor.'

'He mentioned your name,' Harrington replied cautiously, wondering where his friend had got that information from.

'So? What was your impression?'

Harrington wished he hadn't accepted the invitation to this odd party. He might have known, when the Duke spoke about Fonseca, that he was being drawn into something too deep for him. From where he stood he could look across at the group at the far end of the terrace; something about the way they stood appeared significant – he'd seen similar conspiratorial closeness when groups of his students were plotting mischief.

Fonseca might have made a sign behind his back for Harrington saw one of the group looking in their direction.

The man said something to his companions and began to leisurely walk over.

'Your impression,' Fonseca repeated impatiently. 'What did he say about me?'

The man was within yards. Harrington searched for something useful. 'I think he appreciates your understanding of the world situation at this time. The need to be united against the Communist menace and all that.'

To his ears that sounded lame but Fonseca nodded. 'Good. That's good.' The man drew level. 'Senhor Auguste,' Fonseca said, breaking into Portuguese without further introduction, 'is counsellor to a very important person.'

Senhor Auguste - Harrington doubted it was his real name - was tall and upright, in his fifties, with fair hair cut severely *en brosse*. His skin was pale, his eyes startlingly blue. The suit was a dark formal pin-stripe, the tie was crimson with a narrow blue stripe. He might have been in an accident at one time for there was a thin diagonal scar under his right cheek bone. Counsellor to a very important person, Fonseca had said. Harrington thought it likely the important person wore elastic-sided boots.

Auguste bowed his head and offered his hand to be shaken. 'Delighted to make your acquaintance, senhor padre.' His Portuguese was easy and fluent but Harrington detected something foreign in the crisp accent the man imparted to the usual soft slur of the language.

'Padre Harrington is going to tell us about his recent meeting,' Fonseca said.

'It was a private conversation,' Harrington demurred. 'I don't think his Royal Highness would expect me to speak about it.'

'A confession, was it?' Fonseca sneered. 'I didn't know Windsor was a Catholic.'

'No,' Harrington tried to be reasonable, 'but it was of a confidential nature.'

'Stuff that!' Fonseca turned to his companion. 'Tell him.'

Auguste smiled. 'I think the padre is to be admired for his discretion, Antonio. However,' he spoke directly to Harrington, 'I have to point out we're talking about matters that may concern this country's security.'

He paused before adding inconsequentially, 'I understand the English College has quite a special history in Portugal. A privileged place in the nation's affections, you might say. It would be unfortunate, wouldn't you agree, if that privileged status were to be in any way compromised?'

Harrington recognised the implied threat. 'The Duke said that some people wanted him to go back to Spain.'

'And what did he think about that?' That was Auguste again. Fonseca, standing back, arms folded across his chest, looked on silently.

'He said Spain had been severely ravaged by the war.'

'True,' Auguste nodded. 'The Communists brought down ruin on the country.' He waited patiently for Harrington to continue.

'He's been offered hospitality there but I had the impression he didn't consider Spain to be in his best interests.'

Harrington was thinking furiously. A privileged status, the man had said. What could they do to the college? Cancel their residence permits? It had always been English College policy never to interfere in Portuguese political affairs, a policy Harrington knew had been maintained throughout the difficult days of the nineteenth century and the violent revolutions prior to Salazar's take-over of power. He'd seen the laconic entry in the college diary dating from one attempted coup d'état in 1927: *Rifle rounds through the library windows, lecture continued as normal.* It was a policy that had served them well, but perhaps at this moment, he thought, it needed some refinement.

'The Duke wondered,' he said, trying to remember exactly what the man had said, 'at least he gave the impression that he was considering the possibility of staying here in Portugal, where he'd be on hand in any eventuality. He thought that perhaps someone,' he nodded in Fonseca's direction, 'Senhor Antonio, perhaps, might be able offer him hospitality.'

'It was Espírito Santo's idea,' Fonseca said quietly to Auguste.

'But His Royal Highness; was he in favour?' Auguste put the question directly to Harrington. 'In favour of making this country his residence for the time being?'

'He thought that Portugal would be a strategically placed location in the event of his being recalled to take up the reins again. That was the gist of it.' He looked into their faces, trying to gauge the effect of what he was telling them.

The pair exchanged glances. Auguste smiled.

Harrington thought it best to add a rider. 'It's not every day a person like me has the honour of being in the company of someone as important as the Duke. Quite likely I've misinterpreted some of what he said. In any case I understand that he's to be appointed Governor General of the Bahamas.'

'I'm sure your recollection of the conversation is perfectly accurate, padre.' Auguste glanced at Fonseca and turned back to Harrington. 'So, thank you so much for sparing us your valuable time.' He offered another dip of his head and gave his hand to be shaken.

'The chauffeur will drive you to the station,' Fonseca told Harrington, 'in time to catch your train.' He wasn't expected to stay for the cutting of the cake.

He'd been called upon to take the role of what the theatrical world would call a spear carrier, Harrington mused, as the train chugged its way back to the city, a useful idiot in a game of international politics. Britain was on her knees, as any fool could see, and Botas was weighing up the probable outcome, waiting, playing the game he was best at. Harrington had read in that morning's *Diário* more of the popular speculation that Churchill, for all his war rhetoric, would soon find it convenient to come to terms with Hitler, thinking it more important to preserve the Empire in some form or other rather than lose everything in flames.

He shivered as the train drew into Rossio station. A game of these dimensions carried more consequences than he cared to consider. What a fool he'd been to imagine there'd be any possibility of him gaining some advantage for himself. If Windsor did return to the throne; he wouldn't remember a half-hour conversation with an insignificant priest on the lawn of the Casa de Santa Maria.

39

The first Harrington knew about Fielding carrying out his intention to enlist was when Martin Blount summoned the staff to a special evening meeting. 'He's entirely determined,' Blount told them, 'and I saw no purpose in trying to persuade him to change his mind.' Harrington thought Martin Blount sounded weary, as if old age had suddenly caught him unawares. 'We can only hope his example won't be followed by anyone else,' the college president added, glancing round the little group and seeing no such hope in their eyes. Harrington understood his dilemma. If the call of patriotism won over the desire to be ordained, the college would be emptied and Blount's position would become hopeless.

'So what are we going to do about Fielding?' That was Cope, ever the realist, and it was a fair question. Royal Mail and Booth Line ships were no longer sailing, and the train had been out of the question since the fall of France. 'The aeroplane?' Cope asked. Despite everything the BOAC Dakota was still flying a regular weekly route between Bristol and Lisbon. He immediately answered his own question: 'There's a waiting list as long as your arm.'

'There is one possibility,' Blount said. 'Mr Marchant was here at Mass on Sunday, as you may have noticed.'

Bill Marchant worked part-time for the British Council; Harrington had been to a very interesting lecture he'd given on the English Impressionists. But there was a bit of a mystery about him. Working for the Council couldn't earn Marchant more than enough to keep him in cheap wine, as Cope had once colourfully remarked, yet he owned a yacht he kept in the harbour at Cascais.

The story Harrington had heard about the yacht was that Marchant had a rich uncle with a sheep ranch in Australia and Bill was his only living relative. The uncle had paid for the yacht and Marchant had chosen the boat's name - *Esperança* meant Hope in Portuguese - in the expectation of the proceeds of his uncle's estate coming to him in due course.

Inevitably, Maria Winter peddled another story about the boat. According to her, Marchant was something big in the secret service and used the boat as cover for his activities. But then, Harrington thought, Maria Winter delighted in conspiracy theories, the more outlandish the better. Either way, it was well known that even after the outbreak of war Marchant sometimes sailed the Portuguese registered vessel single-handed as far as Gibraltar and smuggled back luxury goods that were hard to get hold of in Lisbon.

Blount was explaining how he proposed to get Fielding off their hands. 'Quite by chance, Mr Marchant mentioned that he's making another of his voyages to Gibraltar, leaving this coming Friday, the day after tomorrow. I took the liberty of asking him would he accept a passenger. He's agreed to take Fielding along with him.'

Harrington had to suppress a smile. This little plot had been cooked up the previous Sunday but only now was Blount letting them in on it. Mother Teresa at the Convent of Divine Mercy wasn't the only one to act high-handedly. Decisions about the running of the college were supposed to be taken collegiately by the staff, a procedure the President ignored when it suited him. A little devil prompted Harrington to ask: 'I suppose Fielding knows about this?'

'Fielding has chosen to leave us,' Blount said coldly. 'He's hardly in a position to dictate the manner of his leaving. As to what he does when he gets to Gibraltar, that's not our concern. I suppose he'll be able to sign up there or go back to England in a Navy ship. Fielding's told me that he'll be returning to the college as soon as the war is over.' He sighed. 'Be that as it may, I doubt we shall ever see him again.'

'I wonder, Michael,' he went on, 'if you'd be so good as to escort Fielding to Cascais tomorrow? I understand Mr Marchant plans to leave very early on Friday morning. Something to do with the state of the tide, so he says.'

'Is that all you've got?' Harrington asked the following morning, looking at the cheap little suitcase, when he met Fielding in the Arches. Blount had asked Arthur Cope to order a taxi to take them down to the station at Cais de Sodré.

'I'm told Mr Marchant says I have to travel light.'

It was odd to see Fielding standing there in the shabby clothes he reserved for holidays at Pêra. 'I've just brought a few bits and bobs. I haven't very much and these,' he added, pointing to his jacket and trousers, 'are my only civvies. I suppose I'll get properly kitted out when I actually sign up, or whatever they call it.'

'I don't suppose they'll give you Waiting Days,' Harrington said in an attempt to lighten the occasion. The custom had begun in the early days of the college; a three-day sounding-out process by which strangers seeking entry as students were vetted in an attempt to guard against the possibility of an English government spy getting in among them. In modern times Waiting Days provided an opportunity for the new arrivals to acquire something of the flavour of the city while their minders welcomed a three-day break from lectures.

Fielding grinned nervously. 'No such luck. It'll be square-bashing from the word go, I suppose.'

213

'You'll survive,' Harrington tried to encourage him, 'and when they see what you're made of, they'll put you to good use, I'm sure.'

'I hope so, sir.' He hesitated. 'I was quite surprised, as a matter of fact, that Father Blount gave me leave to go so easily. I thought he'd put all sorts of difficulties in my way.'

He sounded rather bemused. Not surprising, Harrington thought. The poor fellow had geared himself up for a fight and Blount had thrown in the towel before the bell had gone for the first round.

The Cascais train was crowded with people excited about going to the Portuguese World Exhibition in the Praça do Imperio in Belém. 'I've not visited,' Harrington said brusquely in reply to Fielding's question. 'I know the exhibition was in the planning long before Hitler decided it was worth plunging Europe into war, but all the same there's something strange about a demonstration of national pride just now, even in this neutral country.'

His dismissive attitude put paid to any further conversation. Though in a way he admired Fielding for finding an honourable way of escaping from the college, Harrington felt that joining the armed forces was a desperate action. He wondered if Fielding's silence meant he, too, was beginning to think along much the same lines.

They disembarked from the train at the Cascais terminus and walked the few hundred yards, past the parish church and the town hall, to the harbour. 'I imagine that must be Mr Marchant's yacht,' Harrington pointed out the elegant lines of a sleek sailing vessel moored to a buoy among the dozen or so fishing boats.

Fielding didn't reply *He's got the same idea as I have,* Harrington thought. The boat didn't look very big and he could imagine that in any sort of rough weather they'd get tossed around unmercifully.

'There he is.' There was a man leaning against the harbour wall, wearing a blue shirt and dark trousers, his rather long blond hair swept back over his forehead. He was talking to an older man, formally dressed in a suit and leaning on a cane. It was too fanciful to imagine that Marchant's friend might have been one of the men on Fonseca's terrace but all the same something about his posture suggested to Harrington an air of superiority and a concentrated attention on whatever the other was telling him.

'He's obviously busy at the moment so I'll leave you to introduce yourself and I'll say good-bye here.' Harrington fumbled in his wallet as he spoke. 'Here. Take this. My father gave it to me when I left home to come to the college. You might need it one day.'

Fielding looked at the coin he'd been given, heavy in his hand, and was blushing when he looked up. 'Thank you, sir,' he stammered. 'I've never had a sovereign before.'

'Don't spend it all at once,' Harrington admonished him with a smile.

'Father Blount's given me quite a lot of money, five pounds, but I'll keep this carefully. Perhaps I'll be able to give it back to you one day.'

They shook hands and Harrington watched Fielding walk off, *like a lamb to the slaughter*. It wouldn't end well, of that he was certain.

40

'You seem out of sorts, my darling,' Beta observed as she and Harrington sat together on the sofa in the Lapa apartment. She'd snuggled up to him only to be disappointed by his awkward response. His body remained tense even as she touched him, shifting away from her as though he wanted to avoid contact.

'What's the matter?' she asked.

The brittle note in her voice alerted Harrington and tried to pull himself together for her sake. 'It's this bloody war.'

'But darling,' Beta said, 'it doesn't concern us. Why worry?'

'That's where you're wrong, Beta. It does concern us. At least, it concerns me.'

'But how?' She sneaked her arm around his shoulder but he ignored it.

'You know, this morning, I've just seen our most promising student pack his bag and go off to join the armed forces. What are the chances of him coming out of this alive?' He sighed. 'The waste, Beta, the utter waste of it!'

'Tell me about it,' Beta murmured. It would do her lover good to unburden himself and she was ready to listen.

'I had to take him down to Cascais. There's an Englishman, Bill Marchant, he has a yacht there and he's sailing to Gibraltar.' He shook his head. 'You might know the man, he's one of Maria Winter's crowd.'

Beta didn't recognise the name. That wasn't really surprising; Maria tended to keep her guests in carefully sequestered groupings. 'Anyway, he volunteered to take Fielding with him to Gibraltar, to sign on.'

'That's very noble, Mickey, surely, to give himself in the cause of his country?' She wondered if Mickey hadn't heard what she'd said; so lost he seemed to be in his own thoughts.

'There are times,' he said, 'when I wonder about what we're doing in our college, whether it's right to keep our students cooped up, but to lose men to the war isn't good. It was the same in the last show. Students abandoned their studies, went to fight, never came back.'

Beta had heard Mickey express doubts about the college before. Personally, she thought it would be a serious loss to the colour of Lisbon life not to have those young people in their distinctive black habits and red stoles strolling through the streets. But she had to sympathise with Mickey's obvious hatred of war. 'My father,' she said, 'nearly went to fight in 1916. But the family was going through one of its more difficult patches and I was only little. Mother persuaded him to stay. If she hadn't he might have been killed, too.'

She kissed him. 'You mustn't let yourself get upset, darling,' she said gently.

'I know just how futile it is,' he responded, not easily comforted.

'Mickey, sweetest,' Beta murmured, 'I know just what you need.'

'You wouldn't believe what I did as I left him,' he said as she eased his jacket from his shoulders, 'I gave Fielding my sovereign.' He used the English word.

Beta paused in her work of undressing him. 'Your *sovereign*? What's that?'

'A gold coin, a bit like the old *cruzado*. My father gave it to me when I left home to come to Lisbon as a boy. In case of necessity, he told me. It's worth quite a lot now but I've always kept it safe.'

Beta was impressed. 'It was so thoughtful of you,' she whispered, 'but why, if it was so precious to you?'

'I wish I knew,' Harrington confessed. 'Maybe I envied him in a way.'

'Don't tell me you've decided you want to join up, too?' Beta asked in dismay.

'No. no, it isn't that. But I've got to admire someone who knows what he wants and has the courage to go through with it.'

It had been his last memento of his father. Harrington couldn't imagine how many weeks of scrimping, pennies painfully saved from meagre wages on the Salford docks, that sovereign represented. There'd been times, as a student, when its conversion into Portuguese currency would have provided him with useful addition to his funds, but he'd never succumbed to the temptation to hand it over to the money changers in Rua Aurea. And now he'd given it away to someone who might be dead within weeks.

41

Time rolled by with no word of Fielding. Blount was growing gloomier by the day. 'There might be a war on but I know for a fact mail is still getting through from Gib. And no sign of Marchant either. Were we wrong to entrust our boy to him?'

There was no answer to that, Harrington had to admit. He'd made discreet enquiries of his own, at the Embassy, about Marchant. Miss Singleton had been professional, saying only that as far as anyone knew Mr Marchant was in good standing with the authorities both back in England and here in Portugal. Harrington hadn't known what to make of what seemed to him a singular lack of enthusiasm in her endorsement. *As far as anyone knew.* What for God's sake did that mean? And was he being over sensitive in detecting a certain frostiness in his regard? He felt he'd inadvertently trespassed on forbidden territory.

On the last Sunday before the whole college decamped to Pêra for the summer break Harrington was in the college chapel for High Mass. The congregation was the usual mixed bag of Bairro Alto faithful and the more devout of the Anglo-Portuguese community. A glance up at the tribune opposite the organ loft confirmed that Maria Winter was occupying her usual vantage point, along with a handful of her immediate clan.

During the course of Knox's sermon, Harrington – he was sure he'd heard it at least twice before - distracted himself by looking around at the chapel's dusty décor, not all that much better, he thought, than the tawdry decorations in the chapel of the Divine Mercy convent. The college had never been rich enough for the sort of decoration to be found in the wealthy churches of the city but it would have been all the better if Beta were sitting up there in the tribune instead of the formidable Dona Maria.

When Beta learned the college chapel was open to all and sundry for Sunday Mass, Harrington had had a hard job in persuading her not to attend the celebration. 'I'd be very discreet,' she'd assured him when he'd explained that Maria Winter was a regular worshipper. He was tempted to give in - it would be delicious to have Beta so close - but the thought of what she might let slip in casual conversation after Mass deterred him from giving way.

He was shaken from his reverie by Knox, sermon finished, pushing past to regain his place in the choir stalls 'I saw you nodding off,' his colleague hissed. Harrington didn't think it was prudent to protest that he had been lost in contemplation of earthly delights.

As he'd expected, Maria Winter was holding court in the garden when he finally emerged after disrobing in the sacristy. 'Ah, there you are!' She pounced on him, abandoning her entourage' 'Tell me, Father, have you heard from that rascal Marchant recently? Haven't had as much as a peep out of him since he buggered off to Gib.'

'Marchant took one of our students with him,' he told her, thinking she probably knew that already.

'Did he indeed? Whatever for?' she demanded with an astonished look.

'He wanted to leave us,' Harrington said, 'decided to volunteer for service in the armed forces.'

'Silly fool him then. But I'm surprised you let him go with Marchant,' Maria retorted. 'Isn't he supposed to be a bit of a shirt-lifter?' She peered around, short-sightedly, eyeing the students strolling around on the far side of the garden as they waited for the lunch bell. 'I may have got that wrong,' the old lady admitted, 'but everyone knows he's up to something that's no good. When is he supposed to be coming back?'

'Oh, Fielding won't be coming back.'

'Not your lad,' Maria replied irritably. 'Marchant. When are we likely to see him again?'

'We don't know,' Harrington admitted. We're waiting to hear from him too.'

'He usually brings some stuff back for me. Contraband!' Maria squawked dramatically, raising her eyebrows. 'Shame on you, I hear you say, in time of war!' The wicked chuckle that accompanied her outrage told Harrington she wasn't in the least contrite. 'Now,' she changed tack abruptly, 'with France caved in, what d'you reckon, Father, about the way this war is going to go? Is it going to run and run, or are we waiting for something to be sorted out, all smoke and mirrors?'

It was an expression new to Harrington but he could guess at what it meant. 'It seems to depend whether one's an optimist or a pessimist,' he replied, surprised she should be asking his opinion.

'Or how much you're baying for blood,' she retorted. 'One way or another there'll be a lot of that spilt before the end.' She turned about as though to make her way back through the garden to the Arches but stopped unexpectedly. 'The Louçá e Medronho woman,' she demanded abruptly. 'Seen much of her recently?'

He opened his mouth, tried to say something but failed to find the words.

'She doesn't come to my suppers any more but someone said they'd seen her a couple of weeks ago, at the São Jorge. That *Young Mr Lincoln* film. Don't go to the flicks myself but I hear it's supposed to be good. They said they'd caught sight of you there, too. Wondered if you'd met her.'

'Er,' he floundered, 'Dona Elisabete? Yes, well, as a matter of fact, I did. That is, we did bump into each other. Quite a coincidence.' What did she know? More importantly, who'd spilled the beans?

She favoured him with another of her chuckles. 'Incognito you were too, according to my informant. Mind you, I don't blame you, Father. That dog collar,' she sniggered, 'must be a bit of a strait-jacket at times, eh? But tongues will wag if you're not careful. I don't listen to tittle-tattle,' she declared with lofty mendacity, 'but we all know how people love a bit of scandal.'

She looked around. 'Francis!' she called in a trumpet tone. Harrington saw several students' heads swivel about at the sound. 'Where the devil is the boy when I need him?'

The 'boy', her youngest son Francis, in his early forties, gangling and prematurely bald, hurried over from where he'd been in conversation with Martin Blount. 'Here I am, Mama.'

'You mustn't keep me waiting around here all day,' the old lady told him sharply. 'It's about time you earned your keep. Take me to the car.'

Francis offered his mother his arm and smiled wanly over her head at Harrington. The poor man was hen-pecked at home as well, so the rumour mill ran, his wife having proved to be a junior version of her mother-in-law. As a friend had once remarked, Francis' plight was one of the best advertisements for the benefits of celibacy.

'I'll say goodbye then,' Maria allowed herself to receive a kiss on the cheek, 'and mind what I say, Father.'

Cope joined him. 'Maria's on good form today,' he observed as they watched mother and son vanish through the doors into the Arches.

'What was she saying to you?' Harrington demanded sharply, still severely shaken by the woman's observation, warning, or whatever it had been.

'She was asking about Marchant.'

'She was asking me the same thing. I told her he'd taken Fielding to Gib.'

'We should have heard from him ages ago.' Cope could have been referring to Marchant or their former student. 'I hope he's all right. That boat. *Esperança's* a nice enough vessel I suppose. All right for a trip round the bay, but I wouldn't fancy my chances in her myself. I like *terra firma* under my feet any day. Ah well, can't stand here gossiping. I must go and see what they're up to in the kitchen.'

He'd been seen, with Beta. It was inevitable, really, Harrington supposed. Lisbon was not a big city and he and Beta were frequenting much the same territory as Maria Winter's crowd. Hers was a friendly warning; there were others out there who would be sharpening their gossip knives.

42

Harrington had been looking forward to seeing Beta more often during the summer but she'd reminded him again that it wouldn't do for Ana to catch him in the apartment.

'I know you think I let her get away with too much,' Beta had told him when he'd complained she was letting her servant rule the roost, 'but living at such close quarters under the same roof it's not easy to maintain one's distance and she's very good to me.'

They could arrange to meet somewhere and have lunch any day of the week, provided he wasn't wearing his clerical armour, as she'd called his black suit and dog collar, but their têtes-à-têtes in the apartment would continue to be confined to Thursdays.

Harrington arrived at the apartment early on the first Thursday of the summer break, full of expectation, only to find her in a strange mood. She kept getting up to make some pointless adjustment to an ornament or move one of the chairs an inch or two. He was about to ask, as discreetly as he could, what the matter was when she stopped fiddling with the pleats in one of the curtains and came to sit herself down beside him on the sofa.

'Mickey, darling!' she said breathlessly. Her face was flushed and her hands when she grasped his were warm and damp. 'Mickey, sweetheart, 'I've the most wonderful news! I know you'll be delighted. It'll be a boy, I'm convinced.'

'What on earth d'you mean?' he demanded. 'What boy?'

'I did the test,' she said, 'you know, the one with the rosary. It's supposed to be infallible. It'll be a boy,' she repeated, 'and that's what you'd wish, I'm sure.'

'I don't understand. A rosary?' Harrington demanded unsteadily. 'A boy? What on earth are you talking about?'

'Don't they do this in England?' Beta demanded. 'It never fails, apparently. You hold your rosary over your belly and you let it rotate. Clockwise, it'll be a girl; the other way, it's a boy. My rosary spun anti-clockwise like a merry-go-round!'

What he'd wished for, she'd said. She might as well have slapped him across the face. She was supposed to be looking after that side of things; Harrington distinctly remembered her saying as much, ages ago, when he'd first expressed his anxiety on that score - it might have been the second time they'd made love. When she'd said that ladies had means he hadn't liked to question her further, hadn't wanted, if he was to be honest, to think about it.

'You're pregnant?' he asked, his voice weak.

She beamed at him. 'It's far too early to tell the world but I knew you'd want to know as soon as possible. I missed my last monthly, and that's something I never do, you could set your clock by me, and now I've done the test.'

'It can't be,' he moaned, feeling a familiar cold dread void in his stomach. 'It's not possible.'

'I was beginning to wonder about that,' she said candidly, 'but thanks be to God, we can now say that there's nothing wrong with me and,' she added with a fond smile, 'quite clearly nothing wrong with you either. Not that I ever doubted you.'

'This is some sort of joke, isn't it?' Harrington demanded hopelessly, turning to face her properly. 'Some sort of game? You said that side of things would be all right. You promised.'

'Did I?' she answered dreamily, 'I don't remember. Perhaps I did. I must have forgotten.'

She said she'd missed her period. He wasn't sure how significant that was. Weren't there feminine ailments that suppressed the normal flow of things? 'There's got to be some other explanation,' he said boldly. 'You're not pregnant at all.'

'Of course I'm pregnant!' she exclaimed indignantly. 'I told you, I did the rosary thing.' She reached out one hand to caress his cheek, the other to draw his hand to the soft swell of her belly, no rounder under the silky blue dress than he remembered it from previous explorations.

'But... ' But nothing. Why ever had he imagined that a divine exemption had been granted in his case? Sex was a game of consequences, ordained by the working of the Natural Law.

'I understand,' Beta whispered softly, understanding nothing, 'it's so much for you to take in, so much to think about, so many plans to make. But don't worry, darling! It's all in hand. I've an uncle who's got an estate up-river, on the other side of Vila Franca de Xira. It's not large, but the house is pretty. It might need a little modernisation. And there's a good well. My uncle doesn't live there any more – he's got a house in Setubal – so I'm sure he'd let us have it. There's a farmer who looks after the fields, the sheep and the cows and so on. I'll care for the baby, with the help of the nanny, while you're busy,' she concluded vaguely, her imagination failing her at this point, 'with things around the estate. I'll sell this apartment, of course.'

Harrington was aghast. 'You haven't spoken to your uncle, have you?' This is the way his world was going to end, with word of his fall from grace passed from mouth to mouth like a contagious disease.

'She shrugged. 'No. But don't worry about that,' she dismissed the question. 'I'm sure he'd do anything for me, for us.'

Dona Elisabete Louçá e Medronho would arrange everything; Dona Elisabete, socialite, impoverished aristocrat, down to her last luxurious apartment in Rua do Prior, with an understanding uncle - not yet informed of his niece's great good fortune - who had a little estate somewhere up-river that he'd willingly hand over to them in due course.

'Darling Mickey,' she had her arms around his shoulders now, her face close to his, her scent permeating the air around them, 'Mickey, I know, I understand how you must be feeling. Such news, it's overwhelming for you. I could scarcely believe our good fortune at first.'

That really roused him. 'Good fortune! What on earth do you think you've done to me? A child! How could you?'

She sat back. 'What do you mean, what have *I* done to you? *Our* baby, Mickey! This is what you've done to me, with me, for us.' She caressed his cheeks. 'I thought you'd be so pleased to have a child, the fruit of our love for one another.' Her face crumpled. 'I should have broken the news to you more delicately, I was thinking selfishly, only of my own joy.'

'Your joy!' Harrington said bitterly, refusing to look at her. 'Oh God! Why me?' It was the most fervent prayer he'd made in a long time.

'Our joy,' she corrected herself. '*Medronho* I despise, but *Louçá e Harrington*, that's got a ring to it, to compare with the Taylors and the Fladgates, the Symingtons and the Winters, families who've brought lustre to Portugal.'

He knew it wasn't the moment to remind her that the noble Harrington clan had migrated from a bog in Kerry to a Salford back-to-back, and the only claims to fame he possessed were an uncle who'd taken up the gun against the British and a half-hour spent in private audience with a former king.

'You don't understand, Beta,' he said as calmly as he could. 'You know priests can't marry like normal people. I'm sorry but you'll have to get it adopted,' he declared as roundly as he could.

'Your child? Adopted?' She stared and then laughed at his little joke. 'Oh! I understand what you mean, and you're right. We've got to regularise our union as soon as possible.' She paused, with a finger to her lips. 'I wonder,' she said. 'One of Dona Louleira's relatives was ordained some years ago. I believe he's something on the Cardinal Patriarch's staff now. If I asked Dona Louleira to introduce me he'd arrange things for us, I'm sure.'

'God no! You mustn't go near him. Adoption,' he insisted. 'I mean it. It's the only way.'

She ignored his protest. 'You said you're not normal, Mickey? This,' she patted her belly complacently, 'says otherwise. Which means there's no reason why this one,' she patted her belly, 'should be the last.'

He almost gagged at the thought. 'Normal. I meant...' he struggled to explain to this foolish woman, 'You know perfectly well, there's a requirement for priests, a Church law.'

'Pouf! So much for your law! She caressed her belly again. 'We've a superior law, you and I, and he's here, inside me.'

Harrington only escaped by making all sorts of excuses; the need to plan ahead, make important decisions, whatever came into his head, trying to ignore her expressions of dismay and confusion at his precipitate departure.

Marriage, of course, that's what she had been leading up to all this time. How naïve of him to have ever imagined she'd one day settle for being his *governanta,* his housekeeper in a shady clandestine little arrangement in some village backwater.

She didn't realise, of course, how impossible it was to think about marriage. It wasn't merely the obstacles posed by Church law; quitting the priesthood would be a degradation for him worse than being cashiered might be for a military man. It would mean being cut off, ostracised by former friends and colleagues, the butt of seedy little jokes.

Harrington suddenly remembered what Fonseca had said, on St Monica's day last year, at the feast in the village square: about the country priests and about the motherless women crying out for new-born babies. At the time he'd wondered whether Fonseca wasn't talking from personal experience; Antonio wouldn't have been the first wealthy landowner to take some of his rents in kind. He probably knew of a convent in some town well away from the capital - Mafra or Torres Vedras - with nuns who knew how to be discreet about the lapses of the gentry.

He could approach Antonio for advice, presenting the matter as something he'd come to hear of in the course of his pastoral duties. The nuns would respect Beta's privacy and he'd impress on her that it was vital to keep his own part secret. It was the only way out of the dilemma, if he could persuade Beta to go along with it.

43

Beta knew she could have handled the news more circumspectly. If she had fallen pregnant in the early days of their acquaintance she didn't now know what she might have done but as the months had gone by she'd resigned herself to accepting barrenness, a dreadful fate for any woman. But now, at last, this!

Mickey was a delicate creature, unworldly, innocent in so many ways, she shuddered to think of that dreadful misunderstanding over Heinzi. It was part of his charm but it also made for careful handling and she should have known better than to break the news of the baby in so forthright a manner. He'd come round in the end, of that she was sure, but in the meantime she'd have to tread carefully.

She decided that before bearding Uncle Francisco about the use of his quinta she ought to go and refresh her memory of the property. Despite the enthusiastic description she'd given Mickey, her only previous visit to the farm had been when, at ten years old, after her uncle's wife had died of the Spanish flu, she'd accompanied her father there to pay their condolences. Uncle Francisco had lived ever since in what she remembered as a grim old Setubal town house and things on the estate might have changed a little over the years.

The taxi was the one she always used for her journeys to the convent. She thought Villa Franca wore a drab unfriendly face and she was all for immediately pushing on across the river to the Quinta dos Cinquo Irmãos, as Uncle Francisco's estate was called, but after they'd crossed the bridge and her driver asked which road he should take she realised that her twenty-year-old memory had failed her completely.

They'd come to a halt at a crossroads. Over on the other side, Beta saw in the shadow of a massive palm tree a ramshackle single storey whitewashed building doing business as a café. There were a couple of metal tables on the pavement and a half-dozen chairs occupied by some of the local worthies putting the world to rights over cups of coffee.

She told the driver to pull over. 'Not for a drink,' she said, seeing the incredulous look in his face. 'We need to get directions.'

Nobody seemed to recognise the name of the estate and she was beginning to wonder whether, as well as losing her way, she'd got the name of the place confused in her memory. Then one old peasant with a face burnt to the colour of a chestnut came to her aid.

The man dragged off his long black woollen bonnet, scratched his bald head. 'Quinta dos Cinquo Irmãos? Five Brothers' Farm? Ain't called that no more, don't call it nothin' these days. But there's a story they used to tell,' the old man reminisced, ready for a good long chat. 'The five brothers, they ran the farm together until they all went mad, fell out and shot each other dead. Or it may be as how it was named after the five umbrella pine trees that used to grow near the house.'

He was clearly ready to embark on more folklore until Beta cut him short and asked for precise guidance about the road they had to take. 'Down along that way,' he said, pointing, adding helpfully when the taxi driver asked him how far, 'a couple of hours by ox-cart. Maybe three.'

In the car, they covered the distance in little more than fifteen minutes. Beta dimly remembered the entrance to the estate as being quite splendid. Viewing it now she saw the fine wrought-iron gates had gone and the supporting pillars leaned drunkenly. The gravelled drive, no more than a rutted and weed-infested track, wound round slight dips and hollows in the land, every turn and twist revealing more neglected fields; here a miserable patch of cabbage, there a few rows of poorly tended vines. There had been lemon trees and olives, Beta recalled; perhaps they were now represented by the wizened skeletons she saw over to her right on a shallow south-facing ridge.

She saw the pine trees first and then she saw the house. It was perfectly true, as far as her memory served her, that the house had once been pretty. Now leprous stains spread across the patched and peeling stuccoed walls and the dead eyes of its empty windows stared sullenly at her from under broken roof tiles. She could see the front door was roughly boarded up.

First impressions, she told herself firmly. The place mightn't be as bad as it looked. She was about to get out for a closer inspection when the driver turned in his seat and laid a hand on her arm. 'The dog,' he warned.

A huge shaggy-coated Estrela mountain sheepdog was standing at the corner of the house. Triggered by the slight movement of the car door, the animal suddenly bounded forward, its mane of dark hair bristling, barking madly until it reached the vehicle, where it stood with teeth bared, uttering a menacing low-pitched snarl.

Beta looked at the driver for inspiration but he only shrugged his shoulders.

'If we spoke to it nicely?' she suggested.

The driver snorted. 'I don't think it speaks our language, senhora. And it's not alone.' He pointed.

She saw there was someone now standing where they'd first seen the dog. Wearing a soiled blue overall and with a broken shotgun tucked casually into the crook of his arm, the man stared in their direction and quite deliberately clicked the barrel into position before walking leisurely to the car. He reached a hand to the dog and spoke a word to make it lie down quietly at his feet.

Beta cautiously wound down her window a little and got as far as wishing the man a good-day before he cut in. 'Private property. You can clear off right away.'

'My uncle Francisco is the owner,' Beta riposted.

'Francisco Pacheco? The old bugger sold this off years ago. It's mine now, and I say clear off.' There was no argument, no explanation, only the dog, the man and the gun.

They were back on the outskirts of the town before either of them had much to say. 'Up to no good, that's obvious,' her driver said.

'But what?' Beta wondered.

He shook his head. 'Do you see much of your uncle these days?' She confessed she'd rather lost touch over the years, and the driver grunted. 'You should check up on him,' he said, 'see if he's all right. What we saw back there, that kind of welcome bodes no good to anyone.'

It was true, Beta thought. Portuguese land owners were reasonably tolerant about people passing over their property. Her mother had always welcomed to her garden unexpected visitors who'd caught sight of the lovely flower beds that were her pride and joy. It was a matter of common courtesy to entertain such people, offer refreshment, chat about mutual interests. To be greeted by a ferocious dog and a man with a gun was quite foreign to the national character. 'Do you think there's something criminal going on back there?' she ventured to ask.

'Could be, senhora, though God knows what it might be. Mind you, Vila Franca's a funny place, right enough,' he

233

conceded. 'The town used to have quite a reputation at one time.'

He was evasive when she asked for details. 'That side of the river used to be a recruiting ground for the Viriatos,' he told her. 'Perhaps some of them have come back, looking for a bit more adventure, using your uncle's old place as a base.' He gave her a shrug of resignation. 'You wouldn't know what to think.'

So there wasn't going to be a rural idyll for herself and Mickey. She tried to comfort herself with the thought that Mickey might not in any case have adapted very easily to country ways and, if she were to be totally honest with herself, she wondered whether the isolation would have suited her either. The best one might have hoped for would have been a banal round of bucolic neighbours and coarse entertainment far removed from the refinement of the city.

Ana Bigode had prepared *arroz de pato,* shredded duck-breast with creamy rice, one of Beta's favourite dishes, taken with a couple of glasses of a light red wine. 'I've taken the liberty of sorting out some of your dresses,' the maid told her as she served up the food. 'There were a couple that needed a bit of attention, a few stitches and a little pressing.'

'That's kind of you,' Beta replied carefully, unsure of what exactly to read into Ana's straight-faced solicitude. There were times with Mickey when dresses had come off worst as passions got the better of decorum. She'd put the damaged garments at the back of her wardrobe, intending to see to them herself some time. Ana must have routed through her things to find them, which was not her normal behaviour.

'And padre Harrington called while you were out.'

'Oh? What did he want?' Beta replied nonchalantly.

234

'Nothing important, he said. He brought you some flowers. I know you don't much like cut flowers but shall I put them in the hallway?'

'Thank you, Ana,' Beta said, hoping that she was still keeping her voice neutral. 'He's very kind.' What a pity she'd been out. His unexpected visit must mean something. A change of heart, she hoped, on his part.

'Indeed, Dona Elisabete, very kind, I'm sure,' Ana replied in a neutral tone.

If there was any trace of sarcasm in that reply, Beta was determined to ignore it. Mickey was right. It was not the maid's business to interest herself in her mistress's affairs.

The flowers, chrysanthemums, were certainly not her favourite, reminding her of funerals she'd attended at Prazeres cemetery, but the thought had been kindly. Perhaps Mickey was beginning to come to terms with the prospect of paternity.

She drank her wine while she pondered on the total failure of her expedition. If there was to be no country estate for them to settle into, could they live in the apartment after the wedding? She thought not. Quite besides any other consideration, it would mean jettisoning Ana. To have her in daily attendance on herself and Mickey would be too much to contemplate.

The Brazilian option? In her heart of hearts she knew it would be a step too far for her precious Mickey. As for Angola, she was afraid that country might bring out some hidden missionary zeal in him, not at all what they needed.

England? Mickey was terrified of being exposed here in this Catholic country but England, she'd been told, was a godless place where religious sentiments counted practically for nothing. Mickey was an educated man who could easily find employment, in teaching perhaps.

The sale of the apartment would surely bring in enough for the purchase of a house somewhere in that wet and windy island. She'd seen pictures, in books about England, of cottages with lovely gardens. She could become a country woman, with her brood around her while Mickey educated the rural young.

Or, better still and remembering what Abe Eldridge had so often jokingly proposed, there might be another option. They could look to the USA, a land of boundless opportunities where a person's background was less important than a person's potential.

Ruminating on such a tantalising prospect sustained her through the rest of the evening.

44

It wasn't the sort of task Beta thought she could entrust to Dr Tomás Cabreira, the lawyer she generally used for confidential matters. There was nothing for it but to go in person to the offices of the shipping agents Macmillan e Cavaleiro Lda in Rua dos Remolares down in Alcântara, chosen, she had to admit, mainly because of the English-sounding half of the name.

She was dismayed to find a crowd thronging the entrance to the shipping office, miserable-looking people clutching reams of paperwork as though their very identities were bound up in the printed word, and muttering to each other in a pot-pourri of language.

The French she recognised and partly understood despite the uncouth accents; the German – well, her acquaintance with the Legation helped her recognise the sound if not the sense. As for the rest, it was the babble of faraway countries. She'd heard something of the plight of such people, displaced by the upheavals taking place in the farthest reaches of Europe as a result of the war and Hitler's policies as regards Jewish people. Now here they were in Lisbon with the same idea as she had.

Beta began after all to regret not confiding this task to her lawyer. One of his clerks would have done the job just as, if not more, efficiently without her having to subject herself to the indignity of rubbing shoulders with these poor souls.

Despite the company's name, when she managed to squeeze her way to the desk she found herself confronted by a harassed Portuguese functionary whose desk was littered with untidy heaps of paperwork. She drew herself to her full height and adopted her most patrician accent as she impressed on him the urgency of her request.

'You want to go where?' the clerk demanded incredulously. 'You know there's a war on out there, senhora? Cruising's off the agenda for the duration.' He dipped his head to the paperwork on his desk as though to dismiss this crazy woman who thought that giving herself airs entitled her to special treatment.

'This isn't to do with a holiday, senhor,' she replied icily. 'Perhaps I should be speaking to your superior, senhor Macmillan?'

The clerk's laugh took her aback. 'Senhor Macmillan? You'd have to scale the holy stairs to heaven, if you want to speak to senhor Macmillan. He's been dead these fifty years or more. If he is up there,' he added inconsequentially. 'Some say you'd have to address your remarks to the other place.' He leaned back in his seat and eyed her frankly. 'Not a holiday, you said?'

'I'm not looking for a cruise. I'm considering relocating completely.'

'Lock, stock and barrel?'

Beta nodded. 'Indeed. I hear many of our people are doing well for themselves in the States and, I might say, I'm not without means.' If the clerk thought there was a bribe somewhere in the offing she wasn't going to disabuse him.

'Well,' the clerk drawled, 'there's still one or two mixed cargo and passenger vessels doing the New York run. Mind you, you'd have to put up with,' he nodded to the throng behind her. 'It wouldn't be too bad, I suppose, if you had a first class cabin. You'd need a visa.'

'I don't believe that would present a problem.' She smiled. 'My name isn't unknown at the American Embassy.'

'You get yourself a visa,' he said laconically, 'and then come back and we can begin to talk about getting you a passage.'

She wondered how many of the desperate women who came before his desk the clerk had taken advantage of. Looking around as she left the office, she could see that beneath the tattered clothes and worn faces there were not a few women who might become easy meat to such a venal operator. Language wouldn't be an obstacle for in that kind of transaction actions spoke louder than words. She felt herself defiled merely by being in the same room as such an odious person.

She'd exaggerated slightly in claiming to have contacts in the United States Embassy on the Avenida das Forças Armadas but she was sure Abe Eldridge would help her. It wasn't as though she were a refugee; she could pay her way easily enough and, a necessary detail, make sure that Mickey, if only his pride allowed, would also be financially acceptable to the Immigration authorities on Ellis Island.

45

The following Monday Harrington came back to Lisbon from Pêra on an early ferry with Arthur Cope who had some legal business to attend to, about a property the college owned in Rua do Cabra. He hinted that his own still ongoing Masonic business was going to occupy him for a day or two and Cope wished him good luck.

Beta's announcement had thrown him into a quandary. He loved her, of that he was absolutely sure, but a baby was altogether another matter. He'd been so pre-occupied with their intimate relationship, and her assurance that everything was taken care of, that the prospect of a baby had quite vanished from his mind. That had been simplistic he recognised. The imperative now was to find some sort of resolution.

He could have used the college telephone but he thought it was safer to make his call to Antonio Fonseca from the public telephone booth in the main Post Office in Restauradores, though after the way he'd been treated at Carmelita's birthday party Harrington wasn't sure what sort of reception he might expect.

Luckily, Fonseca seemed back to his normal genial self. 'What a pleasant surprise, Father!' They were speaking in English. 'I thought you were staying in that rural slum across the river. I hope you're going to honour us with your presence soon?'

'Well, it's a bit delicate, Antonio,' Harrington explained. 'I need your advice over a problem I've come across in the course of my pastoral duties.'

'My advice, Father?' Harrington could hear both puzzlement and interest in Fonseca's voice. 'I'm not the one you should be turning to on theological matters.'

'Oh, it's not a theological problem, it's more to do with...' He hesitated. 'I don't suppose you remember our conversation last year, at St Monica's feast?'

'We talked of so many things, Father. Oh, you mean, about the country priests and their *governantas*? You've got a priest with a special problem, have you?'

There was a note of cynical laughter in Fonseca's voice that Harrington didn't much care for. He would have to step delicately. 'A lady, actually. Look,' he said, 'I can't talk about this over the telephone.'

'Come to the Quinta, Father. You know you're always welcome here.'

'As I say, it's delicate. I'd rather not intrude.'

Fonseca was totally cooperative. 'You know Lawrence's Hotel in Sintra? What time is it now? Ten? Meet me there in an hour's time.'

Lawrence's Hotel seemed to Harrington the perfect place for a meeting of the kind he had in mind. Perched on its rocky ledge, close by the Monserrata Palace and allegedly the oldest hostelry in Portugal, the hotel exuded a faded elegance. Lord Byron had stayed there, and he could believe that the comfortably shabby sofas gracing the lounge might well have been the very ones to accommodate that notorious if aristocratic bottom.

He'd had to hurry to catch the train but he managed to get to the hotel just in time to choose a quiet corner before Fonseca bustled in. The lounge, he supposed, would normally be bustling with foreign holiday-makers, but this day there were only a couple of men in suits - commercial travellers, to judge by their bulging briefcases and the sheaves of paper they were assiduously studying. They were far enough away not to present any problem.

'What's all this about then, Father?' Fonseca demanded pleasantly as he sank into the armchair opposite Harrington. The obsequious reception he received from the staff when he flicked a finger in the direction of a hovering waiter demonstrated he was a familiar visitor. 'Coffee,' he ordered, 'and my usual.'

'As I said,' Harrington explained, 'it's a pastoral matter. From time to time, in the course of my duties I come across distressing cases.' He offered a smile he hoped conveyed both the sympathy of a good confessor and the prudent counsellor's need for discretion. 'People sometimes think being a priest means one has all the answers at one's finger-tips.' Harrington sighed. 'I only wish it were true.'

The waiter interrupted at that moment to set down the coffee, a bottle of Hennessy and two glasses. 'Sorry, Father,' Fonseca addressed Harrington with perfunctory politeness, 'You were saying?'

This was Fonseca's world, Harrington realised. It would be necessary to work with and not across the grain if he were to get anywhere with him. 'Well, you see, I'm rather out of my depth with this one and I wondered whether I could ask your help. As I mentioned on the telephone, it involves a lady.'

Fonseca shot him a quizzical glance. 'A Portuguese lady?'

Harrington nodded. 'She's pregnant and I remember you saying that there were always desperate women crying out to adopt.'

'She wants to give her baby away, this friend of yours?'

Harrington did his best to ignore the faint lines of a smile around Fonseca's lips. 'The lady,' he stressed the word, 'wishes at all cost to avoid any scandal.'

'She might have thought about that before she allowed herself to get pregnant.'

'Indeed,' Harrington said with a resigned shrug, 'but what's done is done.'

'And now she wishes to make it all go away. Is the lady married?'

'No,' Harrington shook his head. 'No,' he said, 'and marriage isn't an option. A prior commitment on the gentleman's side, you understand.'

'If it's not too late, there are remedies,' Fonseca said slowly, 'practised by women who know about such matters.'

'No!' Harrington spoke too vehemently and tried to check himself. 'No, I couldn't agree to anything like that.'

'You might not,' Fonseca said cynically, 'but you'd be surprised how many women are ready to choose that option. So,' he took up his coffee cup, 'abortion's out of the question. I only mentioned it because one has to consider all possibilities. Pregnancy isn't something one can hide very easily.'

He read the expression on Harrington's face. 'All right. In that case,' he said, putting down his cup and reaching for the Hennessy, 'the little intruder has to come to term.'

'But an adoption could be arranged?' Harrington insisted. 'Discreetly?'

'Most things can be arranged, with care, and money. How far is she advanced?'

Harrington considered how best to answer before he replied. 'The lady wasn't precise,' he said, 'but at a guess I'd say she's in the early stages as yet,' he forced a smile, 'though, as you might imagine, I'm far from being an expert in such matters.'

Fonseca set down his glass and put steepled hands to his pursed lips. ' In Valença do Minho there's a small convent. The Sisters of Magdalene.'

Harrington had never heard of them.

'That's hardly surprising, considering the nature of their special vocation. They only have one house here in Portugal and, I believe, another couple in Spain. Or, at least, they used to have, before the war.'

Fonseca took another sip of his coffee before continuing. 'As you probably know, Valença's a small walled town, on the northern border with Spain. The convent's actually built into part of the town walls. It's a very picturesque location, with lovely views over the river. And the Sisters are very kind to ladies with problems.' He smiled. 'Between you and me, one or two of them have had problems of their own in the past.'

It sounded to Harrington as though the Sisters of Magdalene and their convent might be just right for Beta. 'Valença. It's certainly remote,' he said.

'Most certainly,' Fonseca agreed straight-faced. 'And the good Sisters understand perfectly how to respect the confidential nature of their work.'

'I wouldn't want anyone to think less of the lady. She's been placed in an impossible position.'

Fonseca nodded. 'Ah yes, indeed. As you said.' He dipped into the inside pocket of his jacket, drew out a small notebook and scribbled an address. 'Here, he said, 'handing over the torn page, 'if your lady would care to get in touch, I'm sure Reverend Mother would give her every kind attention. Mention my name. I do hope everything goes well for you.' The smile he gave Harrington was almost crocodilian.

46

Peter Fielding stood on the deck of the Tagus ferry, watching the majestic panorama of Lisbon creep slowly ever closer. He could see the broad expanse of Black Horse Square and the triumphal arch leading to Rua Augusta. Over to the right the castle of St George crowned the hill containing the ancient centre of the city, and looking to his left he could make out the funnels and tall masts of shipping in the Alcântara docks.

It was illogical, he supposed, to expect the scene to look different than it had done six weeks earlier. He was the one who'd changed and not, he thought, entirely for the better. What had happened to the young idealist who'd clambered on board Bill Marchant's yacht in Cascais harbour, his ears burning at hearing himself being patronisingly described as *a soldier boy for King and Country*?

After his initial seasickness, the voyage to Gibraltar had been uneventful apart from meeting a tuna boat off Cape St Vincent. Marchant's Portuguese was fractured and Fielding had taken over, bantering and swapping jokes with the crew whose thick southern accent was laced with what he guessed might have been Arabic idiom. They'd mocked him for being an *alfecinha*, a lettuce eater, the slightly derogatory slang name for a native of Lisbon.

It turned out that the boat had been stopped a couple of days earlier by a cruising German U-boat. The captain had bartered a bottle of schnapps for a ten kilo tuna. 'They didn't bother us,' the fishing boat's master told Fielding, 'though I don't reckon we got much of a bargain. That German stuff was okay but I'd rather have a bottle of *aguardente* any day. Still, you don't argue with someone whose got a bloody great deck gun pointing at you.'

The news there was a U-boat on the prowl made Marchant very nervous despite the fact that *Esperança* was flying the Portuguese flag. 'If we do meet them,' he told Fielding after they had got under way again, 'God help us if they want to come aboard. In any event, you're the one that'll have to do the talking. I'll keep my trap shut and try to look native, wear a hat to cover my blond curls. Where the hell did you learn to speak the language like that?'

Fielding could understand Marchant's nervousness - it wouldn't be funny to have the enemy at such close quarters — but he thought it unlikely anyone would stop a lone yacht like *Esperança*. 'We shall have to make sure we keep the flag flying,' he said in an attempt to reassure his companion. As for the language, 'We had lessons,' he explained, 'when we first arrived in college and then, well, I'm just a parrot.'

On arrival in Gibraltar's harbour, Marchant had hardly finishing making *Esperança* safely moored before he said he could put Fielding in touch with just the right person. 'In the meantime, take things easy and see the sights.'

The Rock was a bewildering place. Hordes of Royal Navy and Army personnel rubbed shoulders with a motley crew of civilians whose language flitted indiscriminately from English to Spanish and back again. The narrow streets were much like any Fielding was familiar with from Portugal but the fish and chip shops whose smell permeated those same streets in the evening, the branch of Woolworth's and the red post-boxes bearing the cypher of British monarchs - he saw one dating back to Queen Victoria - provided a bizarre contrast, as did the policemen's uniforms and the defiant signs plastered across the windows of bars and shops. *British We Are, British We Stay* seemed to him to be a sort of talisman against what he'd heard was the policy of clearing Gibraltar of all but the most essential of dock workers. Apparently, the luckier deportees might find themselves in temporary accommodation in Madeira, those not so lucky would have to live out the war in some drab London suburb, if the ship carrying them didn't meet a torpedo on the high seas.

After an uncomfortable night in the dormitory of a naval barracks he'd found himself being interviewed in a bare dusty room on the second floor of a palatial eighteenth century building crawling with military of all shapes and sizes.

If it was an interview: it had been very informal. The bespectacled grey haired middle-aged man wore what Fielding supposed was a naval uniform though it bore no insignia. He said his name was Hamish and he offered a cigarette from a packet of Senior Service which Fielding politely declined.

Hamish had wanted to know about the English College. 'I've always admired you RCs,' he said after Fielding had described the daily routine, 'the way you take orders from the top brass and get the job done. Life in the armed forces ought to be a doddle for someone like you.'

There was no real answer to that. He'd never thought of life in college as being particularly arduous or restricting but then he'd never really known anything else.

Then Hamish had moved on. 'I hear you're quite a dab hand at the Portuguese.'

'I get by,' he replied modestly. Bill Marchant must have said something about the encounter with the tuna boat.

'We're looking out for people with that sort of gift. People who can get about without drawing attention to themselves.'

The conversation had taken a more serious tone at this point. Fielding might like to do a little job for an outfit Hamish helped to look after. Both the outfit and the job were undefined at first and when Fielding had timidly enquired for further information he'd been amiably told that though he could be guaranteed the work would be interesting, in the Service one did what was required of one without asking too many questions. 'Not so different from life in that college of yours, eh?' Hamish had added with a grin. Fielding hadn't liked to argue about that.

Maybe I should have pressed the issue, he reflected now as the ferry nudged into the landing stage at Cais do Sodré. He stepped ashore, and walked along the Avenida da Ribeira das Naus as far as Black Horse Square, which he crossed diagonally and passed under the triumphal arch into Rua Augusta.

When he'd obediently said he'd do whatever was demanded of him, Hamish had decided to open up a little. 'We're Navy,' he said, 'loosely speaking. In a way, not entirely orthodox. *Special Intelligence in Neutral Countries.* Quite a mouthful, so we prefer to talk about SINT. And we interpret "neutral" quite widely. At the moment we're especially interested in Twenty-four Land.'

He'd seen Fielding's raised eyebrows. 'That's what we call Portugal. Your old stamping ground. We think you might fit in nicely, what with you looking the part and speaking the language so perfectly. The top brass have concerns about the fragility of Portugal's neutrality and what chance there might be of Salazar offering the Nazis facilities in the Azores or in the Algarve. One of these days we might have to encourage some sort of underground resistance.'

'It wouldn't come to that, surely? Britain's oldest ally?' Fielding had hesitated. 'Would it?

'Salazar will do whatever he thinks will ensure his safety and the security of his precious New State. France has capitulated, with half the country occupied. Italy's in with the Nazis, Spain is Germany's friendliest neutral. We're hanging on here in Gib by our toenails. What would you think was the wisest course of action if you were Dr Salazar?'

Put like that, Fielding couldn't argue. The idea of rooting in the undergrowth for possible Portuguese subversion sounded a daunting task but Hamish had reassured him. 'You wouldn't be alone. One of many, as you might say. Part of the team.' Then, casually, as an afterthought, 'But there's one little thing you might do for us in Lisbon first.'

Peter Fielding, secret agent: it was laughable, like something out of one of those novels Father Harrington sometimes lent him. There had been days of training, political education, conducting surveillance, learning how to write in what was called Open Code; seemingly innocuous reports about cork manufacture, wine production, forestry, that concealed the fruits of intelligence gathering. It was, he'd thought, like something out of a Boys-Own adventure until the day he was given instruction in unarmed killing. Death could be brought about quite easily, he discovered, if you knew how.

He'd tried in vain to find out what it was they wanted him to do in Lisbon. Nobody would tell him anything. 'It'll all come clear when you've spoken to your Control in Lisbon,' Hamish had assured him. 'Gloria will deal with all that.'

47

Harrington used the telephone booth in Lawrence's Hotel to contact Beta who was delighted to hear his voice. They arranged to meet that afternoon in Estoril at the Copper Kettle, a tea room he thought Beta might like. He had visited once before. The place was run by an eccentric but amiable middle-aged Devonian expatriate woman given to wearing frilly blouses and gingham skirts. Before the war, she'd told him, she'd relied almost exclusively on the custom of discerning British tourists. Now she was struggling to draw in enough customers to keep the place going at all.

'I've never in my life seen anything like this,' Beta said as she gazed in wonder at the decorations; kettles of all sizes, all in burnished copper, hanging from the ceiling or sitting on shelves along with porcelain boxes, each marked with the variety of leaf within. The coloured engravings of hunting scenes along the walls she thought were 'so very English.' Harrington didn't like to ask whether that was a compliment to the quality of the artwork or a comment on the barbarity of the English landed classes.

The fare was clotted cream and scones, which Beta thought delicious, with Assam tea to drink. The plates they were eating off and the cups they were drinking from were bone china, hand-painted with posies of wild flowers; so delicate, Beta declared in mock alarm, she was terrified that she might break something. 'Are there many places in England like this?' she wanted to know.

Maybe Devon was littered with such establishments but Harrington had to admit he wasn't familiar with them. It would be hard to imagine anything like the Copper Kettle in the grimy streets of Salford, where spit-and-sawdust corner pubs were more the order of the day; dens of iniquity, according to his mother, places of refuge for his father, when he'd sneaked out for what he used to call 'a swift half.'

'I went to Macmillan e Cavaleiro the other day,' Beta announced as she used a dampened forefinger to mop up the last fragments of scone crumb.

'What on earth for?'

'It was only a preliminary enquiry. I didn't tell you, but the day you brought the flowers I'd been to have a look at Uncle Francisco's estate, the one I thought might suit us.' She used her napkin to delicately wipe a smear of cream from her upper lip. 'It wouldn't have done, Mickey. The place has gone to rack and ruin. You'd never have enjoyed being there.'

Had the estate been never so grand it wouldn't have done, as far as Harrington was concerned. 'But what possessed you to go to Macmillan e Cavaleiro?' he demanded again.

'Well,' Beta replied, 'if you are absolutely determined that we can't make a life for ourselves here in Portugal,' she offered a little sigh of resignation, 'we shall both have to make sacrifices.'

She leaned forward to place her hand on his. 'England, I'd thought at first. A little place in the country, Mickey.'

'Beta,' Harrington began, keeping his voice as calm as he could, 'England's at war. The Germans are carrying out massive bombing raids. There's every possibility that if Churchill doesn't soon see reason, the country will be invaded and no matter what the Prime Minister may pretend, the British army in its present state would be no match for the Wehrmacht.'

'Oh, I know all that,' she assured him blithely, 'and I wouldn't want to be anywhere near where I might be bombed. But a small country village, Mickey. With you teaching, doing what you do already.'

I don't think the average English village school would have much time for Catholic theology,' he replied wryly.

'But then I began to think of another possibility,' Beta continued. 'Somewhere we could both make a fresh start.' Her eyes opened wide. 'America! Think about it Mickey, the land of opportunities!'

Harrington stared at her. 'America? Why on earth would I want to go there?'

'The three of us,' she replied dreamily, 'in a land far away from the war, a land crying out for new people, wide open to all sorts of possibilities, where what you were before doesn't matter, only what you might become.' She looked fondly across the table at him. 'And, Mickey, I know someone in the American Embassy who could get us visas, *at the drop of a hat!*'

Harrington ignored the English expression. 'I don't think you appreciate what an upheaval it would be.'

'Oh, I do, I do!' Beta exclaimed. 'But wouldn't it be exciting? I know my English isn't good, Mickey, but I could improve, with you to teach me.'

'We wouldn't know anyone. I'm middle aged,' he complained, 'and I'm too old to be uprooted.'

As well as being cut off from all he had so far known in his life, it was the open-ended commitment that marriage entailed, not where they might live, that he was really afraid of. As lovers, they each had their private spaces to retire to. Sharing their lives at close quarters would be quite different; waking daily with her beside him in the morning; coming home after a day's work – of what kind he couldn't begin to imagine - to be greeted by her, communicating trivial as well as great concerns, laying each other open to their daily swings of mood. He wasn't sure he could live like that.

Beta carefully folded her napkin. 'So,' she said slowly, 'we seem to have reached an impasse. But there's the baby to think of, Mickey.'

'I know, and I've been making some enquiries of my own.' He began to explain.

Afterwards, they walked down the narrow cobbled street, past the harbour where fishing boats bobbed in the afternoon swell and crews busied themselves with tangles of nets and gear; past the Hotel Parque that had been more or less commandeered by the Germans and the next door Palácio, haunt of the British, all of them spying on each other, according to Maria Winter; past the long sloping green lawns and flowerbeds that led up to the Casino. The August sun was strong, the sky bleached almost white.

'And if I went to this convent in Valença?' Beta asked.

'They'd take you as soon as you like and they'd care for you until the baby's born. In the meantime they'd set about arranging the adoption. No one would need know anything.'

She didn't have much to say in response, except to comment that she thought there was a relative on her mother's side who used to live in Valença, 'though she probably died years ago.'

They sat in silence side-by-side in the train all the way back to the city but when they arrived at her stop and he made it clear he would be staying on the train to the end of the line, she turned to him and said earnestly: 'America. Think about it. You aren't too old and it's still not too late, Mickey.'

'I think you might be better off without me,' he said. 'If the baby were adopted you could make a new life for yourself, with someone who could look after you, offer you all the things I couldn't give you – a proper home, the chance of making a proper family.'

He kissed her full lips, not caring if other people in the carriage were staring. 'I still love you,' he whispered, seeing the unhappiness in her face.

48

Hamish had instructed Fielding that on arrival in Lisbon he should take a room in the Pensão Boa Vista, behind São Domingos church off the Praça da Figueira at the top of Rua dos Franquieros. 'There's a chap called Alberto Pedrosa runs the place. He's on our payroll. Mind you, he might be on the German payroll as well as the PVDE, but we pay better.'

Rua dos Franqueiros was in the Baixa, an area Fielding knew well, the eighteenth century rebuild of Lisbon Low Town, after the great 1755 earthquake. The Pensão Boa Vista was no better or worse than the boarding houses he'd used on his journey through Spain and up from the Algarve. He showed Manuel his doctored British passport that gave 'salesman' as his occupation. He'd asked Gus, his gritty-voiced mentor in the basement room that had become his training base in Gibraltar, what he was supposed to be selling and hadn't been entirely satisfied with the laconic reply he could sell what the fuck he liked. Pedrosa hardly bothered to look at the document. 'The cops will want to see it,' he said, 'but they won't give you any problems.' He handed over the key to a room on the second floor.

Fielding dumped his scuffed pigskin suitcase on the bed. He'd been terrified, all the way through Spain, of being stopped and interrogated by the Guardia Civil who hung around at nearly every street corner, carbines slung on shoulders, a visible reminder that Generalissimo Franco was in charge of everything now. A close inspection of the suitcase might easily have revealed its secret compartment housing the Mauser automatic and a couple of spare magazines, not the sort of accessory for a salesman to have by him.

As it was, though he'd seen the mixture of hatred and fear of the green-uniformed militia in the eyes of passers-by, he'd not been challenged. The nondescript clothing he'd been issued with might have been his salvation, helping him to blend in with the locals, or it may have been sheer luck that no one expressed the slightest interest in him.

He had been scarcely more relaxed on the journey up from the Algarve; the PVDE had, he knew, a well-deserved reputation for brutality and, as his briefing in Gibraltar had taught him, their spies were everywhere.

At the little desk in his room, beneath the hand-tinted picture of the Virgin of Fátima, Fielding penned a few words on the postcard he'd bought at the tobacconist's in Figueira. *Darling Gloria, Arrived safely, weather glorious. The Boa Vista is charming. Looking forward to meeting you soon. Your loving Aunt Betty.*

The address was in the Mouraria, the ancient district beneath the castle. 'It doesn't matter what rubbish you write,' Gus had told him, 'but make sure you sign it *Aunt Betty.*'

Gus: Fielding had never discovered any other name for the hard-bitten crop-haired instructor, nor to what branch of the Navy he might have belonged but he thought the man's grating voice, relentlessly issuing directions, criticism and the very occasional hard-earned praise, would remain with him for ever.

The nonsense he'd scribbled on the card seemed to work. The reply came the next day in the form of a note hand-delivered by an urchin. 'Cheeky young blighter,' Pedrosa told Fielding as he handed it over, 'wanted an escudo for his trouble. Sent him off with a couple of *tostões* and a flea in his ear.'

Twenty cents wouldn't buy the boy much more than a bag of boiled sweets but Fielding expected the lad would have got something more substantial from Gloria, who declared she would be delighted to meet dear Aunt Betty for lunch in O Grande Elias in Trafaria on the other side of the river. Fielding had passed the waterfront restaurant often enough though he'd never been inside. It had the reputation of being rough and ready but serving great food.

She would be wearing a Barcelo Cockerel in her lapel, the note said. He'd recognise that easily enough; the bird was part of Portuguese mythology. A pilgrim on his way to the shrine of Compostela was arrested in Barcelos on suspicion of murder. Condemned to death, he'd pleaded his innocence, declaring that if no one else would witness for him, the cooked fowl on the magistrate's table would stand up and crow. Whereupon it did. The image of the brave little bird had become almost a national emblem.

49

As he pushed open the restaurant door and breathed in the mixed aromas of food, alcohol and tobacco, Fielding could see what a cosmopolitan crowd patronised the place; suited businessmen, dock workers in greasy overalls, off-duty policemen, even a gaggle of raucous-voiced women market traders swapping coarse jokes over plates piled high with steaming rice and pork.

The décor was basic, a stone-flagged floor, sturdy wooden chairs and tables covered in plain white cloths. The bar, panelled in dark wood, ran the width of the restaurant and behind it a range of mirrors reflected the bottles and faces of those customers who preferred to take their lunch liquid and on the hoof. The tiled walls echoed to the hubbub of well-oiled voices and the frantic traffic of orders being passed to the unseen toilers in the kitchens. The scene reminded Fielding of the old saying, *never get between a Portuguese and his food.*

A woman sitting alone at a small table in the far corner raised a hand in welcome. Even from where he stood he could make out the cheeky little bird, with rosy cockscomb and flamboyant tail feathers, sitting in the lapel of her grey coat. The wave was clearly meant for him. He navigated his way between the seated diners and around a couple of waiters with laden trays until he arrived at her table.

'I've ordered sole but I'm told the sardines are good.' She touched her glass. 'Dry Martini. You might prefer a beer.' She got the instant attention of a passing waiter. 'The senhor would like to order.' Her Portuguese was English-accented but fluent.

'I'll have the sardines,' he told the waiter, 'and a bottle of Sagres beer.'

The hat she was wearing was a frivolous little thing with a wisp of veil that served no useful purpose and her hair was an artful tangle of dark curls. The grey coat hung open to reveal a blouse of a paler grey, the top button undone. Around her neck she wore a thin gold chain from which dangled a plain cross. She was, he guessed, not all that much older than himself, late twenties perhaps.

'Did you have a good journey?' she asked politely.

'Interesting,' Fielding said, his eyes flickering around the noisy room. It seemed safe enough to be talking in English.

'You needn't worry about the beetles,' she said with a smile.

'I wasn't,' he began, glancing at the tiled floor.

'That's what we call the PVDE. They don't dare show their faces in here.'

That was reassuring. He had to lean over the table to hear clearly what she said. 'What do I call you?' he asked.

'We can dispense with Gloria,' she said. My name's Diane. Diane Singleton. I take it you'd prefer not to be called Aunt Betty?'

The waiter slapped Fielding's beer on to the table. 'Food will be along in a minute.' They both assured the flustered man that there was no hurry. Miss Singleton toyed with her Martini and Fielding started on his beer.

Rather to his surprise, over the sole and the grilled sardines, Diane didn't say a word about his mission. Instead, like Hamish had done, she asked about life in the college. 'Background information,' she explained. 'I want to get the feel of the place.'

'It sounds positively Spartan,' she said after he'd told her about washing in cold water; studying by oil lamp in the evenings; wearing an overcoat indoors in the winter because there was no heating in the college; how the students were expected to take charge of the kitchen and the laundry. 'But surely there are servants as well?'

'Of course.' He laughed. 'They're a mixed bunch. The porter, Cordeiro, has been at the college since Adam was a lad. José's getting on a bit. He ran away from his village because he thought he going to be put under a spell by the local *Senhora dos Santos*.'

She frowned.

'Wise woman,' he explained. 'Or witch.'

Diane was intrigued. 'Do they still have witches in Portugal?'

'So I'm told, in the villages.'

'And what does José do when he's not warding off the evil eye?'

'He's the professors' major-domo. He's a pompous old fellow but he's devoted to the college. Never married. He's fond of talking about an older brother who was a sailor and drowned when his ship was hit by a torpedo from a U-boat in the last war.'

'He sounds like quite a colourful character. Now, tell me about the professors. What are they like?'

'They've all been through the same mill as us,' Fielding said, disconcerted by the rapid change of subject. 'I mean, they've all been students at the college. They aren't ogres or anything. It's quite a kindly regime, I suppose.'

He'd never before been asked to assess the qualities of his teachers. They were just there, a solid fact, and you accepted them almost as part of the furniture. He couldn't say this to the woman sitting opposite him but she must have sensed something of his dilemma.

'Any favourites?' She smiled encouragingly. 'From what I remember of university, most lecturers can be dry as dust but there's the odd one who stands out from the crowd.'

'Father Knox tends to ramble on in his lectures,' Fielding said, 'and I suppose you might say Father Blount's a bit of an old fuddy-duddy. But he was very understanding when I told him I wanted to join up.'

'Tell me about Father Harrington.'

'You know him?' he asked in surprise.

'I spend most of my time in the Consular offices,' she said, 'renewing people's passports. I've met him a few times. He struck me as rather shy but I liked him.'

As the meal continued she at last began to talk about why he'd been sent back to Lisbon. Fielding didn't believe a word of it. A cock-and-bull story, he told her, the product of someone's over-active imagination. 'Where did you get all this nonsense from?'

She didn't answer that directly. 'Here and there,' she said. 'People tell us things. We try to interpret what they say, sift the wheat from the chaff. Sometimes we find it's the wheat we've thrown away and kept the chaff.' It was all speculation, she admitted, and no one would be happier than she if it could be proved incorrect.

They agreed to skip the dessert, it was only pudding flan, and have coffee and brandy instead.

'Look at it this way,' she said, 'it's just a little exercise, something to cut your teeth on. Get this sorted out and we'll give you something more challenging to do.'

'Why don't you just haul him in, if you think he's up to no good?' Fielding asked.

'It's not quite so simple as that, here in Portugal. What he's up to, what he *might* be up to,' she amended, seeing the look on his face, 'isn't illegal here as long as it doesn't harm Portuguese security. Then again, he's a Catholic priest in a Catholic country. That gives him a certain status.' She examined the bill that had been left with the coffee.

'I'll pay for that,' Fielding said. It was the first time he'd ever bought a woman a meal. He'd been given money in Gibraltar, more than enough for his needs.

'That's a barbaric habit,' she said as he hissed to catch the attention of the waiter. 'I know it's the way it's done in Portugal but it's still barbaric.'

'They clap hands in Spain,' he replied. 'Different countries, different ways, I suppose. You can't change their customs.' All the same, smarting slightly under her criticism, he left ten escudos, an extravagantly large tip, under his saucer before they went outside.

A cool breeze came off the river. Diane threaded her hand under his arm as though they were enjoying a moment of familiarity. 'Look,' she said as they stood admiring the view of the city on the far side of the Tagus, 'if we're going to get to the truth we need to do some planning.'

She squeezed his arm as if to reassure him 'You'd better move out of the Boa Vista. That address you sent the postcard to,' she said. 'I shouldn't be doing this and I'd probably get cashiered if our bosses found out, but you can stay there with me. Just tell the old lady next door, senhora Magricela, that I sent you. She's my landlady and she'll let you have the key.' She laughed. 'She's always saying I need a man in my life and she'll love you. Make yourself at home. I'll be in quite late.'

50

Fielding didn't know the Mouraria well, a winding labyrinth of steep cobbled alleyways, cats and stray nondescript dogs, with lines of washing strung from side to side from upper windows, where decaying mansions rubbed stuccoed shoulders with hovels. At night, with only the occasional lamp to illuminate the narrow streets, he imagined it would be a nightmare to navigate and even in daylight he had some difficulty in finding Diane's little house off the Calçada de Santo Andreas.

She must have warned senhora Magricela of his coming. 'Dona Diane said I had to look out for a dark good-looking bearded stranger,' the old lady told him with knowing nods and winks as she gave him the key. 'Mind you treat her proper, the poor woman. She works all the hours God sends, always out and about. It's all on account of the book, you know.'

He couldn't make sense of what the old dear was saying about the book but didn't like to ask, just accepted the key and assured her that he would take good care of Dona Diane.

The house was filled with a domestic clutter that spoke to Fielding of this being a very private retreat. The tiny kitchen boasted an ancient wood-burning stove and cupboards filled with a miscellany of crockery. In the living room, stacks of books were untidily heaped on the shelves. A couple of armchairs, one had underwear lying across its back, looked as if they'd come from a second-hand shop. The large wooden table by the window doubled for the purposes of office and dining to judge by the folders and clutter of cutlery on it. Three mismatched upright chairs were pushed haphazardly under the table-top. A couple of the pictures on the wall facing the window were cheap Impressionist prints. There was another very simple unsigned oil still-life that Fielding thought might be valuable. A steep narrow staircase led to the upper regions but he resisted the temptation to explore further.

Make yourself at home, she'd said. She hadn't mentioned anything about sleeping arrangements so he left his suitcase against the wall by the living room table and tried to make himself comfortable in the armchair that didn't harbour underwear.

It was nearly ten when she came in. 'A hard day at the office,' she told him, kicking off her shoes. Without apology she whisked away the offending garments from the chair and shoved them in a wicker basket by the kitchen door.

'I don't feel like cooking,' she said. 'How about bread, cheese, *presunto*, olives and figs, and some red wine?' After busying herself for a few minutes in the kitchen to the accompaniment of a stream of patter about office trivialities, Diane emerged to set food on to the table and gave Fielding a plate. 'Don't stand on ceremony,' she ordered.

He helped himself, piling slices of the cured ham and a handful of olives on his plate, picking a couple of figs from a majolica-ware bowl and cutting himself a slice of the soft mountain cheese. It all looked delicious and tasted even better. The little rolls were a bit stale but he was used to that: always delicious fresh from the bakery in the morning, chewy by evening.

Apart from the few brief weeks of his home-leave five years earlier, and then the females at the table had all been family, this was only the second time – and in the course of a few hours - Fielding had ever shared a meal with a woman. How oddly exciting, he thought, to be in this house, a secret world apart from the college that was just a couple of miles away, with Diane sitting opposite him.

'Senhora Magricela, said something about a book. What was all that about?'

Diane grinned. 'She's a duck, isn't she? I'm only renting the house for a short while. Just think, Peter, me, a respectable English lady, here in this insalubrious end of town.' She grinned mischievously. 'I love it by the way. You meet some marvellous people once you get to know your way around. I told her I'm writing a book about by-gone Lisbon. It takes me out and about, all hours. Research, you see.' She saw his face. 'Well,' she said, 'I could hardly tell her I was a spy, could I?'

They both laughed.

She was a SINT operative, had probably undergone a far more arduous training than he'd experienced in Gibraltar, but here in her very untidy little house, he was very much aware Diane was also very good-looking. Fielding remembered what Father Harrington had said to him, about the *what ifs* in life, and how he'd answered so confidently that he'd be coming back to complete his studies for the priesthood when the war had ended. He wasn't sure how he'd reply if that question were put to him again.

Diane, curled comfortably in the other chair and obviously ravenous, was making short work of the contents of her plate. 'I've been thinking how to tackle him,' she said between mouthfuls. 'Consider this. You're a deserter, on the run from Gibraltar. You didn't like it, you tell Harrington; you were upset they didn't properly appreciate your sacrifice. Now you need his help. Birds of a feather, so to speak.'

Fielding, too, had spent time thinking about what she'd told him in O Grande Elias. He'd found it difficult to believe old José had been involved. According to Diane, he was in the habit of visiting his sister who kept a small florist's shop off the Rotunda at the top of the Avenida. He'd been coming back to the college one afternoon when he'd seen *padre Arrington* going through an office door over which hung a German flag. He'd mentioned this curious thing to Cordeiro and in return the porter had gleefully told him about the funny letters *padre Arrington* had been getting lately. José couldn't see any connection but he didn't like Germans after what they'd done to his brother, couldn't understand why *padre Arrington* should be consorting with them, and had begun to do a bit of unofficial snooping. 'What made him really suspicious was when your Father Harrington started sneaking out of the college in civilian clothes. He decided there definitely was something going on. So he became a *bufo*, an informer, like half the inhabitants of this crazy town. He came to the Embassy, not knowing who he should speak to but ended up with me,' Diane had concluded with a half smile.

It all still seemed fanciful but had begun to appear less implausible. There were odd little eccentricities Fielding had noticed lately, the departures from orthodox teaching in his lectures, occasional signs of unusual irritability – like the time Father Harrington had got cross because Cordeiro had handed over the task of delivering the post. And then there was Father Harrington's conviction that the war would be over soon: was that wishful thinking or was it propaganda on his part?

None of it added up to very much, Fielding had objected, and Diane had agreed. 'Ninety percent of the time we're running after shadows, but occasionally there's substance in the stories. Look,' she added, 'this is just an exercise for you. It might be something or nothing. Just try to set our minds at rest.'

He accepted that with bad grace. 'There's a difficulty,' he told her. 'It's holiday time. They'll all be over on the other side of the river. I can't just turn up at Pêra and ask to see him.'

'You'll think of some way round that,' Diane said, getting out of her chair. 'Now it's time for bed.'

266

Fielding felt himself blushing. She looked at him as if she could read his mind. She had brown eyes, he suddenly noticed. 'There's a little room in the attic,' she said straight-faced. 'It's a bit poky but you'll manage. I have first go in the bathroom in the morning but once I've gone to work you'll have free run of the place. Make sure you lock up when you go out.'

Lying in bed, Fielding heard sounds from downstairs, a door closing, the flush of the lavatory, a tap running. Just below him an attractive woman was getting ready for bed and his imagination was running loose.

51

It was odd to be rattling around in an empty college. Harrington had spent the better part of a sleepless night turning over in his mind the way he and Beta had parted. If only he'd handled things better, he reproached himself and then was tormented with the realisation that there was no easy way to persuade a lover to go to the other end of the country, have her – their – child, and then give it away. When he'd finally dropped off it had been only to have weird dreams about a baby who lived in his sitting room, growing cuckoo-like until it occupied the entire space.

In the morning, when he staggered bleary-eyed into the professors' dining room he found Cope already eating his breakfast. The bursar was full of the iniquities of the lawyer engaged by their tenant in Rua do Cabra. It was manifestly unjust, he told Harrington, that the same rent should still be paid as was imposed in 1892. 'The man knows a damned sight too much about the small print in the lease,' he complained.

Harrington let him ramble on, grateful that his colleague didn't expect him to contribute more than the occasional expression of support while his own thoughts were still fully occupied with Beta and the child. Hard though it was, he couldn't see any other solution than the one Fonseca had advised. Marriage was obviously out of the question and it would only harm both of them to continue their clandestine relationship. This way, once she'd had the baby, she could take up her normal life and maybe find someone who could give her what she really wanted. As for himself, he was reluctantly beginning to think a return to England, despite the dangers that might present, would offer the clean break they both needed.

What about Koenig? He'd made it clear often enough that he'd carry out his threat if his demands weren't met but what could he do, Harrington wondered, *if I'm in England, now we're at war with Germany?* It was small comfort to think that safety lay in being so far away from the one he loved.

Back in his room Harrington found another heart-marked letter waiting for him and he decided to off-load it as soon as possible. He looked at his watch: half-past nine. The Augsburger office would be open and even if Koenig were not in, he could leave the letter with the Valkyrie. He didn't know whether she would open the damned thing or not and he didn't care.

He said hello to Cordeiro in his cubbyhole, thanking him for delivering the mail, and had just come down the steps to the street to turn left with the intention of walking along to the Calçada de Gloria to take the funicular down to Restauradores when he heard someone calling out to him: '*Olá, o senhor padre Arrington!*'

He stopped dead in his tracks, alarmed to see a bearded figure approaching him from the foot of the college chapel steps.

'*O que quer você?* What do you want?' Harrington demanded brusquely, ready to brush off an importunate beggar.

'It's me, sir,' the stranger said in English. 'Peter Fielding.'

Harrington peered closely at the figure in front of him. 'Good God! It can't be! Is it really you? You're supposed to be in Gibraltar. What on earth are you doing here?'

'I was in Gibraltar, but now I'm on the run, sir. It's a long story.'

Harrington could only stare. It was Fielding, right enough, however improbably. The beard, thick and as black as the hair on his head, made him look so piratical, so much older. 'On the run? What do you mean, on the run?'

'It didn't work out, sir.'

The poor fellow sounded desperate. 'Did Mr Marchant bring you back?'

Fielding shook his head. 'I haven't seen him since he left me in Gibraltar.'

On the run? It didn't make sense. And if Bill Marchant hadn't brought Fielding back, how on earth had he got here?

'It wasn't at all what I'd expected,' Fielding said. 'I volunteered for the Navy but they had me cleaning out the latrines. So I jumped ship, so to speak.' He managed a feeble grin.

They were standing outside the little shop from which senhora Bonito sold oranges in season, eggs the year round, and a variety of the sweetmeats so beloved of the younger college students. Harrington could see her peering out at them, attracted by the sound of their voices, and he nudged Fielding further down the street. Stupid really, he thought. She wouldn't understand a word of what was going on, but instinctively he didn't want to draw attention to themselves.

'We can't have you back,' he said hurriedly. Martin Blount had called all the senior students into the chapel the day after Fielding had left, to explain what had happened. Harrington had been there too and recalled precisely what the college president had said: *We may question whether Mr Fielding has made the right choice but we must respect his decision and pray that the Lord will keep him safe in the midst of the perils he will face.* And now the subject of this heartfelt prayer was standing before him saying that he'd run away because he didn't like having to clean out lavatories.

'I still don't understand. How did you get here?'

'With difficulty,' Fielding told him. 'I managed to buy some pesetas from a dock worker in Gibraltar, then I sneaked across the frontier at La Linea and came up through Spain anyway I could. Buses mostly. There's scarcely any traffic on the roads. I managed to get a train from Seville to Ayamonte. There's a ferry that crosses the Guadiana but the Guardia Civil were checking all the passengers so I bribed a fisherman to get me across in a little boat at night.' He grinned ruefully. 'I got rather wet. And after that, well, I got lifts up to Lisbon.' He grinned as if he expected a pat on the back for being so resourceful.

'But why here, Fielding?' Harrington insisted. 'Why come here, to the college?'

'Where else? It's where I belong, isn't it, sir?' Fielding pleaded, desperate dog-eyed, clearly at the end of his tether. 'At least, that's what I thought. I'm a deserter and if they caught me they could, well I don't know what they could do, but it wouldn't be very pleasant.'

Of course, as a deserter, Harrington realised, Fielding wouldn't have been able to hide in such a tiny place as Gibraltar, and Franco's Spain would have provided no safer refuge. 'We can't have you back in college,' he repeated.

'I understand that.'

'Money. What are you doing for money?'

'There's the money Father Blount gave me before I left,' Fielding told him. 'I'm managing quite well on that for the moment. I've got digs, up near the cathedral. And,' he added with a touch of pride in his voice, 'I've still got your sovereign. I wouldn't want to spend that.'

Harrington supposed he ought to be flattered. 'I still don't understand, Fielding,' he said. 'What are you expecting from us?'

'It's just, well, I don't know. I just wanted to see the old place. I didn't expect to see anyone, I thought you'd all be at Pêra. And then when I saw you, I thought, at last a friendly face. You wouldn't believe what it's been like these last few days.'

'You're lucky to have caught me. I'm only over here briefly. I've got business in town.' Harrington explained. He shifted about irresolutely on the pavement. 'But I've no idea what I can do for you.'

Fielding hesitated. 'I don't suppose,' he said, 'we could meet somewhere? For a bit of a talk?'

'Not here, not at the college,' Harrington hurriedly insisted. It wouldn't do for the couple of servants who were running a skeleton crew to catch sight of the renegade.

'No, sir. I understand that. But there's a lot to tell.'

'I can imagine.' Harrington replied drily. 'But you, turning up like this, out of the blue without a word of warning; it's difficult to take in.'

'I could hardly send you a postcard,' Fielding smiled.

'No, I suppose not, Still, you have to understand, it's quite a shock to see you here when we thought you were signed up with... the Navy, did you say?'

'That's right, sir. Maybe, if I could explain everything, there might be something that could be done?' he pleaded.

As if I don't have enough to worry about, Harrington thought. 'If it would help, Fielding, of course,' he said. There were ties of college life, shared ideals, concern for another's welfare, all demanding a hearing no matter what mess Fielding had found himself in. The sad way Harrington had left Beta the previous day made him all the more anxious to redeem himself in any way possible, in his own eyes at least.

'When I was in Cascais,' Fielding said, 'before we sailed to Gibraltar, Mr Marchant took me to a little restaurant. The name intrigued me. O Golpe de Sorte, The Bit of Luck. The name seemed a sort of omen at the time. If we could meet there?'

Harrington fidgeted uneasily. He made a show of glancing at his watch. 'It's a long way out of town and I've an appointment just now.'

'I didn't mean for lunch. I was thinking of this evening, sir.'

'Oh, very well.' It would be ungracious to refuse, though he didn't know what there was to talk about. There wasn't much he could do to help a British deserter adrift in Portugal.

'At seven o'clock?' Fielding asked eagerly, adding, 'I'm at a loose end now as a matter of fact. Perhaps I could walk along with you?'

'No!' Harrington snapped, and then took a breath. 'No, let's save things for this evening.' He hesitated. 'The PVDE. They aren't looking for you, are they?'

'I've done nothing against the law, not here.'

'That's a comfort,' Harrington said, 'but now, I've really got to go.'

Fielding backed off as if not quite sure how to bring the meeting to an end.

Harrington nodded, 'Well, then, I'll see you later.'

Harrington found it difficult to imagine what it must have been like for Fielding to travel through Spain as a fugitive. Reports in the aftermath of Franco's victory were contradictory but a wandering Englishman who couldn't properly account for himself would easily be taken for a stray from the International Brigade and thus fair game for the firing squad or the garotte. Fielding's stubborn attachment to the college was either a measure of his desperation or spoke volumes for his fidelity; either way, his needs demanded some sort of gesture in return.

52

'You're agitated, my friend,' Koenig said as he took the letter. They were alone in the office; Harrington supposed the Valkyrie had been sent out on some errand or other.

'Do you want to come upstairs? A coffee, perhaps?'

'No,' Harrington replied abruptly. Apart from any other consideration, the memory of that portrait, with the staring maniacal eyes fixed on an apocalyptic Germanic future was enough to make him not want to set foot ever again in Koenig's private quarters.

'Michael, I can see something's troubling you.' Koenig was at his most odiously solicitous. 'Is it the delectable Dona Elisabete?'

'You can damned well leave her out of anything, Koenig. You've got your blasted letter. Be content with that and keep your nose out of my business.'

'Oh dear! Such a spirited defence of your beloved!'

Harrington could have hit him. He strode out of the office just in time to catch a tram.

He got off in Restauradores and was heading for the Calçada da Gloria when he heard raised voices: unmistakably Irish voices. There were three of them, at the tobacco kiosk on the corner; by the sound of it an argument over the price they'd been charged for American cigarettes. He wouldn't normally have involved himself but the woman behind the counter was shrilly defending herself in the few words of English she had, the Irishmen were getting increasingly heated and a policeman standing at the entrance to the Calçada was beginning to take an interest in what was going on.

The argument was easily sorted out, a simple matter of the woman not recognising the Irish pound notes she'd been offered. The men had the look of seafarers and their spokesman, a rangy beanpole with sharp blue eyes and high weather-beaten cheekbones, who said his name was Ryan, was quick to confirm that they were off the *Saint Brendan*, berthed in the Alcântara dock.

'A stinking old tub,' he said. 'We're on our way home to Cork, Father, if the old love will get us that far.' They'd visited Brindisi, Naples and Palermo, Marseilles and Barcelona, 'and we'll be calling in at Oporto and Bilbao, like as not.'

When Harrington asked what sort of cargo the *Saint Brendan* carried the answer was simple. 'Any sodding thing we can get, Father. We've handled everything from sheep to spaghetti at one time or another.'

They'd been stopped and searched, Ryan said, by a Royal Navy ship. *HMS Tuberose,* in international waters off Mallorca. 'They were decent enough about it, mind. Always the perfect gentlemen, his Majesty's sailors.'

'When they fucking want to be,' one of the others muttered.

They were more afraid of what might happen if they encountered any German navy vessels. 'They're not supposed to interfere with neutral shipping,' Ryan told Harrington, 'and we've the Tricolour painted on both our sides, with *EIRE* in bloody great letters a blind man could see in a fog, but it seems some of Mr Hitler's U-boat people are colour-blind or don't have the Gaelic. They got *The Pride of Erin*, off Finisterre, back in June.'

An idea had been germinating in Harrington's head while Ryan was talking. 'I don't suppose you carry passengers on board your ship?'

That provoked hoots of laughter. 'It'd be a crazy one, Father,' Ryan said, 'and no mistake, who'd book a berth on our old rust-bucket, and if anyone was daft enough to come on board they'd be lucky to get where they were going in a month of Sundays.'

Even so, Harrington thought, as he bade them farewell, if a man was desperate enough, what would the Irish authorities have to say to a young Englishman who introduced himself as a deserter from the British Navy?

Harrington knew there were ingenious means of getting back to Britain. He'd even heard of one desperate character who'd got himself shipped across the Atlantic to the USA, had trekked overland to Canada then joined a convoy out of Halifax Nova Scotia to Greenock on the Clyde. But a would-be priest, slipped ashore in Cork, might fare well enough, and Harrington knew the man who might be able to make it happen.

Though it was well over a year since he'd had anything to do with Fergal O'Dowd, now might be the time to put that right. He knew that the Dominican priest didn't get out much and would as like as not be ensconced in his room or in one of the confessionals in church. Wouldn't it be splendid to be able to tell Fielding that a way had been found to spirit him out of harm's way?

53

The half-dozen tables were all empty when Fielding walked into the little restaurant. As he looked round, he thought O Golpe de Sorte was the right place for a cosy heart-to-heart. The walls were covered in blue and white *azulejos* tiles showing scenes from Portuguese maritime history. The frame of the door into the kitchen was festooned with a piece of old fishing net and above it was a neatly crafted model of a fishing boat complete with a guiding eye painted on its prow.

Harrington was right; Cascais was quite a step from the city, the end of the train line and there wasn't much of anything beyond the village apart from the wild rocky coast, which was precisely why Fielding had chosen this to be their meeting place. A few steps out of the village and there would be no one to observe. Observe what, exactly, Fielding didn't care to specify, keeping that thought in another brain compartment, in a drawer he didn't want to open. Pure melodrama, he told himself.

'I remember you!' The proprietor, his generously distributed middle a testimony to his own cooking, was delighted to see him. 'You came in a few weeks back with that English gentleman. I haven't seen him since. How's he getting on?'

Fielding had noticed *Esperança* wasn't in the harbour and had wondered what had become of Marchant, who he'd last seen sailing out of Gibraltar. 'Sorry,' he said, 'we've rather lost touch.'

'Ah well, he'll turn up in his own good time, no doubt,' the proprietor said. 'Table for two? That's no problem. As you can see we're quiet at the moment,' he admitted with a shrug, 'but things will soon be livening up. So, what's it to be? We've some lovely golden bream in today. Or we could do you a seafood risotto, very tasty. Whatever the senhor desires.'

The senhor said that he would like the table furthest away from the door and would wait until his guest arrived before ordering. 'In the meantime, a glass of white wine, please.'

Fielding washed his hands at the little basin in the corner and made himself comfortable on the chair facing the door. The little German automatic wedged in his trousers' waistband dug into the small of his back. '*Never let them get behind you, Sonny Jim,* he could hear Gus's voice in his ear, *Make sure you see them before they see you. And the gun, it hasn't got to snag on anyfink. You wouldn't half look a Charlie if they pumped a couple of rounds into you while you was trying to free your weapon from your knickers, in a manner of speaking.*'

The practice on the firing range was routine, Gus had said, and everyone had to learn how to fire something. To his delight, Fielding had discovered he could shoot pretty accurately at short range with the Webley .455 service-issue revolver but, as Gus had pointed out, it was a clumsy piece of weaponry for an agent to be carrying. The .25 Mauser with the walnut hand-grip was much more suitable for the task. Gus had shown him the little shells. *A poncy ladies' gun, according to some, but with these hollow-nosed beauties it can make quite a hole, if it's used right.* In any case, Hamish had assured him the gun was only a precaution. 'You'll probably never need to use it.'

When they'd met in a noisy little café behind Rossio at lunch time Diane had approved of his plan. 'He'll quite likely open up if you handle him right,' she assured him. 'Take the gun with you though.'

He'd protested he wasn't placing himself in any danger, didn't need to protect himself. 'It's only a training exercise, you said.' She'd given him a sideways look at that. 'What if we are right?

What if he's already run off to tell Koenig about you? You don't know who might turn up. Take the gun.'

'And if I find you are right about him?'

'You'll do whatever you have to do.'

He still didn't think it was necessary, not really. He was only carrying the weapon this evening as a piece of bravado, he told himself, helping to make him feel as though he were a real secret agent.

The proprietor returned with the wine and busied himself arranging the cutlery on the tables, ready for a chat at this slack time. 'The name of the restaurant?' The man chuckled comfortably. 'I'm always being asked about that.' He paused, using the corner of his apron to wipe an imaginary stain off the knife he'd been about to lay before Fielding.

'The Bit of Luck? That was the missus' granny dying and leaving us some money that we never knew she had. Enough to open up this place. Then again, the name suits. It's mostly fish we serve and we depend on the boats for a little bit of luck. We won't ever make a fortune but we're happy here. Nice set of customers, regulars for the most part. And a few foreigners, even with this war on and all.'

'What kind of foreigners?' Fielding asked.

'There's your friend the Englishman for a start. A nice bloke but, like I said, I haven't seen him for a bit, nor his boat. Well,' he laughed at himself, 'without one you wouldn't get the other, would you?'

'Any others?'

'There's an older gentleman. German, he is. He's got a house on the other side of the village. Quite a fancy place.' The proprietor examined his handiwork with obvious satisfaction and laid the knife down on the table. 'Funny really, him and the Englishman, they get along quite famously. Between you

279

and me, I think they're both happy enough to be well out of the line of fire at the present, if you know what I mean.'

'This German, what does he do for a living?'

'Now, that's a thing. There's a bit of a mystery there. There's money, right enough. You've only got to see that house of his to know that much. Keeps himself to himself, he does. Always well dressed, nicely spoken, polite as you could wish when he comes in here.'

At that moment the door opened. 'Excuse me, senhor,' the proprietor said, before bustling forward to greet the newcomer.

'He's with me,' Fielding called after him.

Harrington had hesitated for some moments before crossing the street. He could see Fielding, sitting in the far corner of the empty restaurant, talking to a fat man in an apron, seeming perfectly at ease.

The person he'd met outside the college had been the old Fielding right enough, under the beard and the unfamiliar civilian clothes, but there'd also been something different about him. Not surprising; he was entitled to have a bit of a changed look, after all his experiences, running away from the Navy and risking his neck travelling through unfamiliar and hostile territory to come back to Lisbon.

At least now, Harrington thought, as he crossed the road, thanks to the chance meeting with the Irish sailors and the subsequent visit to Fergal O'Dowd, he'd be able to offer the fugitive good news.

The Dominican priest had been dubious at first. He'd admitted he was familiar with the movements of Irish shipping and counted some of the captains among his friends. But, he pointed out, Harrington's scheme would involve a deal of illegality, both in Lisbon and at the Irish end. Fielding would have to be smuggled on board the ship or passed off as an extra deck hand and then, at the other end, what would the authorities make of a failed priest and fugitive from British justice?

After a good deal of argument O'Dowd had eventually grudgingly agreed to check on the arrival of the next Irish ship and, provided the ship's master was willing to run the risks involved, something might be arranged.

Harrington crossed the street and pushed open the restaurant door.

54

They settled for the golden bream, a bottle of the house white and a tomato salad.

Harrington was full of nervous excitement, bursting to deliver his news. 'I've been thinking hard about your predicament, Peter. Have you any family in Ireland?'

'I imagine I might have,' Fielding replied. 'My grandmother, my mother's mother, had some Irish in her.' He laughed. 'That's where I'm supposed to get my looks from. She claimed there was an ancestor who was a shipwrecked sailor from the Spanish Armada. But if there are relatives still in Ireland I don't know the first thing about them.'

'Oh. That's rather a pity.'

Harrington looked so disappointed Fielding had to ask why that was.

'I thought Ireland might be the answer to your problem.'

'Really?'

'You see, there are Irish ships that come into Lisbon,' Harrington said, 'and I've been talking to someone who's got contacts among their captains, someone who could arrange for you to get a passage to Cork or Galway.'

Fielding was intrigued. 'And what, do you think, would I do when I got there?'

'That's why I asked about family,' Harrington said. 'I thought, if you got to Ireland, you could get in touch with them and they'd look after you until things settle down.'

'I'm sorry? Settle down? What do you mean by that?'

'This war, Fielding, it won't last long. Churchill will see reason. Hitler doesn't want to destroy Britain. And then, when it's all over...'

'When it's all over,' Fielding cut in, 'I'll come back to the college, get ordained and go to a parish in England? If the Nazis would allow such a thing?'

He broke a piece off his bread roll and popped it into his mouth, all the while eyeing Harrington curiously. Close inspection revealed how much of a wreck he'd become in the space of only a few weeks. There were bags under his bloodshot eyes and his clothes hung off him as though he was shrinking.

Fielding had spent most of the day wrestling with precisely how to carry this through and he'd finally decided the only way was to be brutally straightforward, settle the matter once and for all. 'Tell me about your German friend.'

Harrington started. 'German friend? What d'you mean? I don't have any German friends.'

'That's not what I hear,' Fielding said. A dish of ripe black olives had been put on the table. He picked one, extracted the stone and dropped it into the bowl provided. 'Herr Koenig, isn't it? He's something to do with printing machinery?' He was watching Father Harrington carefully as he added, 'As well as being a German secret agent.'

There should have been an expression of amazement, disbelief, or even a burst of astonished laughter. Instead, the last vestiges of colour drained from Harrington's cheeks, 'You're no run-away,' he said in a shocked whisper.

'I'm sorry.' For himself as much as anything, Fielding meant; suddenly desolate at such immediate confirmation of what he'd been so reluctant to believe.

'To think I was going to get you passage to Ireland to save you from court martial!' Harrington said in a hollow voice. 'What have they done to you?'

'D'you realise the mess you're in?' Fielding said. 'There are stories about you and your friend Koenig.'

'All right, I admit I know him. He's not a friend exactly,' Harrington said, apparently prepared to bluster, 'but yes, we've met a few times, for a drink. Is that a crime?'

'I don't know. It depends what was served up, apart from the drink.'

'What do you mean?' Harrington demanded, trying to sound aggrieved.

'Letters.' Fielding picked up the bottle the proprietor had left on the table. There was no label but the white wine was good. 'Another drop?'

Harrington nodded and mechanically pushed his glass across the table. 'What letters?' he asked.

Fielding poured the wine carefully. 'The ones you take to to Herr Koenig.' It was a shot in the dark.

'I don't know who's been feeding you this rubbish, but whoever it is has got it all wrong.' Harrington protested. His voice sounded odd and, in what might have been intended as a gesture of dismissal of the accusation, his hand knocked over his wine glass.

Fielding watched Harrington ineffectually dabbing at the soaking tablecloth. 'Here,' he offered his own napkin. 'Just cover it up.'

The food arrived at that moment. The proprietor didn't seem to notice the spill as he placed the fish on their plates while a young woman - his daughter, Fielding guessed, by the look of her round face and comfortable proportions - brought the boiled potatoes, a dish of fava beans and a plate of sliced tomatoes drenched in olive oil. '*Bom apetite,*' she encouraged as she left them to it, 'and watch out for the fish bones.'

'I'd hoped it was all just stupid rumours,' Fielding said softly.

'I didn't think there was any harm in it, at first,' Harrington whispered, looking at the grilled fish as if wondering what to do with it. 'Love letters, that's what he said they were. From someone he'd met in England.'

'Love letters?' Fielding forced himself to eat some of the fish.

'The bastard was blackmailing me,' Harrington said miserably.

'How did he manage to do that?'

'If you know so much, you probably know about Dona Elisabete.'

'A lady friend?' Fielding made another intuitive leap. This was something Diane hadn't known about but if true it could go a long way to explaining things; blackmail, not treason. 'Dona Elisabete. So that's her name?'

Harrington nodded. 'Dona Elisabete Louçá e Medronho. It's pathetic, isn't it?' Me, a priest, carrying on with a woman. Koenig threatened to expose me if I didn't do what he wanted. So when he asked me to pass those letters on to him, I didn't have much choice.'

Fielding let him concentrate on his plate for a while before putting his next question. 'They weren't love-letters, were they though?'

'Military intelligence,' Harrington mumbled. 'Koenig's an agent for the Abwehr.' Then he looked up. 'But I swear I didn't know that until much later.'

'Was this woman involved in this?'

'Dona Elisabete? Certainly not!' For the first time Harrington showed real animation. 'She's got nothing to do with all this, nothing at all.'

'So Cordeiro was right, in a way.'

'What are you talking about?' Harrington asked.

'Do you remember the day I brought up the mail and you were cross with me? There was an American letter addressed to you. I asked could I have the stamp. The envelope had a mark on it, a little pencilled heart. Cordeiro said you'd been getting a lot of letters with that mark. He said you had a lover.' Cordeiro was practically illiterate and most people in college thought he was half-witted but Fielding used to take the trouble to talk to him, listen to what he had to say; mostly a lot of gossip but with a peasant's acute awareness of everything that was going on. Not his fault he'd got hold of the wrong end of the stick.

Harrington pushed away his almost untouched plate. 'I never understood about that American letter. The Americans aren't in this war.'

'No, but they're supplying us with necessities. At a guess,' Fielding said, 'I'd say someone was passing on information about convoy routes across the Atlantic.'

'Oh.' Harrington's head drooped. 'I'd never thought of that.'

'You've had enough?' Fielding enquired. Neither of them had eaten very much.

'Yes, I suppose so.'

'No coffee, thank you,' Fielding said to the girl who came to take away their plates. 'It was very nice but we weren't very hungry. May I have the bill?'

The place was beginning to fill up and the proprietor was struggling to manage. 'Thank you, senhores! Please come again, soon.' The man clicked his fingers at his daughter: 'Another couple coming in. Clear that table, quick!'

55

They stepped out into the warm evening air. It had just turned eight o'clock and the sun was touching the horizon under a bar of blood-red cloud. 'Shall we walk?' Fielding suggested. He needed time to think now that the 'exercise' had become real.

They headed towards the harbour where stacks of lobster pots and coils of net spilled across the pavement. It was low tide, Fielding saw. The tubby little fishing boats lay tipped on their sides in the mud, attached by long ropes to iron rings set in the harbour wall where by some sort of mutual unspoken consent they stopped and leaned against the stonework.

Harrington was the first to break the silence. 'Koenig said the letters would help bring the war to an end. The Duke said more or less the same.'

'The Duke?'

'The Duke of Windsor. He was staying at the Casa de Santa Maria, over there,' he waved in the direction of the fort that hid the villa from view. 'Before he went off to the Bahamas. He came to the college and he wanted my advice about staying here in Portugal.' There was a pathetic note of pride struggling to express itself. 'My advice. Imagine that!'

'You told the Duke of Windsor what you were up to?' Fielding asked, incredulously.

'No, no,' Harrington explained. 'We were talking about the war and he said it was unfortunate people were getting killed but it was all Churchill's fault and the sooner there was an understanding, the sooner it would end. I think he wants to be king again, when the war's over.'

'Wishful thinking. There'll be no arranged cease-fire, no bargaining with Hitler.'

'You can't know that. Not for certain.'

'I wouldn't bet on that.' His job was nearly done, Fielding reflected, as far as SINT was concerned. But he was still curious. 'Tell me about the lady.'

'She's a widow. Her husband was killed in the Spanish Civil War, fighting for Franco. I love her,' Harrington said simply.

'Does she love you?'

Harrington thought for a moment. 'She loves me enough to have my child.'

'She's pregnant?'

Harrington nodded. 'She wants us to get married.'

'You're a priest,' Fielding reminded him.

Harrington didn't answer that. 'Beta says we should go to the States,' he said. 'She knows someone in the American Embassy who could easily get us visas.'

'She's a Nazi?' Since getting out of the college, Fielding had begun to learn just how far the Portuguese state leaned in the direction of Hitler's fascism.

'No, she isn't,' Harrington insisted indignantly. 'She's got too soft a spot for animals to be one of those.'

Fielding didn't think love of animals said anything about political inclinations; he'd heard the Führer was fond of his Alsatian dog. 'About the letters,' he said, 'what you've been up to, that's called aiding the enemy. There's a man called William Joyce on the German Radio. Back in England he joined Moseley's Black Shirts. He was going to be arrested, but he escaped to Germany, and he's been pouring out Nazi propaganda ever since. He'll hang, when we get our hands on him.'

'And you think I'm like that? You've got me down as a traitor?'

'I'm not saying you're in the same class as Joyce, but you're running the same risk.' It was time for a bit of drama. 'I have to tell you,' Fielding was reaching behind him as he spoke, easing the Mauser from his waistband, 'I'm under orders to stop you, one way or another.'

Harrington saw the gun and squealed in panic. 'No,' he cried, 'Peter, you can't!' He twisted about, as if searching for an escape.

Fielding reached out with his free hand and grabbed Harrington by the shoulder, twisting him round and bringing the gun close to his chest. 'I should shoot you here and now,' he said quietly, glancing around to confirm there was no one in sight. 'That's what they expect me to do.' He could feel Harrington trembling under his hand. He was pretty unsteady on his feet himself.

'Is that what they've ordered you to do?' Harrington asked. There was no further attempt to escape, as if he'd come to terms with his fate.

'Not in so many words. But that's what they expect. This woman, you said she wanted you to go to the States with her?'

'Yes,' Harrington said.

Fielding released his grip. 'Would you really have married her?'

Harrington was silent for several seconds. 'I should have said yes when I had the chance,' he said slowly.

Fielding decided. He lowered the gun. 'I'm giving you the chance. There's a train back to Lisbon in a few minutes. You'd better be on it.'

Harrington tried to say something but he was stuttering, couldn't get the words out properly.

'Shut up,' Fielding shouted, suddenly blazing with anger. 'Just shut the fuck up and go to your woman and clear off to the States. To Brazil or fucking Timbuktu for all I care. But there's a condition. You don't ever contact Koenig again. No more letters.' He jabbed the gun against Harrington's belly.'

Harrington swallowed and nodded. 'No more letters,' he echoed hoarsely, 'I promise.'

'I never want to see you again. And here, you'd better have this back.' Fielding fished the gold coin out of his pocket and threw it at Harrington's feet. He turned away, with hot tears in his eyes. 'Now bugger off,' he said without looking back, 'before I change my mind!'

With his legs shaking uncontrollably and his heart thumping, Fielding leaned his weight against the harbour wall and stared blindly out to where the incoming tide was sending wavelets to lap against the stone.

It might have been ten minutes before he steeled himself to turn round. The sovereign had gone and there was no sight of Harrington or the sovereign. He heard the toot of an engine's whistle in the distance. He pushed himself off the wall and automatically took the road that led out of the village and along the coast westwards.

SINT shouldn't have sent him back to Lisbon. They should have given the job to one of their seasoned hands; Gus, for example. He could hear the man now: *One, two. Double tap. To be sure to be sure, as the Irishman said as he put on the second condom.* Making light of killing another human being. *It's you or him, Sonny Jim, when the chips are down. Your choice.*

Harrington had taught him Latin in Lower House. Harrington had introduced him to Shakespeare and Wordsworth, had patiently corrected his grammar, had lent him a copy of Graham Greene's *Stamboul Train* to read one summer over at Pêra. Harrington had given him his father's sovereign - the sovereign he'd thrown back at him just now.

It was getting quite dark and the first stars were sparkling in the eastern sky. He'd walked about a mile without coming any nearer deciding how to explain the outcome of his mission.

He turned about and had walked less than a hundred yards back towards the village when he heard behind him the grunt and rattle of an approaching vehicle. The crumbling road surface at his feet gleamed faintly in the headlights' beams.

The car, he saw it was the popular old Citroen C Type, drew up alongside him. The driver, decked out in a grey jacket, black flat cap and with two days-worth of bristle on his chin, leaned across the passenger seat and stared out at him. 'Heh, mate! You want a lift?'

The back of the little open-topped car was filled with a jumble of rods. 'There's good fishing out on the rocks,' the man said by way of explanation as Fielding pushed aside a basket of fish and climbed into the front seat. Putting the car into gear, the driver added speculatively, 'It's late to be out on foot.'

It was only to be expected that he'd be nosy. 'I needed to walk,' Fielding explained. 'My dad's died, very suddenly. We'd grown apart but he meant a lot to me. You understand?' It was shocking, how fluently he'd learned the linguistics of lies in recent weeks.

He needed to say very little as the driver, who he guessed would be about fifty years old, regaled him with a detailed account of his own father's demise, how the doctors gave up on him, how he'd taken to his bed, how the whole family held vigil around his bedside until at last death had taken him from them. 'Padre Marques was very good to him. They used to play dominoes in the Palmeira nearly every day, in better times. Five years ago it was he died, and me and the wife, we still go up to the cemetery nearly every week to see him.' He hadn't finished. 'Are you married?'

Fielding managed a weak smile. 'There's a girl, but,' he shrugged, 'you know how it is.' *And if you do, it's more than I do*, he thought as he accepted the other's sympathy.

56

The apartment had never seemed lonelier to Beta. All day she'd waited for a word from Mickey but now finally she had to recognise the inevitable, their parting yesterday had been definitive. All that lay before her was the prospect of a convent in the far north and the uncertain mercies of a religious community.

Unwilling to turn on the lights, she wandered about in the gloom; touched the heirloom silverware, ran a finger over the seductive curves of the Indian ivory sculpture, gazed distractedly at the ancestral portraits and the choice pieces of furniture, all the relics of the old house in Evora. None of it meant anything any more. The chess set caught her eye. She'd throw it out in the morning.

Moods could be infectious. She heard Ana being aggressively noisy with the pots and pans in the kitchen, her way of communicating that she too was out of sorts about something.

Beta went to the window overlooking Rua do Prior, where she'd stood so many times, waiting expectantly for Mickey. Strange, she thought, after Garcia she'd vowed she'd never look at another man again, let alone one ten years older than herself and a priest.

What was it had made her reach out so eagerly to him: the challenge of chasing the untouchable? As a child, she'd automatically accepted that priests were sacred. At Mass their hands alone touched the sanctified bread, their lips drank from the chalice of salvation. They dispensed divine forgiveness, they guided the paths of the dying. One might snigger at their foibles, tell tales about the uncertain temper of such-and-such a parish priest, might even heave a sigh over the impossibly good looks of the new curate, but priests were fundamentally different, on a higher plane than ordinary mortals.

And then, there he was, padre Harrington, tucked away at the end of Maria Winter's table, dressed in a badly-cut black suit, with that ridiculous collar clamped round his neck. The conversation at the table was conducted in a mixture of English, of which she understood quite a lot but could contribute little, and Portuguese, of which on the rare occasions when he was called upon to speak, padre Harrington was in admirable command, delivered with a charming light accent.

She'd been at the head of the table, the prize exhibit as she interpreted her placing, on show for Dona Maria's nephews, for she knew perfectly well why she'd been invited. It was only afterwards, when they'd retired to the drawing room and she'd found a seat next to padre Harrington, that they'd had the chance to discover a mutual interest in the cinema. They had been flirting, she quite consciously, he almost completely and innocently unaware.

Beta sighed deeply as she stared into the darkness of the August night. From such beginnings had been spun this complex web that now entangled and threatened to strangle them both.

The thought of the boy, she was convinced the baby would be a boy, being brought up by strangers was unbearable. Suppose she went to live in another town where she wasn't known, Coimbra perhaps? After all, she was a widow whose husband had died a hero in many people's eyes. She'd keep the little one and call him Miguel, keep something of Mickey alive in her heart.

'Supper is served, Dona Elisabete.' It was *Arroz com mariscos*, rice with prawns in the shell, mussels and crab meat and curls of squid. Ordinarily, Beta would have tucked in greedily but this evening all she could manage was an unconvincing attempt to push the food around on her plate so as not to disappoint Ana too much.

Beta heard the apartment door bell ring and looked at her watch. Nearly ten o'clock. She sighed heavily. At this hour it could only be Jacinta Louleira, who had no sense of time, with another urgent litany of woe.

Ana stood in the doorway, clearly flustered. 'I told him, Dona Elisabete,' she said, 'that it's far too late for him to be calling, but I couldn't stop him.'

She was still speaking when Mickey pushed her aside. 'We have to talk,' he said breathlessly.

'Thank you, Ana,' Beta said, trying to stay calm as she rose from the table. 'I shan't be requiring your services any further this evening.'

She couldn't read the expression on his face. Excited? Frightened? Had he come to apologise? What was she supposed to do? His breathing was ragged and his face was blotched red and white. Anyone would think he'd been drinking but there was no smell of alcohol about him.

'I've been threatened with death,' he announced dramatically, 'with a gun in my face.'

'A gun?' she shrieked. 'Are you wounded?' She couldn't see any signs of blood on him.

'He didn't shoot me but I thought he was going to.' Harrington laughed wildly, raggedly. 'He gave me a new life instead!'

'What do you mean, Mickey?' she stammered.

'Exactly what I said, a fresh chance, to begin again.'

That didn't make much sense either but she pulled Mickey to her. She could see he was in no fit state to think straight. 'We must tell the police at once. Did you get a good look at the monster?'

'I can't go to the police.'

'Why ever not?'

'I just can't,' he repeated. 'It's not that sort of thing.'

'My darling,' she said, hugging him tightly. 'Of course you've got to go to the police. There's a dangerous man out there, with a gun. I'll telephone them now and they'll send someone round to talk to you.'

'You mustn't,' he pleaded. 'It was that student I told you about, the one who sailed off to Gibraltar.'

The whole story came out then: about Koenig, the letters, about Fielding, everything, even about the sovereign he'd rescued from the pavement. He couldn't stop, and for once Beta listened to the end without interrupting.

Then: 'What did you mean when you said, "a new life"?'

'They say your whole life goes before your eyes at the moment of death. I'd never believed it,' Harrington said. 'That moment, when he was pointing the gun at me, all I could think of was what a mess I'd made of things. A total mess.'

'Not a mess, darling,' she whispered, shaking her head. 'You've got me and I love you, truly.'

'I know you do. That's why it was a mess,' he insisted, 'because I was only ever really thinking of myself, never really of you.' He took her hands. 'Do you still want to marry a silly old fool?'

57

From the railway station at Cais do Sodré Fielding walked all the way through the city to the Calçada do Santo Andreas acutely aware of the automatic weighing down his pocket. *It's your lifeline, Sonny Jim,* he heard Gus say. *Use it and clean it, as the actress said to the bishop. And keep it ready for the next time.* Well, he hadn't used it but the weapon would have to be accounted for, so he couldn't chuck it down a drain. Though the streets were still busy, no one paid him the slightest attention.

She'd said that it was up to him to decide what to do. But she'd also made sure he was carrying the Mauser when he went off to meet Harrington. Just in case, she'd said. It was clear to him what she'd expected of him.

What could he tell her? That he'd thought it had been enough to put the fear of God into a man who had for months been passing information to the enemy? He'd look all kinds of an idiot if Harrington chose to ignore his threat.

'Well?' Diane said as he opened the door. There was a bottle of brandy on the table in the living room, a bowl of olives and a platter of buttered rolls filled with *fiambre,* English-style ham. 'How did it go?'

'He admitted what he'd been up to, the letters, everything. Koenig was blackmailing him over a woman.'

'Now that's something we hadn't thought of,' she said thoughtfully. 'And?'

'And what?' Fielding demanded.

'You dealt with him?'

'I dealt with him.'

'Good. Discreetly, I hope? No messy details to clear up?'

Her callousness roused him. 'Have you ever killed anyone?'

She returned his gaze impassively. 'No, not yet at any rate.'

'So it's bloody easy for you to sit there and say, good!'

'You might say that.'

'He wasn't harming me, for God's sake!'

'And how many other lives do you think your precious Harrington might have been harming? You did the right thing in killing him.'

'I didn't kill him,' Fielding said.

'But, you just said,' she stared at him wide eyed, 'you'd dealt with him.'

'I did. He's going to the States, with this Medronho woman. He's going to marry her. She's pregnant.'

She stared at him. 'Very clever,' she said sarcastically. 'What a clever way of letting him off the hook.'

'He's no danger to us any more.'

'Oh, really? You're sure of that?'

'Yes. After all, I think I know him well enough after all these years.'

'Easy to say that, Peter.'

'I saw his eyes when I told him. I said I ever see him again I'll shoot him,' Fielding muttered.

'Let's hope that's a promise you won't have to honour,' Diane said, adding in a suddenly practical tone of voice, 'You'd better eat.'

'There's something else,' she said, rather too casually, as she cleared away the plates. 'We only got the news this afternoon. Wreckage from Marchant's yacht came ashore at Cape St Vincent a few weeks ago. We think the Kriegsmarine were using her for gunnery practice.'

Fielding was aghast. 'He was flying the Portuguese flag!' He'd only known Marchant for a few days and had him to blame for the predicament he found himself in, but he'd liked the man. 'There'll be an official protest, surely?'

She pulled a face. 'Protest?' she said. 'I doubt it. Who's going to protest? Salazar must have an extra crease in his arse from sitting on the fence. He wouldn't want to do anything to upset the Führer at this stage, not for the sake of a piddling little yacht and someone who's probably on PVDE's watch-list anyway.'

'It's all such a bloody waste!' he shouted.

'War tends to be wasteful.'

He was about to make a reply when she added: 'We did rather wonder whether he'd been talking out of turn.'

'There was a man,' Fielding suddenly remembered, 'in Cascais, when I went to join Marchant. An older man, very smartly dressed. They were chatting.' He hesitated, adding doubtfully, 'I think he might have been German. The proprietor of that restaurant I took Harrington to, he said Marchant was friendly with a German.'

'There's a man in Cascais, von Karstoff, who runs agents for the Abwehr,' Diane said. 'I wonder? Marchant surely wouldn't have been so stupid?' She shrugged. 'It might have been Karstoff. Anyway, there's nothing we can do. Marchant's another casualty of war. As for you, you sit tight here until you get your marching orders. And by the way, I'll have the gun now, please.'

'No!'

'Why not? It's over, finished with.'

'So you say. All the same, I want to hang on to it for a bit.'

She eyed him speculatively. 'I hope you know what you're doing.'

58

The next morning Fielding waited until he heard the front door slam before he got out of bed. There'd been a street party going on until the small hours; so many people enjoying themselves, singing and drinking. He'd been tempted to sneak downstairs and join them. He'd only ever once been drunk, one summer over at Pêra, an injudicious mixture of sun, cheap red wine and a couple of glasses of *aguardente* at a little beach café at Caparica. It hadn't been a pleasant experience but it was one he'd felt like repeating as he lay awake, listening to the noises from the street below.

He didn't care that he'd failed SINT. He wondered what he'd have done himself if he'd been in Harrington's predicament. Self-preservation was instinctive, wasn't it? Perhaps Harrington shouldn't have got himself involved with the Medronho woman but falling in love was instinctive too, wasn't it? He'd seen something in Harrington's eyes when he'd told him to go. Not fear, something more like enlightenment.

After a cup of coffee and a roll in a café near the castle, Fielding sauntered down to the main Post Office in Restauradores and found what he wanted in the Lisbon telephone book.

What was he doing here? he asked himself as he stood near the doorway to the apartment block in Rua do Prior. He'd had a fanciful notion he might find Harrington hiding with his lady-love but more likely than not he'd be skulking in his rooms in college if he hadn't flown back across the river and was keeping his head down in the house at Pêra. He might even have run off back to Koenig, as Diane had said, despite his promise. Fielding had told her he knew his old professor well enough but he'd already been proved wrong about that. She obviously thought it had been a mistake to have let Harrington off so lightly and perhaps she was right, but what else could he have done?

Fielding was about to head back down to the tram stop on the Avenida da India when a well-dressed woman came out of the building and glanced incuriously at him as she walked past in the direction of a taxi that had pulled up at the curbside a few yards down the street.

'Senhora!' he called out suddenly. The woman turned. He could see she was rather beautiful; black hair, shapely figure under a light blue dress. 'Excuse me, senhora, could you tell me if Dona Medronho lives here?' He indicated the building behind him.

'Dona Louçá e Medronho,' she corrected him.

'I'm sorry,' Fielding apologised for his error. 'Yes, that's the lady I'm looking for.'

'I'm Dona Louçá e Medronho,' she said primly. 'I don't know who you are.'

'Peter Fielding,' he said.

'You're English?'

'Yes.'

'You don't sound English.' She frowned distrustfully. 'For that matter, you don't look English. What do you want?'

'A few moments of your time, please,' Fielding said.

'I'm busy. I don't know you and if you don't go away this instant I'll get my driver,' she pointed in the direction of the taxi, 'to make you go away. If you want your Embassy, it's up that way.' She pointed before stepping in the direction of the vehicle.

'It's about padre Harrington.'

That stopped her dead in her tracks. 'What about him?' She came back and peered hard at Fielding. 'Are you the student who ran away to Gibraltar?' she demanded.

'I volunteered for service in the Royal Navy.' It wasn't far from the truth though *press-ganged* might have been nearer the mark. 'You've got to get him away,' he said. 'I can't answer for his safety if he stays here in Lisbon, in Portugal.'

'Why are you persecuting him?' she hissed, stepping close enough for Fielding to smell her heady perfume. 'What's he ever done to you?'

'He's still in danger. Not from me,' he added hurriedly, 'I only want to help him.'

She hesitated a moment and then called out to the taxi driver. 'I've changed my mind. I'll call you again, later.'

She turned to Fielding again. 'You'd better come in. And I'm warning you, my maid's in the apartment. Ana's built like a battleship and she doesn't take any nonsense from young men like you. The first sign of funny business and you'll have her to deal with.'

Fielding followed her up the steps and into the foyer. 'I'm not going out after all,' she said to the uniformed man who leapt forward to open the lift door.

Once in the apartment she led him through to the living room. 'If you are who you say you are,' she told him as she pointed to a chair he could use, 'you'd better convince me you mean him no harm. I had him here till all hours last night in a terrible state.' She sat down opposite him. 'Now,' she commanded sternly, 'explain yourself.'

Fielding didn't respond at first. Now he was sitting in front of the woman who had been the root cause of Harrington's problems he felt he'd got to try and convince her that she could also be the solution. 'I don't know how much he's told you,' he began.

'You threatened to shoot him,' she replied drily, 'because of some arrangement he had with a mutual acquaintance. Is that enough for you?'

'It's a bit more complicated than that, senhora,' he said. 'The mutual acquaintance, as you call him, is in fact an agent of the German Military Secret Service.'

'So Mickey told me.'

'That makes padre Harrington a spy. He wasn't spying against your country. The PVDE would have no quarrel with him.' They'd probably applaud what he's doing, Fielding thought privately. 'But what he's doing, what he's been forced to do, is extremely dangerous for my country.'

'I don't know why you're telling me all this. Mickey's explained everything. It's all right. We love each other.'

Fielding nodded. 'I'm sure you do.'

'You're a secret agent yourself, aren't you?' she demanded.

Fielding shrugged. 'I suppose you could say that.'

'But an odd sort of agent. You could have killed him last night, but you didn't, and now, what's this you're doing?'

'I owe a lot to padre Harrington,' Fielding said. 'He's a victim of this horrible war. You both are. So am I.'

'You?'

'I was to be ordained to the priesthood next year. I don't suppose that will ever happen now.'

She let that pass her by. 'You say he's got himself in danger. But haven't you absolved him?'

'It's not my place to absolve him, senhora. But maybe you can offer him a sort of absolution. He told me you wanted to go to America.'

'It's all arranged. We're going to make a fresh start. I was on my way to the American Embassy when you met me. There's a man there who'll help us get visas and there's a Greek ship, the *Nea Hellas,* due in port next week, sailing to New York.

I've spoken to the agents already this morning. It's perfectly possible.'

'Be on it,' Fielding said. 'It's very likely the Nazis will be looking for him if he stays in Portugal.'

'And you. What are you going to do?'

'I'm going to tidy up a few loose ends.'

59

Fielding glanced across the Avenida da Liberdade to where the swastika flag hung limply over the doorway of the Augsburger office. *Got to have your plan worked out, Sonny Jim,* he heard Gus in his ear admonishing him, *no use going off half-cocked.*

The door under the swastika flag opened. A big blonde woman stepped out, squinting in the bright sunshine, perched a pair of dark glasses on her nose and set off down the Avenida. *In Portugal,* Fielding thought, *even the German war machine stops for lunch.*

He kept watching the doorway. If the secretary was entitled to take time off, what about the boss? No one else emerged. He waited a few moments longer and then crossed over the broad avenue, dodging a tram on the way. There might be other staff in the office but that was a chance he'd have to take.

There was a sign on the door: *Aberto.* Still open for business then, and the door yielded to his touch. He entered, closed the door and turned the sign over so it told the outside world the office was *Fechado.*

He looked around. There was a staircase on the far side but the large office itself was no more than a single room. The secretary's desk was an advertisement for German efficiency; not as much as a pencil out of place. The office walls were decorated with photographs of different kinds of printing machines and in one corner there was a small beautifully restored antique hand press, testimony, he supposed, to the long tradition of German technical excellence.

Fielding looked around for a bell to signal his presence. Nothing. He coughed discreetly, the diffident throat-clearing exercise of a Portuguese peasant up from the country.

He heard footsteps on the stairs and a voice calling, '*Wer is da? Quem está ai?*' Bi-lingually wanting to know who was disturbing the lunch-time peace. A nattily dressed plump little man appeared, halting on the bottom step, equally ready to either send the intruder off chastened for his impertinence or to welcome a valued customer.

'Senhor Koenig?'

'What do you want? We don't have any work for casuals.' One sight of the clothes he wore and Koenig had got Fielding instantly weighed up.

'You are senhor Koenig?'

'Yes. What of it?'

'It's about the English priest,' Fielding said.

'What about him?' Koenig stepped forward with a frown on his face.

'Padre Harrington,' Fielding said. 'You've been using him.'

'I don't know what you mean,' Koenig said, irritation mingling with a small dose of apprehension. 'What are you? PVDE? I'll have you know I'm a German citizen and I'm a friend of your superiors.'

'I'm not a beetle.'

Koenig's eyes narrowed. '*Polícia Judicaria?*'

'Not them either. Different party altogether.'

Koenig came another step closer. Fielding could smell garlic on his breath 'Who the hell are you? Show me your *mandato!*'

'I don't need a warrant,' Fielding said, this time in English. 'Father Harrington's going away, to where you can't touch him,'

Koenig blinked. 'You're not Portuguese!' He took a step back, fumbling for something inside his jacket.

Fielding was quicker. *Two taps,* he heard a voice say as he fired. *Don't forget, Sonny Jim, one, two; that's the way to do it, as Punch said to Judy.*

Koenig fell back over the edge of the desk, mouth and eyes wide open in a comic expression of astonishment; two extra holes in his face and a spray of blood and tissue all over the secretary's paperwork. Fielding's ears were ringing from the detonations that had seemed deafening in the confined space of the office but the *ding* of a passing tram's bell was a reminder that the outside world continued on its way, oblivious to this tiny drama in the Augsburger office.

Fielding pocketed the Mauser, turned back the card in the door window to *Aberto*, and left. The secretary would be in for a nasty surprise when she returned from her lunch but that couldn't be helped. As Diane had said about Bill Marchant, she was another casualty of war.

Fielding set off for the long walk down the Avenida da Liberdade, his mind empty of anything coherent. He wasn't in a hurry and no one paid him the slightest attention. Before he got to Restauradores he turned left and cut through to Rua das Portas de Santo Antão, the narrow little street that was home to a few antique shops and one or two eating places.

He looked through the window of one restaurant, the Faisão Dourado. Apart from a couple of long tables filled with men noisily tucking into a hearty lunch the place was strangely empty for that time of day.

'What's up?' he enquired of a waiter standing beneath the gaudy sign of the golden pheasant at the door, a cigarette hidden in his cupped hand.

The man looked left and right before muttering out of the corner of his mouth, 'Fucking beetles. Some sort of fucking celebration. Another poor sod in one of their fucking jails, no doubt. They're all pissed.'

PVDE. They might be even more pissed when they were called out to deal with remains of an assassinated German salesman and spy. Or did the Abwehr have its own disposal team?

From Antão he passed through the Largo de São Domingos and up into the depths of the Mouraria. He suddenly discovered he was hungry, bought a *bifana*, a slice of grilled pork in a bun, in a corner café and washed it down with a bottle of Sagres. He let himself into Diane's safe house, went up to his room, flopped on the bed and fell almost immediately into a dreamless sleep.

He woke to the sound of a door shutting, the clatter of something falling in the kitchen and the accompaniment of an exasperated 'Shit!' Diane was home early. Fielding prised himself off the bed and went downstairs to join her. 'It needs cleaning,' he told her by way of greeting as he threw the gun down on the living-room table. 'I shot Koenig.'

She nodded. 'Well, that does rather put a lid on things.' Quite cool, as though she'd expected the news, she stood facing him, arms by her side, her large brown eyes fixed on his.

Fielding didn't hesitate. He strode forward, put his arms around her and kissed her. Diane didn't resist, so he kissed her again.

60

They stood at the rail of the upper deck of the *Nea Hellas* watching the crew casting off the last cables that held the ship to the Alcántara dockside.

A thin cold early morning wind blew off the river, making Harrington shiver, though Beta, muffled in a soft silk scarf, seemed to be revelling in the bracing atmosphere.

He could still scarcely believe the whirl of frenetic activity of the past few days was over and that he and Beta were now cocooned in a blanket of safety, about to cross the Atlantic aboard this single-funnelled steamer, not much bigger than the vessel that had brought him from Liverpool all those years before.

The air was full of noise, mainly from the rail of the lower deck, where hundreds of fellow passengers, men, women and children were excitedly jabbering in a half-dozen languages, shouting farewells to less fortunate ones waving them goodbye from the dock. Many of them might have been the same people Beta had told him she'd seen crowding the offices of Macmillan e Cavaleiro.

Down there somewhere in the crowd, Harrington couldn't see them but he knew they were watching, were Fielding and that Singleton woman from the Consular office who had pulled strings with her opposite number at the US Embassy to get them visas and places on board the Greek Line ship.

The four had met briefly the day before in Beta's apartment amidst a chaos of packing cases and rolled up carpet; everything to go into storage until he and Beta had established themselves in America. The farewells had been necessary but awkward;

how did one say good-bye to people who only a few days before had been contemplating one's elimination? Fielding had taken control of the situation. 'It's a new beginning for us all,' he'd said. 'No use looking over our shoulders at what might have been.'

Harrington's leave-taking from the college had been painful. Martin Blount wore an air of bewilderment, seemingly unable to comprehend what his colleague was about to do and making Harrington more than ever guiltily aware of the deception that had become so much a part of his life in the preceding months. 'You can have everything,' he told Blount, 'books mostly, I don't have much else besides.' The college president had brushed aside the offer in his distress. 'It's the end of everything for you, Michael,' was all he could say.

Harrington wanted to tell him that it might be the beginning of everything but he doubted Blount would understand. To anyone outside the priesthood what he and Beta were undertaking was no more than a rather abrupt change of career. Diane Singleton had said as much to him when they'd met: 'I'm sure you'll find something interesting to do in the States,' adding with a suspicion of a grin, 'Just make sure it's nothing to do with the US postal service.'

He'd worried she might have let something slip to her opposite number at the US Embassy, making him *persona non grata* in Uncle Sam's backyard. 'I'd been tempted,' she admitted, 'but Peter persuaded me you were more of a victim than a spy.'

Beta had been quite taken with Fielding. 'Such a capable young man. And isn't he lucky?' she added coquettishly. Harrington had been slow on the uptake. 'Diane,' she said, 'how appropriate. The Huntress. Well, she's found her quarry.'

It was difficult to imagine Fielding as a quarry, more of a hound. The earnest scholar he'd known for so many years had been transformed into something at once more mature and infinitely more dangerous. Nothing had been said explicitly but Harrington had a shrewd idea his former student had something to do with what had been announced in the *Diário*. The assassination of a respected German businessman was attributed to the work of a communist cell.

The memory of that night at the harbour wall in Cascais was still vivid in Harrington's memory. He longed to ask, yet dared not, whether Fielding really would have pulled the trigger, but Beta was right about Singleton being a huntress and Fielding had indeed been her hound. Whether he would remain her faithful dog was entirely another matter.

He took Beta's hand and felt her fingers pressing into his. 'In a few days,' she whispered back, 'we shall be in a new world, all three of us.' She patted his hand against the gentle swell of her belly by way of reminder.

A new world, a new life, he thought, and for all of them the end of any kind of innocence.

THE END

Afterword

There was an English College in Lisbon, closed now and converted into luxury apartments, but *End of Innocence* is entirely a work of fiction. Names, characters, places and incidents are either the product of the author's imagination or are used fictitiously. Any resemblance to actual persons, living or dead, businesses, companies, events is entirely coincidental.

Acknowledgements

I owe an immense debt of gratitude to the seemingly inexhaustible patience of James Essinger who has proved himself to be far more than my literary agent.

Joe Swann, Mike Horrax, Tony Flynn, Bill Dalton and the late Philip Gummett are among so many people who have at one time or another, consciously or unknowingly, had their brains picked for scraps of information. I am grateful to Sue Massey for some timely legal advice and I would never have finished the work without my sons' encouragement and without having my wife Maben at my side.